Dear Reader

The novels

by such authors as Kathleen

Rosemary Rogers, Johanna Lindsey, Laurie McBain, and Shirlee Busbee are accountable to one thing above all others: Avon has never tried to force authors into any particular mold. Rather, Avon is a publisher that encourages individual talent and is always on the lookout for writers who will deliver *real* books, not packaged formulas.

In 1982, we started a program to help readers pick out authors of exceptional promise. Called "The Avon Romance," the books were distinguished by a ribbon motif in the upper left-hand corner of the cover. Although the titles were by new authors, they were quickly discovered and became known as "the ribbon books."

Now "The Avon Romance" is a regular feature on the Avon list. Each month, you will find historical novels with many different settings, each one by an author who is special. You will not find predictable characters, predictable plots, and predictable endings. The only predictable thing about "The Avon Romance" will be the superior quality that Avon has always delivered in the field of romance!

Sincerely,

Walter Meade

WALTER MEADE
*President & Publisher*

*Other Avon Books by*
**Linda Ladd**

WILDSTAR

AVON
PUBLISHERS OF BARD, CAMELOT, DISCUS AND FLARE BOOKS

MOON SPELL is an original publication of Avon Books. This work has never before appeared in book form. This work is a novel. Any similarity to actual persons or events is purely coincidental.

AVON BOOKS
A division of
The Hearst Corporation
1790 Broadway
New York, New York 10019


Published by arrangement with the author
Library of Congress Catalog Card Number: 85-90670
ISBN: 0-380-89639-7



First Avon Printing, September 1985



Printed in the U. S. A.

WFH 10 9 8 7 6 5 4 3 2 1

For my husband and children, as always—
and for my mother, with love

MOONSPELL

# PROLOGUE

*Ulster, Northern Coast of Ireland, 1692*

The cavern was lit by only the flickering of a torch, with deep shadows draping the ceiling far above like heavy folds of black velvet. Shreds of vapor misted the surface of a deep spring while gentle waves lapped against the smooth stone shore. A sleek shadow moved along the edge of the water, pausing once as if to listen to the silence, before padding with soundless feline grace to an ornate dressing table set against the cavern wall.

Jillian Devlin seated herself before the gold-framed mirror; she did not move when the beautiful cat jumped into her lap, except to idly raise one slender hand to stroke its long, silky black fur. Her fragile, finely sculptured features seemed carved in stone as she gazed unseeingly at her reflected image. Her hair was long and thick, draping her delicate shoulders in shimmering, silken waves like a mantle of fine blue-black satin. Her eyes were large and thickly fringed with long black eyelashes, their pure turquoise color a startling contrast to her creamy white skin. Her nose was small and straight, her lips a soft, full red above a small, square chin that slanted up with a determination that bespoke a will of iron. The expression on her face, so breathtakingly beautiful, did not flicker when a woman loomed behind her in the mirror. Mauve Hennessey was much older than Jillian, perhaps forty years, but her face was comely and unlined, her age shown only in the hint of silver in her long, dark hair. Her eyes were dark and luminous and glittered as she spoke.

" 'Tis ready now, child."

She spoke in Gaelic, the ancient tongue of Ireland, and Jillian dropped her gaze to the wooden bowl Mauve held. She wrinkled her slim nose in distaste as she stared at the thick, grayish substance it contained.

"Then let's get on with it," she said quickly, looking away as Mauve stirred the vile liquid.

Mauve hesitated, looking closely at her lovely young charge. "I do not believe this can work, Jillian. 'Twill be difficult to hide beauty such as yours from the man. And 'tis a risk you take considering such a deception—"

"Beauty is but a curse to a woman," Jillian interrupted in a low voice. "It makes her the pawn of greedy, lustful men, as it did to my mother. We must disguise my face before I am forced to marry the Englishman, or he'll possess my body against my will, as well as my lands."

She shuddered as she spoke, and Mauve looked at her with pity. "But Jillian, you cannot stop this marriage; the English king has ordered it."

"Nay, I cannot prevent the marriage, but I can keep the Englishman away from me until my brothers can return to Ulster."

Mauve shook her head sadly, then placed a gentle palm upon Jillian's shoulder. "Brian can never come home. You know the king has exiled him from Ireland forever." Her voice softened. "And Pierce is dead; you must accept that, child. He was lost when the English warships sunk his French vessel just after your father died. There were no survivors; Brian said as much in the letter he smuggled to us."

Jillian's teeth caught her lower lip as she fought to control the rush of tears burning her eyes. She would not believe that her beloved Pierce was dead, she vowed determinedly, no matter what Brian's letter had said. Her family had already been hurt too much by the English. Wasn't it enough that her father, Hugh Devlin, had died at the Battle of the Boyne River three years ago, fighting with King James against William of Orange? James had been their last hope for a tolerant Ireland, and although her father had been a Protestant, he fought for the rights of the Papists, knowing that otherwise there would be no end to the strife and bloodshed.

Her older brother, Brian, had fought as well, before he had been captured and forced into exile when William had crushed the last Irish resistance the summer before at Limerick. And all because of the English tyrants! How she hated them! She clenched her fists, and Ebony stirred restlessly in her lap as she sought to subdue the terrible anger inside her.

"Pierce is not dead," she told Mauve firmly. "And very soon King James will invade England and reclaim his throne from William, and Brian will be free to come home."

Mauve saw the stubborn set of Jillian's fragile jaw and suppressed a sigh. "Nevertheless, now you must obey King William's command and marry the English lord or lose the Devlin lands forever."

Jillian shivered in renewed anger. "It is not fair," she cried bitterly. "These lands have belonged to my father's family for a century and to my mother's ancestors before that. The English have no right to take them from us!"

" 'Tis a wretched fate indeed," Mauve answered calmly. "But there is nothing to be done about it. You must marry Justin Spenser, Earl of Wellingford. And you best be grateful that the king was merciful with you. He could very well have given Lord Spenser the lands outright, since your father and brother fought against him—and he *would* have, if your family had not been Protestant. At least the Englishman can protect you from

Sean Flanagan. He has already begun to invade our property now that we have no armed men to protect us."

"Perhaps I would prefer Sean Flanagan to this Justin Spenser," Jillian muttered bitterly. "At least he is an Irishman."

For the first time Mauve's black eyes flashed with annoyance. "Do not talk like a fool, girl," she snapped impatiently. "Your very life would be in danger with that devil. Did his men not maim my poor son, Donal? Cut out his tongue, they did, and Donal only thirteen, his only crime walking upon Flanagan lands. Sean Flanagan is evil, and he will not rest until he has destroyed everything Hugh Devlin held dear. And you would be wise not to forget that."

Jillian looked down in shame, knowing Mauve spoke the truth. She'd heard the story many times from her father and brothers. Her father and Sean Flanagan had been neighboring landlords when their feud had begun, both young, handsome, and rich, heirs to miles of the wealthiest Protestant lands in Ulster. But Jillian's mother, Maire Hennessey, had changed their lives forever. She was a peasant, a devout Catholic, but her raven-black hair and blue-eyed beauty, so very much like Jillian's, had fascinated both Hugh and Sean, and their love for her had caused a conflict between the two families that continued to the present day.

It had started on a dark and moonless night when Hugh and Sean had left a tavern and encountered Maire upon a deserted lane. Drunk, Sean had given chase, determined to have the maiden who obsessed him, and Hugh had been forced to draw swords against his friend to defend Maire's honor and had wounded Sean with a deep slash across his cheek. Sean had held his face, eyes black with rage, and as blood had trickled through his fingers, he cursed Hugh and Maire in fury, swearing eternal vengeance upon the Devlins. Eventually Hugh had married the gentle Maire, and despite their differences in faith and social station, they had been happy together, Maire giving him two sons before she died giving birth to Jillian.

But her mother's death had not ended the blood feud, and ever since Jillian could remember, she had been protected from the barbarous Flanagans. Her father had often warned Jillian that her uncanny resemblance to her mother would be dangerous should Sean Flanagan ever see her. The only Flanagan she had ever met was Patrick, Sean's only child, and no one knew of their friendship, not even Mauve. They had been children when Patrick had wandered onto the Devlin lands while stalking a stag and had fallen into a bog. Jillian came upon him and managed to pull him free. They became friends, meeting secretly from time to time to play. Patrick was nothing like his father; he was a gentle and kind boy who lived in dread of his father's temper.

Jillian sighed deeply, then raised solemn eyes, watching Mauve study the concoction in the bowl. She carefully tested its consistency before she sprinkled a bit of sand upon its surface. Jillian had no doubt that Mauve could fashion a clever mask for her to wear. She was a healer, her skills with herbs and medicines legendary in Ulster. Many peasants in the surrounding villages considered Mauve Hennessey a witch, and often Jillian had seen both men and woman cross themselves in fear when Mauve passed them in the lane. But Jillian had learned much from the woman who'd raised her since birth, and she knew that Mauve was good and kind, using her skills not for evil spells but for good deeds and healing the sick.

Jillian watched warily as Mauve's fingers dipped into the bowl, tensing as the warm substance touched her cheek. She squeezed her eyes shut, cringing as Mauve spread the odious mixture evenly over her flawless white skin. A moment later she opened her eyes and stared in fascination at the scaly, disfigured appearance of her cheek.

"It is horrible," she breathed, but a slow smile spread across her features. The smile was fleeting as a sudden dreadful thought came to her. "It will come off, won't it?" she asked Mauve worriedly, and Mauve chuckled as she applied more of the thick mixture.

"Do not fret, it will peel away without pain

or effort. And it will make your own skin even softer and lovelier than it already is."

Jillian smiled again and relaxed. "Our plan will work, Mauve, I am sure of it. The English lord will not be so eager to share my bed after he learns that I have had the pox. No man would willingly bed a monster, not even an Englishman."

Mauve carefully smoothed more of the mask over Jillian's clear skin, her face thoughtful. "And what if Brian never comes back? What will happen then?"

"He will come back," Jillian replied stubbornly. "And until he does, I will use the Englishman's soldiers to protect the Devlin properties from Sean Flanagan. He will not dare attack us with an English earl in control. The Spensers are powerful in England and good friends to William and Mary. We will be safe enough until Brian returns. At least the Englishman can serve a purpose while I am forced to have him in my house."

Mauve did not answer, and the cavern became quiet again as they lapsed into silence. But deep inside Jillian, suppressed resentment smoldered in a fiery glow. Her helplessness to direct her own life caused her the most torment. She had not met this Justin Spenser she was to wed, but she knew he had fought at the River Boyne where her father had been killed. That was why the king had awarded him the rich Devlin estates. Jillian's teeth clamped tight. All her father had wanted was tolerance, justice for every Irishman. She squeezed her eyes shut as bitterness oozed from her heart.

"Damn the English!" she gritted through clenched teeth.

"Do not think of it, Jillian. It does no good," Mauve said quietly. "We are Irish, and we are women. We have no rights."

"I am tired of having no rights," Jillian said softly. "I am tired of being a woman."

Ebony moved in Jillian's lap, and she hugged the cat close, welcoming its warmth as she stroked its soft back. The cat purred and rubbed against her mistress, then lifted her head to stare at Jillian. Slanted turquoise eyes, the color of Jillian's, studied the suddenly alien face above her, then she settled comfortably back into the folds of Jillian's velvet skirt, lazily licking her paws.

Jillian looked back to her reflection as the last patch of her fair skin disappeared beneath Mauve's grotesque handiwork. Mauve wiped her fingers upon her apron and smiled. "There, your beauty is gone. I do not think this Justin Spenser will desire you now."

Jillian smiled back at her as she gazed in awe at the blotched, pockmarked face. A cold chill suddenly rose the hair upon her neck, and she shivered.

Mauve saw the fear in her wide eyes and laughed.

"Hush, child, let me show you how easy it comes away." She lifted with her fingernail the solidified mask where it touched Jillian's temple and pulled gently.

Jillian breathed easier as the mask was peeled free, making her skin tingle and glow as if renewed. She raised her fingertips to the softness of her cheek, then found Mauve's eyes in the mirror.

"It looked so real, it frightened me. Surely the Englishman will never guess it is a disguise."

"Aye, but it will not bear close scrutiny by him. You must wear a veil, and you must be careful that he does not see you except in deep shadow."

"I will be very careful," Jillian said, lifting her small chin. "Because I will never let the Englishman touch me. Never."

# ONE

Justin Spenser looked out over Lough Swilly, raising his forearm to shield his eyes against the sun glittering off the blue-gray water. Far across the wind-ruffled waves his merchant ship lay at anchor several miles south of the small town of Lybowdin. They'd only arrived in Ireland the night before, but he had set out for the Devlin properties at the first light of dawn, concerned about their late arrival in Ulster.

He had ridden ahead of his brother and the Spenser men-at-arms, and he stood in his stirrups, scanning the trail along the cliffs that lined the lough. A brisk wind blew from the north, rippling thick black hair away from his forehead. His face was dark, tanned a deep bronze from his last voyage to the American colonies, making a vivid silver of his gray eyes by contrast. He twisted in his saddle for a better view, his muscular shoulders straining against the brown leather jerkin he wore over a simple linen shirt. The unpretentious clothing only emphasized his lean and powerful build. He placed one sun-darkened hand on the hilt of the sword at his hip, smiling as his youngest brother, at the head of a long column of men, topped the rise of the nearest hill.

Justin watched Ryan approach, glad he had persuaded the boy to leave the glittering life of the Royal Court to accompany him to meet the Devlin heiress. At twenty-one, Ryan was the youngest of the Spenser men, a full ten years younger than Justin. Their other brother, Aaron, was between them at age twenty-five, and their only sister, Catherine, was nineteen. Philip Hammond rode at Ryan's side, a tall, gray-headed man of fifty, who had served the Spenser family since before Justin was born.

"We'll stop here and rest," Justin said as they drew to a stop beside him, then grinned at Ryan's look of relief. Philip bellowed the command to the horsemen behind them, and Justin swung easily off his white Arabian stallion and led him toward a nearby stand of trees. He flipped his reins over a branch and watched his brother's slow, painful dismount.

"It's about time you decided to stop," Ryan grumbled. "I'm sore as hell." He was tall, with the same broad-shouldered, lean-hipped physique as Justin, although he stood a full head shorter than his older brother. He had the Spenser curly black hair, but his eyes were brown, almost amber and, at the moment, devoid of their usual lazy humor.

"You're too soft, Ryan," Justin told him, sitting down and relaxing against a tree. "I told you not to spend so much time chasing the women in London. This ride with me should toughen you up a bit. These men"—he gestured to where his men had settled into small groups among the trees—"can sail a ship halfway around the world, then ride all night without a complaint uttered. After you take command of them you will be as tough as they are."

"I prefer spending my nights with a warm, willing woman, thanks just the same," Ryan answered, lounging down beside him. "And according to your reputation around Whitehall, so do you."

Justin laughed. "I don't have time to court women for more than a night at a time, especially the twittering, empty-headed ones who surround the king and queen."

He rose and looked out over the vast rolling hills stretching inland from the lough. Ryan watched him, shifting uncomfortably on the hard ground. He was softer than he thought, but Justin had driven them hard to arrive in time for the wedding.

"If I didn't know better," he said with a grin at Justin, "I'd say you were driving us so unmercifully because you're overanxious to bed the Irish wench."

Justin's silvery eyes remained on the far horizon. "Bedding the heiress is only another duty, as is the marriage itself. I'm more concerned with reaching Devlin Manor before she is humiliated by the absence of a groom. The wedding is to be held this very night, and we have a hard ride ahead of us to make it on time."

Ryan grimaced at the thought of staying in the saddle all day, then looked up as Justin spoke again.

"And what do you think of Ulster, Ryan? Did I not tell you it had a strange, wild beauty?"

Ryan followed his brother's gaze to the patchwork of tilled fields and green meadows that eventually melted into a hazy purple, where white clouds lay in mounds against a clear blue sky. "Aye, it is beautiful enough, I suppose, but if I were you, I would be more concerned with the beauty of the woman I am to take into my bed this night."

Justin turned to look down at him, then swung his arm in a wide gesture toward the horizon. "I am marrying for that, not for any woman. Whether she is pretty or plain makes little difference. As my wife she will bear my sons, but I expect little else from an arranged marriage. The Devlin riches will help us regain the Spenser lands that were confiscated by Cromwell when father remained loyal to the Crown." He paused, then walked back and sat beside Ryan. "Besides, Jillian Devlin should be most eager to have me here as her husband. The king said her family wars with a neighbor. Our presence will keep them at bay. She will no doubt be grateful to me for that."

Ryan's eyes sparkled devilishly as he watched Justin raise a skin of water and drink. "It is said that the Irish hate the English since William defeated them at the Boyne."

Justin glanced at him, then shrugged, wiping his mouth with the back of his hand. "She is a woman," he said arrogantly. "She will do as I tell her. And if she is ugly and unpleasant, I will be glad to return to England and leave her to herself. If she is beautiful, all the better. It matters little, one way or another, as long as the Devlin cattle and linen fill our holds on your next voyage to America. I daresay I'll rarely see the woman."

"Eleanor will be glad to hear that," Ryan said wickedly, thinking of the scene the beautiful woman had created on the deck of his brother's ship before they set sail from England. "She certainly made it known that she will settle for no other husband but you."

Justin made a derisive sound. "She will settle for no other title than Countess of Wellingford, you mean. I've had enough of that one after the foolishness she pulled in front of my men. But come," he said, rising. "Because of her I am in danger of missing my own wedding."

Ryan muttered under his breath as Justin strode away, calling an order to Philip Hammond. He rose stiffly and climbed gingerly into his saddle, wishing for a padded cushion to put beneath his backside. He watched Justin as he rode to and fro on Caesar, checking the baggage wagons and gifts he was bringing to the Devlin heiress. He was still surprised that Justin had agreed to the king's request. Justin was not, and had never been, the marrying kind. Ever since he could remember, Justin had been off on voyages to the Orient or the American colonies. The only woman with whom he had ever had more than a casual affair was Eleanor Marlowe, and that was mainly because of Eleanor's single-minded pursuit. He grinned again as he spurred his mount and fell in beside Justin, remembering Justin's face as Eleanor had wept and cursed like a fishmonger until he ordered her carried bodily off his ship.

They rode hard all day, through the warmth of the early June sun, down rutted coach roads, past green, waving corn and golden fields of barley. They passed several tiny villages but saw few of the inhabitants other than dirty-faced urchins in tattered rags standing solemnly before crude huts of sod and branches. At midafternoon they reached the high wall of gray stone that marked the boundary of the Devlin demesne, and they drew to a stop at the entry gate where fierce stone eagles guarded the road. In the distance the multitude of chimneys of the Devlin estate were detectable above the trees.

"The Devlins are wealthy indeed," commented Ryan as they led their retinue through the eagle sentinels and walked their horses down a wide avenue that wound through open green meadows toward the wood that hid the house from their view.

"The king's reward for standing with him

at the Boyne is a generous one," Justin agreed. "But we must remember that the Devlins are of the nobility themselves, and the girl will no doubt be proud. My men will behave as English gentlemen while we are here and treat the Devlin household with respect." He glanced down at his dark breeches, now dusty and travel-stained. "We must seek out a stream presently where we can bathe before we reach the manor. I intend to arrive before my bride looking presentable."

They mounted and rode on in silence, and Justin looked around the pastures, dotted with fat black cattle and occasional flocks of sheep. It seemed most strange that he would soon control all the rich lands before him, as well as the vast Spenser holdings in Kent. He had been the head of his family since his father died when he was eighteen, making him the Earl of Wellingford and leaving him all the responsibilities that went with the title. But his duties did not stop him from leading a free and easy existence. He often left Aaron to attend to the Spenser estates while he spent his energies running the extensive merchant fleet he inherited from his mother's family. Life at sea suited his thirst for adventure, and fortunately, Aaron's serious nature and love of farming had made it possible for Justin to enjoy the thrill of the sea for a time.

But William's offer had been too lucrative to ignore, even though marriage had always been an alien concept to him, despite Eleanor's outspoken ideas on the subject. She was a passionate woman, and beautiful, but too spoiled and selfish to make a satisfactory wife. He never really considered marrying her. Or anyone else, until William had told him of the Devlin heiress. Her riches would do much to rebuild the Spenser holdings, and perhaps it was time to leave the sea voyages to Ryan and raise a family. He thought often about the girl once the arrangements had been finalized. It would be a pleasant surprise if she were pretty, or even sweet-natured, but as he had told Ryan, it mattered little. There were few men who did not have mistresses as well as wives, especially if they married for land. If Jillian Devlin was young and healthy and could give him sons, that was most important to him. He wanted an heir.

Justin's thoughts fled as he saw a figure emerge from the wood at his left. He drew sharply back on his reins, and Caesar pranced sideways for a few steps at the abrupt halt. They had not seen a single person since they entered Devlin land, and he turned his horse toward the peasant standing at the edge of the trees, wishing to ask him about a stream where they could freshen themselves.

When the man saw Justin turn toward him, he began to run toward the woods, and Justin turned to Philip Hammond.

"Stop him," he ordered, and his sergeant barked a command. Two men left the ranks behind them and galloped after the fleeing serf. They caught him easily, and Justin waited, frowning slightly, as they escorted the cowering man back between their horses. He was dressed in a crude shirt and breeches of homespun wool, but his clothes were clean and in good repair, much better than the shabby garments of other serfs they had passed before they crossed onto Devlin land.

"Are you of the Devlin estates?" Justin asked him, and both he and Ryan exchanged surprised looks as the serf dropped to his knees before their horses, his hands clasped together in entreaty.

"Have mercy, sire," he begged in a shaking voice. "I am but a cowherd. I have done no harm to the Flanagans, I swear it."

"Calm yourself, man," Justin said, a trifle impatiently. "We are not Flanagans. I am Lord Spenser, betrothed of the Lady Jillian Devlin."

A flicker of fear flashed in the peasant's dark eyes, and Justin's frown deepened when the man quickly touched himself with the sign of the cross. He was obviously terrified, as much of the Devlins as of the Flanagans, Justin thought. Apparently the accounts of the feud between the two clans were not exaggerated. But it was Lady Jillian Devlin's name that caused the peasant's frightened reaction, and Justin leaned toward him.

"Why do you quake with fear at the mention of my bride?" he asked sharply. The peasant did not look at him, his hands nervously twisting his shapeless wool hat. "Speak up man," Justin demanded, and the peasant jerked frightened eyes to the men surrounding him.

"Some say she is a witch," he muttered quickly, afraid of rousing wrath in the big, dark-skinned Englishman. "She and Mauve, the woman who attends her."

Justin could only stare at him incredulously, but Ryan threw back his head and laughed. "Lady Jillian a witch? And I suppose she rides a broomstick and has warts upon her nose."

A few of the men laughed, but Justin glared at his brother.

"What does this witch look like, then, man?" Ryan continued, still grinning.

The peasant licked at his lips, his face still afraid. "I am but a lowly servant of the fields, milord, and the Lady Jillian does not leave the manor, but I have often heard of her magic, and one of our crofters has seen her change into a black cat."

"A cat, you say," Ryan said, turning to Justin. "You have little to worry about now, brother. If she does not please you, you can bid her to change herself into a cat and be gone."

Justin gave Ryan a dark scowl, having little patience with talk of witchcraft and magic. He had never lent credence to such things, feeling that only the most ignorant and superstitious listened to such tales. If the Devlin heiress were accused of such things, he would put an end to the gossip after they were married.

"Enough!" he said sharply to Ryan, then looked back to the peasant. "Is there a stream nearby where we might bathe?" he asked.

"Only the river beyond the Devlin Manor," the serf answered.

"There must be a creek or pond near here," Justin insisted, "before we reach the house."

"None but the Enchanted Pool." The peasant's voice dropped lower, and he crossed himself again. His next words were a mere whisper. "But evil spirits dwell there. No one goes near for fear of being cursed."

Justin continued to frown, ignoring Ryan's grin. He'd heard that Ulster was a backward place, but he had little tolerance for ridiculous fears and pagan beliefs. "Don't talk nonsense," he said irritably. "Show us the way."

The peasant was clearly dismayed as he was prodded forward by one of the guards. He led them across the nearest field and into a thickly wooded deer park that stretched for several acres alongside the road. The forest was thick and dark with much undergrowth where they entered, and the air seemed dank and chill after the sunny fields. The man continued to hang back, then stopped suddenly, his eyes wide and terrified. Justin followed his pointing finger to where a dark blue patch of water could be glimpsed through the trees.

"Yonder lies the Enchanted Pool, milord, and Devlin Manor is through the wood on the far side."

The serf slowly backed away as he spoke, his eyes on the water ahead of them. "But beware the spirits there. Men are cursed if they enter the water."

Justin was aware, and irritated, that several of his men twisted uncomfortably in their saddles, glancing warily at the ground fog shrouding the trees around them.

"Come," he said, touching his heels to the stallion's flanks. "It grows late."

Before the men guarding him could react, the peasant bolted, tearing frantically toward the dense undergrowth to one side of them, as if pursued by the devil himself.

"Leave him," Justin called as Philip Hammond moved to order his capture. "He has served his purpose."

His horse picked its way through the brush and bracken, and Justin ducked beneath a low-hanging branch. "The Irish are an ignorant lot," he said to Ryan. "And the war between the Devlins and the Flanagans makes it worse. It will be up to me to end the bloody business, as well as superstitious talk of witches. I'll not let helpless women be hanged as used to happen in England."

When they reached the pool, they stopped their horses at a small clearing where soft, emerald-green moss covered the ground, and the men behind Justin and Ryan were unnaturally quiet as they looked out over the water. The overhanging vines and limbs made it seem as if the day had darkened prematurely, and curls of mist rose above the blue surface of the pool like smoke from a gigantic witch's brew.

"We'll stop here," Justin said, and dismounted, missing how the more superstitious among his men followed the peasant's example of crossing themselves.

Justin handed his reins to Philip, then unbuckled his sword and laid it aside as he gazed over the water. "I am going to bathe. The Lady Jillian will no doubt have prepared a welcome for us, and I will not disappoint her by appearing before her like a dirty vagabond." He looked at Ryan, who had settled back against a tree. "And I'd like you to do the same. Especially since you will be standing up with me."

"Later, brother, I'm too tired to move. Besides, you're the bridegroom, not I. The heiress won't care how I smell."

Justin snorted as he took off his vest and unbuttoned his shirt.

"Don't forget to watch out for the evil spirits, big brother," Ryan called, and Justin gave him a sour look before he stripped off his breeches and walked toward the water.

A few of the braver souls among their ranks had already entered the pool, standing waist-deep as they splashed water up over their beards and hair, but Justin bent to retrieve a bar of soap from his saddlebag before he waded in to join them. He stopped in his tracks, surprised that the water was warm. He had not realized that it was a hot spring, and it felt soothing to his tired muscles. He smiled, taking his time as he lathered his hair and skin, enjoying the unexpected pleasure. Most of the other men had left the water, and Justin walked out deeper, laughing to himself as he remembered the peasant's fears. Enchanted pools, witches, curses, he thought derisively. The Irish were indeed an ignorant lot.

# TWO

Jillian tossed her head and retraced her agitated footsteps alongside the edge of the spring. She was alone in the cavern now, waiting for word of the English lord. He was supposed to have come the day before, and the wedding was planned for this night. She was hoping fervently that something dire had detained Justin Spenser, such as a death in his family, or better yet, his own death. She was overcome with nerves, fully aware of the magnitude of the hoax she and Mauve had planned. But despite her inner misgivings, she knew it had to be done. And the more she thought of it, the more she enjoyed the picture it evoked.

She stopped her pacing, and her soft laugh sounded in the quiet cave. It would be worth the discomfort of wearing the mask to see the Englishman's face when he lifted her veil. She could almost picture him, the important Justin Spenser, powerful Earl of Wellingford and confidant to William of Orange. He was probably a stodgy old coot, dressed like a preening peacock in gaudy, effeminate attire of satin and silk and lacy ruffles.

A sudden vision of the English lord fleeing his monster bride, his long ceremonial sword dragging the ground behind him, brought another laugh tinkling into the air. Perhaps she should drag one foot as if lame, she thought in wicked delight, but her smile faded as she heard an unexpected sound.

She whirled to see Donal Hennessey enter the cavern from the shaft that led to the manor. Donal was well over six feet, and his massive shoulders and bulging, muscular arms made him seem huge. He had inherited his mother's keen intelligence and black eyes, and he had been Jillian's friend and protector for as long as she could remember.

"What is it, Donal?" she said, and he moved his fingers rapidly in the sign language Mauve had taught him after the Flanagans had cut away his tongue and left him to die. Jillian watched his hands intently. "So he has come."

Donal nodded, and Jillian looked at him for a moment.

"Where is he now?"

He signed that he was nearing Devlin Wood.

"Go to Mauve, Donal; tell her where he is and that I'll come shortly for her to fashion the mask. Then go to the tower and watch for the Englishman. When he nears the house, come tell us."

Donal hurried off to do her bidding, and alone again, Jillian stared dejectedly over the water. So the time was finally at hand. The charade would begin soon, the mask would be set in place, and she would not be able to remove it. The thought was repugnant, and she looked again at the lacy shreds of mist upon the surface of the water. The spring would be so warm, and it would feel good to let it soothe away the tension in her limbs and relax the quivering of her nerves.

She sighed and took a deep breath, longing to breathe fresh air for a change. For weeks she had stayed indoors, in keeping with their story that she had been ill. Only the most trusted house servants knew of their plan to trick the Englishman, and they had been sworn to secrecy.

Outside, the spring formed a pool in a peaceful glade hidden in a quiet wood. It was one of the few places she could go to be by herself without fear of the Flanagans capturing her. The peasants called it the Enchanted Pool and were afraid to go near. Jillian herself had had much to do with the legend of the pool; many of the fearful tales had stemmed from the day she swam through the underwater passage leading from the cavern to the pool, surfacing unexpectedly and frightening a passing peasant. He had run for his life, sure that evil spirits had surfaced from hell.

Jillian smiled at the memory. Yes, she decided suddenly, she would go there. It would be the last chance for her to swim for a long time, because after the Englishman was settled at the manor, she would have to be very careful. She began to unlace the stiff stomacher of rose-and-gold brocade. Her soft, pink linen gown was soon a heap upon the floor along with her petticoats. When she stood in only her sheer shift of lawn, she walked upon a raised stone shelf that led to the deeper water, sighing in pleasure as she sank to her shoulders. Now that she'd made up her mind she was eager to be outside again, and she dived beneath the surface. Her brothers had taught her to swim when she was hardly more than an infant, and she pulled herself through the dark water with strong, even strokes, her goal the faint, circular glow where daylight suffused the water.

Outside, Justin Spenser stood in the water, his back against a large boulder near the center of the pool. The water was deeper there, and he swam for a time, enjoying the peaceful quiet and warmth. He glanced toward his men's encampment, but the boulder hid them from his view. He stood very still, closing his eyes as he listened to the soft music of wind in the reeds lining the shore. A few birds twittered overhead, and Justin let his mind wander until his thoughts fell on the woman he would wed in a few short hours. What he had told Ryan earlier was the truth. He considered the marriage too good an opportunity to ignore, although he would have much preferred to choose his own wife. He had never yet met a woman he could not kiss good-bye without looking back, and it was unlikely that the heiress would be any different.

He had fought with William of Orange

against James because he felt James's determination to bring back the Papist faith to England would lead to another civil war, and the Puritan rule under Cromwell had cost his family dearly, both in lands and rent. But his decision had been most lucrative, and with William's obsession with his war with France, no doubt the Spenser ships and men would be called upon again to help the king, thus bringing further gains to the Spenser holdings.

The Devlin wealth was well worth the sacrifice, and he was more curious about the heiress than he intimated to Ryan. After all, the woman would bear his children and his name.

He opened his eyes at a sudden splash nearby, thinking that perhaps a fish had jumped, then gaped in complete astonishment when, not a yard in front of him, a young woman rose like Aphrodite from the dark waters. For the first instant Justin was too stunned to react and could only stare in awe at her delicate profile as she tilted her face to the sky. Long black hair clung to her back like a rich length of shiny, black satin, and the sheer gown she wore was plastered against her bare skin, provocatively revealing every curve of her slender body.

Justin slowly stood, his eyes never leaving the vision of loveliness before him, and at his movement, a bird took flight from the trees above him, alerting Jillian to his presence. She whirled toward him, gasping in fright, unable to move as she stared in shock at the man a mere arm's length away from her.

Their gazes locked, and Justin stared into huge eyes the color of the finest turquoise. She was easily the most beautiful woman he had ever seen, and for those first few seconds as she stood so still with the gray mists rising around her slim, high-breasted body, he was not quite sure she was real. He was afraid to move, afraid she was a vision that would disappear.

The strange, silvery color of the man's eyes seemed to hold Jillian against her will, and in that tiny space of suspended time, she knew that he was very big with strong, well-defined features and skin darkened by the sun. His black hair was plastered away from his forehead, and his chest was bare and molded with muscles.

The realization that he was naked brought the return of her wits. Sudden fear clogged her throat, making a scream impossible, but she spun, intending to escape beneath the water.

Justin realized her intent, and before she could flee, he had her from behind, one strong arm like a band of iron around her small waist. Jillian cried out in panic as he drew her back against his hard chest, his forearm just beneath her breasts, and she struggled desperately, her kicking legs impeded by the water as he held her well off her feet.

Justin was smiling now, glad to find that she was truly real and not a figment of his imagination. He kept a firm grip on her, determined that he would not let such a beauty escape him. He pulled her closer, more than aware of her wet shift catching around her waist, baring shapely white legs.

"I won't hurt you," he murmured against her ear, half intoxicated by the sweet fragrance of her hair.

Jillian intensified her struggles, recognizing the cultured speech of a true Englishman. She kicked furiously, her heart beating a wild cadence as he turned her until her breasts pressed against him.

"Let me go," she hissed angrily in Gaelic. Justin looked down into her furious face, aroused still more by her nearly naked body squirming and sliding across his own bare loins. He could not understand her words, but her fierce struggles told him what she wanted. He swallowed hard, his voice hoarse with rising desire. "Hold still and I'll let you go."

Realizing that she had no chance against his strength, Jillian finally lay still against him, her chest rising and falling, and Justin found himself most reluctant to release her, even after she quieted. He loosened his hold, catching her wrist instead, and Jillian backed up at once to the full extent of their outstretched arms.

The pure turquoise beauty of her eyes was enough to take Justin's breath, and his eyes caressed the exquisite loveliness of her flawless white skin and trembling red lips. His eyes flickered down to a strange blue stone on a golden chain, rising and falling with each frightened breath. She seemed to Justin a wild creature of indescribable beauty, untamed, untouched, unreal, and desire rose with unbelievable force to run rampant through his blood.

"Who are you?" he breathed. "Where did you come from?"

Jillian did not answer, fear constricting her throat as she stared into his eyes, burning now with silvery fires. Her pulse accelerated, and her whole body went rigid as he reached out and ran his fingertips along the creaminess of her cheek. She jerked as if burned, her eyes darting around desperately, and Justin knew she was close to panic. He sought to control the passion that engulfed him.

"Please," he said softly. "Don't be afraid. I swear I won't hurt you."

He smiled, wanting to reassure her, and as Jillian felt his fingers loosen, she jerked her arm with all her strength. She was free for an instant, but he immediately had her again, this time swinging her at the waist until her back was against the boulder. He laughed as he braced both hands against the rock on either side of her, imprisoning her between his arms.

His face was very close now, his warm breath fanning her cheek, and Jillian put her hands as a feeble barrier against the wide, muscular expanse of his chest. Even the feel of her soft palms upon him ignited more fires in Justin's core, and he looked down at her face, his eyes drawn irresistibly to her mouth. "I won't let you escape, my little beauty," he whispered very close. "Not until I know who you are."

Jillian only stared at him, her eyes huge, and it suddenly occurred to Justin that she might not understand him. "Do you understand English, my lovely?" he murmured, lightly nuzzling her ear.

His warm mouth against her earlobe initiated an unknown stirring deep within her body, but she ignored it, her eyes catching fire at the humiliation of being toyed with by an Englishman. Rage rose within her as she pushed violently against him. "I understand that the English are bloody swine," she spat out in clear English, made musical by her lilting Gaelic inflection.

Justin laughed. "Yes, I'd say you know my language well enough."

Jillian flushed with fury as he smiled down into her eyes. She wrenched her face away, but he took her chin and forced her to look at him. When he spoke, his eyes were on her lips. "You have nothing to fear. I only want to know your name."

He could not take his eyes off the tempting red of her lips, and before Jillian could answer, he gave in to his desire, and his mouth came down upon hers like a hot brand. He stifled a groan as he tasted the sweetness of her. Somewhere in the vague reaches of his mind he knew he should stop, but she felt so good pressed against him, tasted so good, that his body continued to rule his actions.

Jillian felt herself lifted closer against him, helpless to prevent what was happening. His mouth twisted insistently over hers, burning her lips, her skin, with an oddly gentle force, until her anger was replaced by some inexplicable wonder. She had never been kissed before, never been touched by any man, other than her father and brothers. She was not prepared for the feelings of pleasure fluttering alive deep inside her; the hard, muscular strength of him took her reason away from her.

His hands were moving lower now, and she twisted, shocked, as he cupped her naked hips, clamping them intimately against his lean thighs. She felt weak, disoriented, drained of fight when his mouth finally left hers to begin a fiery path down the side of her throat to press hot kisses beneath her ear.

"You are real," he breathed hoarsely. "I wasn't sure at first."

His eyes glowed like silver coals as he looked down at her, and she could only stare up at him, her blue eyes wide with confusion. But the spell between them was broken abruptly as they heard loud splashing, followed by Ryan's voice. "Justin? Where are you?"

Justin turned slightly to look toward his brother, leaving Jillian to stare at him in dismayed realization. Justin! Could it be? Could this be Justin Spenser, the man she had sworn would never touch her? Fear whipped through her entire body, and she twisted desperately, managing to elude him as he lunged for her. Before he could stop her, she was free and stroking with all her strength toward the underwater opening to the cave.

Justin forgot Ryan and went after her, laughing softly as she dived. He stopped where he was and tread water. She was much too beautiful to let get away, and he waited, smiling, his eyes on the rippled surface, as he tried to decide where she would surface. She could not go too far; the pool was not that large. His grin began to fade as seconds ticked by, and she did not reappear. Ryan called his name again, but Justin ignored him and moved forward, his eyes dark with concern. The girl could not hold her breath much longer.

He frantically searched the water that had gradually returned to a calm blue mirror.

"No!" he cried suddenly, diving where she disappeared, knowing the girl had to be in trouble. He swam through the clear water, his eyes open, searching the sandy bottom for her. Lacy, green fronds of underwater plants waved eerily in the blue silence around him, but there was no sign of the girl. He searched as long as he could, his chest burning, then surfaced, gulping in great breaths of air before he dived again. He came up again, gasping, looking around frantically for help.

"What in the devil are you doing?" asked Ryan quietly from where he leaned against the boulder behind Justin. "Diving for pearls?" He grinned, but one look at his brother's terrible expression drained the amusement from his face. "What is it, Justin?"

"There was a girl here. She swam out there and went under."

Ryan's eyes jerked to where Justin pointed, then he dived into the water, joining his brother in his desperate search. Twenty minutes later he tiredly pulled himself out and onto a low rock. He sought to regain his breath as he watched his brother dive again and again. When Justin finally surfaced and leaned against the boulder in utter exhaustion, Ryan said quietly, "It's no use, Justin. She's not out there, or we would have found her. The water is as clear as glass. Perhaps you were daydreaming. You haven't had much sleep. . . ."

"Don't be absurd," Justin said blackly. "She was real." His eyes were bleak, his mouth set in a grim line. "I touched her. I spoke to her."

His fingers curled into hard fists as he fought down the sickness, the disgust with himself. She was young and innocent and beautiful, and because of his lust, she had drowned.

# THREE

Jillian fought toward the surface and came up inside the cave, gasping for air. Her heart hammered with fear and exertion, and she hugged her arms around her waist, watching the water behind her as she waded quickly toward the shore, in case the Englishman found the underwater opening. She looked around for Donal, hoping he had returned. But the cave was empty. She left the warmth of the water, dripping a trail on the stone floor. The cave was very cool, and she shivered as she crossed to where her long, woolen Kerry cloak lay on a stool.

She wrapped it tightly around her and raised the hood, glancing warily toward the pool. The surface remained calm and unbroken, and she went to warm her hands at the large bronze brazier in the middle of the cavern. She stared at the rods of smoldering turf, beginning to shake from delayed reaction.

Just the fact that the man had been Justin Spenser was enough to send a freezing fear through her veins. The man who held her so tightly was no greedy old man, no easily duped fool. He was young and vital and handsome and had made no pretense about his desire for her.

And what was worse was that he had affected her. She had never experienced the sensations that awakened within her when he kissed her with such hard, relentless passion. A quivery spasm shot through her loins even at the thought, and she shivered with self-disgust. Damn him for the arrogant way he used her, as if she were made for his pleasure! Her own inexperience with men had made her victim to his touch. No doubt she would experience the same feelings if any man kissed her. She grimaced, viciously rubbing the back of her hand over her mouth. She had been very lucky that the other man had come when he had. Otherwise she might have been dishonored by the English earl. It showed the kind of man he was and the kind of debauched life he must lead. He was despicable, she thought furiously, contemptible, seducing maidens just before he was wed. He would never get the chance to touch her again, but she must be much more careful because he obviously desired her; his silver eyes had glowed with it.

A curious, slow-burning rage overwhelmed her, and in a sudden burst of fury she snatched up a flagon of wine and hurled it across the cavern. It hit the wall with a crash and tinkling of glass, just above where Ebony lay curled upon a chair. The cat shrieked in terror, then shot like a black streak from the cave, but Jillian ignored her, staring angrily at the dark liquid as it ran in branching rivulets to form a red pool upon the floor.

Her jaw hardened into a determined slant as she vowed silently to make a fool out of the arrogant English dog who roamed the woods to prey on defenseless maidens. If she had to wear Mauve's terrible mask forever, she would never let him take her to his bed.

But, unfortunately, Justin Spenser was not stupid as she had hoped, and Mauve must take special care with her disguise if they were to fool him. She had very little time now to prepare herself for their meeting.

She walked across the cavern and lit a taper on a wall torch. She entered the dark tunnel that led to the old Norman part of the manor. The flickering of her candle sent eerie, jumping shadows preceding her. The passage was very old, built by the Normans as an escape route from marauding invaders. The floor felt cold to her bare feet as she hurried along to the spiral steps hewn into rock that led into the old tower. She climbed quickly to the platform and peered through the hole into the chapel. When she was sure it was deserted, she removed a panel hidden behind a heavy brocade tapestry, then stepped through and carefully placed it back into position.

The chapel had not been used since her mother had attended private masses there before her death. Jillian hurried down the narrow aisle, past rows of gold candelabra with tall white tapers that had been set in place for her own wedding. She hardly paused when she reached the spacious hall that connected the manor with the stone tower and the banquet hall.

Devlin Manor had been built against the gray stone edifice in 1607 when the first Devlin came to Ireland after Queen Elizabeth had granted him land for the plantation of Ulster. But Hugh had completely redone the house soon after his marriage, so the wide hall that Jillian hurried through was resplendently fashioned with carved oak panels where great ropes of hand-wrought wooden fruit and flowers surrounded large gilt-edged portraits of her ancestors.

She stopped and knelt upon the parquet floor before a dark panel covered with cherubs and roses, then pressed her finger to a wooden rosette near the bottom. The wall moved, opening a narrow space, and when Jillian entered, the door slid closed behind her. During the days after the Rebellion of O'Neill, when Cromwell and his armies had sought to crush the Irish Catholics, Hugh had been terrified for his wife's safety and had built an intricate network of passages within the walls of his estate. Although the Devlins had never been forced to use them, Jillian and her brothers had found the dark labyrinth fascinating, and during her childhood they had played many games of hide-and-seek there.

Inside the dark, narrow hall, Jillian lifted her candle and ran up the steep stairs that led to the second-floor bedrooms. She was cold and uncomfortable now, and eager to bathe and get out of the clammy shift she wore.

Mauve turned quickly when Jillian stepped out from behind an embroidered tapestry in her own bedchamber.

"Jillian! Where have you been? Donal has seen the Englishman and you have not . . ."

Her voice faded away as Jillian tugged off her cape and dropped it upon the floor. She stared in dismay as Jillian crossed the soft Persian carpet to the fire, where Mauve had prepared a steaming hip bath. She quickly stripped off the wet shift before she stepped into the warm water. It felt wonderful to her chilled skin, and she looked up as Mauve came closer, disapproval evident in her dark eyes.

"I went for a swim," Jillian said, answering Mauve's unasked questions.

Mauve looked at her in disbelief, then snorted with contempt. "A swim, is it? Well, how nice for you. I hope you enjoyed yourself while Donal and I paced and worried ourselves sick because the English lord is already in the wood. What if he insists upon meeting you when he arrives? It will take time to apply the mask."

Jillian stared into the fire, watching as flames darted and licked in a golden dance around the logs. "I have already met the Englishman," she said, her voice low.

Mauve stared uncomprehendingly at her. "I am in no mood for jests, Jillian. I have had little confidence in this plot of yours from the outset."

"I am not joking. He was at the spring where I swam. He grabbed me and I could not escape."

Mauve gasped, her hands going to her breast in horror. She stared at Jillian with wide eyes. "But you were nearly naked," she breathed, looking at the transparent chemise in a wet heap on the floor.

Jillian shivered and sank deeper into the water. Mauve's voice gentled into a whisper. "Did he dishonor you, child?"

Jillian turned to her, her turquoise eyes as hard and cold as winter frost. "No, but not for want of trying. If one of his men had not called to him, I would no doubt have lost my maidenhood."

Mauve sank weakly into a chair near the hearth. "You were very foolish to go there alone. Only good fortune protected you."

Jillian did not answer, and Mauve continued, her eyes on Jillian's profile. "I suppose you will now give up this scheme, for if he has seen you, the mask will serve no purpose."

"I am now even more determined that it will work," Jillian told her firmly. "He does not know who I am. I only know it is he because he was called Justin by his man."

Mauve shook her head. "He will search for you, and 'tis more than likely that he will recognize you now."

"We will just have to be more thorough with my disguise. He will not guess."

Mauve frowned as Jillian's eyes seemed intent upon avoiding her own. "And what sort of man is this Justin Spenser?" she asked Jillian. "Is he weak and greedy as you had envisioned?"

Jillian was quiet for a moment as a brief memory of hot male lips upon the side of her throat sent ripples down both her arms. "No, he is big and arrogant and thinks only with his loins." Her voice grew bitter. "He wanted me only because my looks pleased him. If he thinks me ugly, he will leave me to myself. He is obviously in the habit of taking many women at his whim, and he will not miss his wife as a bed partner."

Mauve knew Jillian very well, and she noted the slight flush that had crept into her fair cheeks and the darkening of the clear blue eyes as she spoke of Justin Spenser. "Perhaps you found him attractive as well. Is that the reason you do not look at me?"

Jillian whipped her head around to face Mauve. "No, it is not! I hate him more now than I did before. He is contemptible, and never again will he touch me as he did today. I will die before I let him."

Mauve stared at the twin spots of color upon Jillian's exquisite face, knowing intuitively that Jillian was more affected by the Englishman than she would admit, or possibly even knew herself. And that in itself was very dangerous.

"You must work to make my appearance uglier," Jillian said slowly. "And something must be done with my figure. He held me close against him and explored my body with his hands." She hesitated as sensual shivers coursed across her skin. "Now come and help me wash my hair, then I want you to be on hand to meet him. Use your cleverness to devise an excuse, then take him into the drawing room where I can listen to your conversation from behind the wall panel."

Mauve nodded as she helped lather Jillian's silky black hair, but she knew the meeting at the spring boded ill for their plans. Even more frightening was her fear of what Lord Spenser's reaction would be to such a trick, in the event that he should uncover it. Was he a man who would overlook such deviousness in his wife, or would he mete out a punishment as harsh as the English usually imposed upon the Irish?

# FOUR

Justin Spenser rode silently alongside Ryan, his face carved in stone. Ryan glanced at him, wishing Justin would not blame himself. He still wondered if the girl had been a figment of his brother's tired mind. It seemed impossible for them not to have found her body in a spring of such size and depth.

"It's not your fault, Justin. You could not know the girl would drown," he said, and when Justin did not appear to be listening, he shook his head and did not speak again.

Justin had heard Ryan, but his brother's words of comfort did not assuage the terrible guilt in his heart; he could not come to terms with the senseless death he had caused. The maiden had been so young, so incredibly beautiful, and it knifed his heart that she now lay lifeless somewhere in the dark, quiet depths of the pool. A sudden, vivid image burned into his mind, and he saw her beneath the water, her silky black hair waving spectrally in the currents, her lovely eyes open and staring. He shuddered, his stomach churning with sick regret.

He had been such a fool. If he'd not grabbed

her like he had, frightened her so badly, she would still be alive. It was not his way to use his strength like he had with her. He had never before kissed any woman by force, nor made love to one who was not willing. But she had been so lovely, and he wanted her with a passion he had not known before. Disgust rose within him, disgust and helpless rage at his behavior.

He squeezed the leather reins tightly in his fist, a muscle twitching in his lean jaw as he fought off his emotions.

They had left the thick wood, and the well-manicured lawns of Devlin Manor swept out in a verdant carpet before them. He signaled to Philip to halt the men.

The house was immense, a great Palladian mansion of red brick and white plaster that rivaled in size his own estate in Kent. A circular dome rose behind a massive portico supported by six gigantic white columns, with tall windows reaching out in symmetrical grandeur on each of the three floors. Behind the main edifice, a huge, round Norman tower of gray stone rose imperiously above the slate roof with countless chimneys.

"The Devlins' wealth is not exaggerated," Ryan muttered softly, admiring eyes on the magnificent structure before him, and Justin gave a slight nod of agreement. He spurred his mount toward the cobblestone drive that circled to the main entrance of the manor.

The portico was graced by a series of stone steps, and Justin slowed his horse as a woman moved to the long balustrade, accompanied by a young man whose immense size dwarfed the woman beside him.

Mauve watched the Englishman approach, full of apprehension as her eyes followed the men who led the impressive entourage. They drew up at the base of the staircase, and her heart stilled as her gaze met the steady, silver regard of the larger of the two men in front. She had no doubt in that moment that he was Justin Spenser, Earl of Wellingford, although the man with him had the same proud, aristocratic bearing. She took a deep breath as they dismounted and handed their reins to a tall, bearded man with gray hair, then stepped forward to meet them as they climbed the steps.

At closer inspection she saw that the two men resembled each other, both tall and handsome with strong, even features. But there could be no mistake about which held the position of authority.

"Lord Spenser," she said, smiling as she gave a small, respectful curtsey. "Welcome to Devlin Manor. I am Mauve Hennessey, attendant to Lady Jillian. She begs your forgiveness for not meeting you, but she is resting in anticipation of the ceremony."

Justin's eyes narrowed as he looked closely at the woman dressed in a conservative gown of black silk. She was undoubtedly a cultured lady, but some innate intuition alerted him to a certain reticence in her manner. "I understand," he said. "I hope the Lady Jillian will excuse my tardy arrival, but my ship's departure was unavoidably delayed."

Mauve's eyes went to the other Englishman, who had smiled slightly at Lord Spenser's last words, and when Justin saw her interest, he proffered an introduction.

"This is my youngest brother, Ryan. He will stand with me during the ceremony."

The younger man smiled engagingly at her and bowed slightly. "I am most pleased to make your acquaintance, madame," Ryan said with the charm he reserved exclusively for women. Mauve inclined her head and smiled in acknowledgment, then looked to Donal.

"And this is my son, Donal, milord. He will show your servants to their quarters." She gestured to Donal, who moved to where Philip waited with the men.

Justin watched Mauve steadily, thinking she looked too young to have a grown son, and Mauve looked into the unreadable gray eyes, a breath of unease stirring in her breast. He was very intelligent, his eyes quiet and assessing, as if he could read her very thoughts. He would be very hard to play the fool, she thought worriedly as she led them into the manor and across the huge foyer. Justin looked admiringly around the wide hall with its magnificent staircase that rose in two graceful curves to a wide landing, before it wound again to the next floor. He walked to the foot of the polished steps, lifting his eyes to the dome three full stories above him. A window had been fashioned there, a stained-glass pastoral scene of rolling green meadows and deep blue lakes, and the late-afternoon sun streamed through the leaded prisms, slanting patterns of vivid color on the walls around them.

"Devlin Manor is very beautiful, Madame Hennessey, but I must confess that I am most anxious to meet my bride. I have brought wedding gifts that I would like to present to her. Might I hope for a moment alone with her before the ceremony?"

Mauve swallowed hard, hoping he would not have reason to suspect her next words. "I am afraid I have grievous news I must tell you, Lord Spenser. But please, come, I have arranged for refreshment after your long journey."

Justin exchanged a look with Ryan as Mauve swept ahead of them and opened tall double doors at one end of the foyer. They followed her into a large drawing room with rich brocade furnishings and heavy crimson draperies of velvet.

"Please sit down, milords," Mauve said, "and I will pour wine for you."

Ryan lounged down in a high-backed chair of gold satin, and Justin moved to a position beside the fireplace of black-veined marble, his eyes still on Mauve. Across the room, in the secret passage, Jillian tensed when she caught sight of the man from the spring. She kept her eye to the peephole, hating herself for the shiver that coursed through her as his deep voice sounded inside the drawing room.

"Madame, I'm afraid you have piqued my curiosity. What grievous news awaits us here? I trust Lady Jillian is well."

Jillian's eyes flew to Mauve, to where she sat demurely before a low table, pouring deep red wine into tall silver goblets. There was a slight pause before Mauve responded.

"She is much better now, but I'm afraid Lady Jillian has been very ill these past two months." She handed a goblet to Justin, then another to Ryan.

"What manner of malady did the Lady Jillian suffer?"

Jillian kept her eyes trained on Justin as Mauve quietly answered his question.

"I am sorry to say it was the pox. A very severe case. It is a miracle that she survived at all."

Justin stiffened, and Ryan's eyes openly expressed dismay. No one spoke for several moments, and Justin frowned down at her in concern.

"We are well aware of the horror of smallpox, madame. We lost both our parents to it," he finally said. "Both Ryan and I succumbed to it as well but with only mild cases."

Mauve looked down. "I am sorry. I did not know of your misfortune."

"It happened long ago when I was but eighteen." He hesitated again, then went on. "And am I to understand that Lady Jillian has fully recovered?"

"Aye, by the grace of God, but we are all distressed that my lady was most severely scarred during the course of her illness."

Ryan looked into his goblet, but Justin's gaze did not leave Mauve, his face completely inscrutable. "That is most unfortunate," he said at last, true sympathy in his voice. He had seen the ravages of a pock-marked face, and when the disease struck young, marriageable women, the ensuing emotional impact was often worse than the disease itself.

"Aye," Mauve said, shaking her head sadly, and Jillian grinned to herself at Mauve's splendid performance. "Lady Jillian is most distressed by her appearance. She refuses to be seen without a veil, even by the servants."

"That is understandable," Justin said. "But her self-consciousness will probably pass with time."

Ryan spoke for the first time. "Perhaps her altered appearance is what gave rise to the peasant's words."

Mauve looked back to Justin for explanation.

"We came upon a cowherd near here, an ignorant fellow, and he said that many believed the Lady Jillian"—he paused and smiled—"and you as well, Madame Hennessey, practice witchcraft. Of course, I dismissed it. I do not believe in spirits and other such ridiculous nonsense."

He was surprised when Mauve did not seem startled or even upset by his words.

"We are certainly not witches, milord, but I cannot deny my knowledge of the spirits."

Justin looked at her incredulously. "You cannot mean that you believe in such tales."

"I have seen many things in my life that I could explain no other way," Mauve replied quietly.

"The cowherd also told us of a spring, which he called the Enchanted Pool." He stopped, but when Mauve's eyes remained lowered, he went on slowly. "I'm sorry to say, there was a terrible accident there today. A young woman drowned."

Jillian gasped from her hiding place, not having thought he might believe her dead. But that could work to their advantage, she mused, and she smiled as she listened to Mauve's next words.

"That is most strange, milord. Most of our people are frightened to go near there."

"She was very . . ." Justin's voice faltered momentarily, and when Mauve looked at him, his eyes moved away from her. ". . . beautiful, with black hair and blue eyes. Do you know of such a woman?"

"No, milord."

"I feel responsible for what happened and would like to recompense her family. I'm afraid I frightened her, and she perished trying to get away from me. I am most distressed that it happened."

"Justin tried desperately to save her," Ryan said. "But we could not recover her body."

Justin turned suddenly, as if agitated, and Jillian held her breath as he seemed to look straight at her. She saw him tense, then stare intently toward her. She poised to flee as he quickly strode toward the wall panel behind which she hid. But as he neared, Jillian saw that his eyes were not upon her but upon the wall to one side of the peephole.

She was dismayed when she realized what he had seen. Her mother's portrait! They had not thought that he would surely see the resemblance! She began to tremble, but she could not look away as Justin Spenser stood so very close to her, his eyes still upon the portrait. A strange expression passed across his face, and Jillian's eyes went to Mauve, who watched him, her eyes guarded.

"This is the woman who drowned," he said suddenly, turning to face Mauve.

Mauve returned his stare, but an idea was beginning to form in her mind. Her answer was calm, belying nerves stretched tight. "I am afraid you must be mistaken, Lord Spenser."

"I am not mistaken. Who is this woman?"

Mauve's voice remained quiet. "That is Lady Maire Devlin, but she died many years ago." She waited, then added, "She drowned in the pool you speak of. It is her spirit many think haunt the spring."

Justin and Ryan both jerked startled looks at her, and Jillian barely suppressed her laugh at Mauve's cleverness. No sound issued from the other side of the wall for several seconds, until Justin turned scornful eyes on Mauve.

"I do not believe in spirits, madame, any more than I believe in witchcraft. The girl today was not a ghost. She was very real, and she drowned before my eyes."

"Then I cannot say who it was."

Mauve watched Justin Spenser pace back, realizing that he was truly distressed by what he thought had happened. He took a deep draught of his wine, not listening as Ryan and Mauve exchanged a few pleasantries about Ulster. His eyes strayed back to the portrait, almost against his will, and a strange, cold chill passed over his flesh. He frowned, not wanting to think about it.

"Is the ceremony to be held this evening as planned?" he asked abruptly, interrupting their conversation, and Mauve nodded.

"Aye, but with your permission, we would like for it to be very private, with only the two of you and myself present. Lady Jillian still mourns for her father and brother and is very conscious of her appearance. Of course, a wedding feast is planned afterward, so that the Devlin household and your men may have their celebration."

Justin nodded, then moved across the room to stare out the window, his hands clasped behind his back. He spoke without looking at her. "I do not wish to seem insensitive to the Lady Jillian's plight, but it will be necessary for me to look upon her."

"Of course, Lord Spenser. My lady only

asks that you view her in private, just before the ceremony."

Justin turned to her, inclining his head in silent acquiescence. "Then if all is arranged," he said, "perhaps you will be good enough to show my brother and myself to our apartments so that we might prepare for the wedding."

# FIVE

Night pressed its velvet cloak against the tall, diamond-paned windows behind Jillian as she sat patiently before her dressing table, watching Mauve apply her mask. She knew that everything depended on the grotesque visage Mauve now fashioned so carefully out of the thick, gray concoction. It had to work, if she were to save the Devlin lands for Brian. She still felt confident that it was only a matter of weeks before King James would regain his throne and reward Brian for his loyalty, for she had heard that he had raised French support. But it must be soon, because she now knew she could not deceive the Englishman forever.

"Lord Spenser is very generous with his gifts," Mauve remarked, glancing toward the bed where Jillian's young maid, Bridgit, was lifting gowns of vibrantly hued satins and velvets from an enameled trunk emblazoned with the Spenser lions.

Jillian followed Mauve's gaze as Bridgit lifted a blue cape of velvet lined with soft fox fur. "I do not think it generous to make a token gesture as he steals my brother's inheritance."

She shivered in anger at the thought of giving over control of her property to an Englishman. Mauve smiled, wondering if her shiver was from anger or anticipation.

"He is a most handsome man, and virile by his looks. I fear he will eventually expect to share his wife's bed, if only to beget his sons."

Jillian stiffened, remembering the desire in his silver eyes and the heat of his lips upon her mouth. Suddenly nervous, she leaned closer to the mirror to examine the mask. Mauve had altered her delicate features, giving her a longer nose and full chin, and now that the mask had begun to dry, it looked quite real.

She looked at herself in satisfaction, only recognizing the blue of her eyes in the ugly face, gray tinged with the residue of ill health. Mauve continued to work on it, making shallow holes in the damp substance, to create the look of cracked scars and pox marks. She finally stood back and studied her handiwork.

"You must remember to draw him into the shadows and to keep your eyes lowered when he lifts the veil. Perhaps it will work after all. He seems genuinely concerned for your welfare."

Jillian made a derisive sound. "He is only concerned for his own welfare. He is no better than other Englishmen, who use women for their pleasure, then discard them."

Suddenly agitated, she stood and walked to the tall, oaken armoire where Mauve had hung her wedding dress. She reached out and lifted one sleeve, running her slender forefinger over the lacy medallions of shamrocks and roses made by hand by Devlin women. The silk was very soft and pure-white, and she was to have worn it to wed Thomas Flynnen, to whom she'd been pledged since birth. He was the son of a landowner to the south, young and handsome with brown eyes full of laughter.

Jillian dropped the delicate sleeve abruptly. But now he was dead, killed at the River Boyne, before they had time to know one another. She forced her melancholy thoughts away, then lifted down the dress and examined the waistband Bridgit had padded with layers of linen. Satisfied with the extra bulk, she stepped quickly into it, allowing Bridgit to button the tiny pearl buttons upon the back. She adjusted the white silk stomacher embroidered with silver threads, then stood quietly as Bridgit quickly laced it at her back. She moved before the mirror, hardly recognizing the short, stocky girl with the pock-marked face that stared back at her.

Bridgit's laughter erupted from behind her. "The Englishman will swoon with shock when he sees what he will marry," she cried in delight, her chubby face alight with amusement, and Jillian had to smile.

"I hope you are right, Bridgit," Mauve said. "But I am afraid that Lord Spenser is not one to be duped for long."

"Any man can be fooled," Jillian said, adjusting her heavy skirt over the underskirt of white satin. "They are all alike, gaping and fawning over any woman with a fair face. He will shy away if he thinks me ugly. He is as much a libertine as the next man; he has already proven it. Now help me with my veil and we will go."

Downstairs Justin stood silently before the altar in the ancient chapel while Ryan sat sprawled in a hard-backed pew beside him. He stared morosely at the gold crucifix on the stone wall behind the altar. He knew his thoughts should be upon his new bride, upon his wedding. But his mind would not release the memory of the small, exquisitely beautiful face that had disappeared beneath the misty water. The look in her eyes haunted him relentlessly. She had been afraid, but there had been something more in the turquoise eyes, a strange defiance.

He shut his eyes, trying to block away the terrible image as Ryan spoke, his voice loud in the hushed silence.

"You must stop blaming yourself, Justin. The girl drowned, but you were not at fault."

Justin's smile was humorless. "Then whose fault is it that she is dead? Her own?"

"It is no one's fault. It was an accident."

Justin looked away, his voice low and tortured. "She was so very beautiful, Ryan. You cannot know how lovely she was without having seen her."

Ryan frowned, never having seen his brother brood so over a woman. Women had never been more than pleasant diversions to Justin, and it worried Ryan to see him in such a state.

Justin turned, and Ryan quickly stood, as the arched door to the chapel opened. Mauve appeared with a black-robed Anglican priest, and as they moved inside, Justin's eyes remained on the doorway. A woman appeared, gowned entirely in white, so heavily veiled it was difficult to tell much about her. She appeared to be small and rather stocky, and Justin stepped forward to meet her, frowning slightly as she stood unmoving in the portal.

Jillian's heart began to pound as she realized he might very well recognize her. She took a deep breath and moved past Mauve and the priest. She was surprised that he did not wear the foppish English attire with ruffles, lace, and bows as she expected, but instead, a long coat of rich brown over dark breeches of the same shade. Beneath his coat he wore a shorter jerkin of gold brocade with a neatly folded jabot of white linen at his throat.

When she reached him, he smiled down at her from his great height, his teeth white and strong in his dark face.

"Lady Jillian," he said, lifting her hand to his lips. "It is an honor to meet you at last."

His mouth seemed to burn into her fingers, and Jillian clenched her teeth in self-disgust.

Justin looked down at the young girl who stood at his side, so very stiff and straight. She was obviously terrified of him, and he suddenly felt very sorry for her. He smiled down at her, drawing her away from Ryan, knowing that he must make no visible reaction to her appearance when he lifted her veil.

Jillian went with him, her nerves aquiver, but thankful that he led her to a shadowy spot where the candleglow was behind her.

"I have brought you a wedding present," he said, and her eyes fell to the small box of embroidered gold and scarlet that he held in his hand. He smiled as he opened it, and Jillian stared at the huge diamond ring. The setting was pure gold, the sparkling jewel held aloft by the twin winged lions of the Spenser coat of arms.

When she did not speak, Justin said softly, "It is very old. It has been passed down in my family, for generations, to the wife of the oldest son."

"It is lovely," Jillian murmured almost inaudibly. Justin winced at the trembling in her voice. She was even more frightened than he had thought, but he would put her at ease. She had suffered enough.

She stood stiffly as he slid the ring upon her gloved finger. Justin hesitated, then reached out and took her veil. Jillian held her breath as he lifted it, keeping her eyes on the gold buttons of his vest for the space of an instant before the veil settled gently back into place. She jerked her eyes to him at once, expecting to read revulsion in his face, but instead, she was shocked to see only a faint trace of pity in the silvery eyes. A sudden fear struck her very core as she considered for the first time that her appearance might not deter him from bedding her.

She could only stare up at him, and he put his hand upon her waist and drew her back to the altar, where Ryan and Mauve joined them. The priest began to speak, and Jillian stood in a daze, barely able to repeat the vows. When the ceremony ended, Justin held out his arm for her, and she laid her fingers lightly upon his sleeve as he led her into the banquet hall, where the wedding feast had been set upon long trestle tables. The servants of the estate awaited them there, eager to see their new master, and they arose respectfully as Justin led her through the quiet crowd, many shaking their heads sympathetically at Jillian's veiled face. They mounted the raised dais at the front of the hall, and when they were seated, the lively strains of a harp and fiddle filled the room. Laughter and loud conversation soon became boisterous as the servants enjoyed the rare pleasure of sumptuous food and plentiful ale.

Jillian sat stiff and unresponsive between the two Spenser men, wishing only to escape to her room. She ate nothing, though her servants served roast capon and fatted beef upon silver trays. She surreptitiously observed the man beside her, confused by his manners and lack of reaction to her disfigured appearance. He remained silent for the most part, although politely attentive to her, and she grew increasingly anxious as the evening wore on.

She had directed that the stewards keep the goblets of the Englishmen brimming with the strong Irish ale, and now it was her last hope to keep him from her. If he would drink himself into a stupor, she might escape him. But to her chagrin Justin drank very little, while Ryan partook of the excellent fare with gusto, draining his tankard often and calling for more. Jillian grew more edgy, as the piercing silver eyes touched her occasionally, as if trying to penetrate the lace fabric of her veil.

Justin watched his bride, feeling only pity for her. She seemed so small and alone, and although the light had been very dim in the chapel, he had been appalled at the terrible damage done to her face. It was unlikely she had been a beauty before, since her features seemed heavy and irregular, but the disease had made her truly hideous. She had obviously suffered very much in the last few years with the loss of her father and brother, the disease, and now marriage to a total stranger. He was vaguely surprised to find that her appearance did not overly concern him. He had not expected to find a beautiful bride awaiting him. Marriage contracts rarely combined both wealth and beauty, and only a fool would expect it. More often, the most beautiful women were peasant girls, like the one at the pool.

His thoughts moved away from the veiled woman at his side and settled on the deep regret that plagued him. He had never known a woman to turn him to fire, to take away all reason. To his own disgust his loins tightened now, as he relived the moment when she arose from the depths, her firm, young body molded by the wet, clinging chemise.

He gritted his teeth, forcibly turning his attention back to his bride, wanting relief from his own dark thoughts. Jillian sensed his sudden renewed interest and tensed already rigid shoulders. Justin's eyes fell to where her fingers clenched around the carved arms of her chair, thinking that she seemed more terrified than was warranted, since he had not shown anger or disgust at her disfigurement. He could not really understand it, but they had not spoken ten words, and he decided to try to calm her.

Jillian jumped when Justin's large palm settled gently over her hand, and she quickly pulled it away. He did not seem offended but smiled kindly at her.

"You are very quiet, Jillian," he said, his face so close that she could feel the warmth of his breath stir her veil. She clasped her trembling hands and swallowed her agitation before she murmured, "I am very tired, milord, 'tis all."

"You have not fully recovered from your illness. It is not surprising that you are exhausted. Would you like to retire now?"

His calm suggestion sent Jillian cold with dread, and she jerked frightened eyes to him but could not read his expression. His silvery gaze seemed only concerned, but she dared not agree, for fear that he meant to accompany her to her bedchamber.

Justin saw her stiffen and grow wary at his words, and he was more than aware of what she feared. He spoke softly, so only she would hear.

"You need not fear me, Jillian. I am not so heartless as to force myself upon you before we have become acquainted with one another. I will not come to you until you are ready to receive me."

Jillian stared at him through the gauzy veil, amazed at his words. She never paused to consider that he might voluntarily give up his marriage rights, especially after his lustful behavior at the spring. She could not believe his words, and she was filled with suspicion at his motives. She searched his face, trying to see subterfuge, but his eyes were compassionate.

A great burden lifted from her heart, for if he meant to leave to her the time of consummation, it was the answer to her prayers. It stood to reason that her altered appearance had effected his sudden charitable decision. There was little doubt that if she had appeared before him without the mask, as she'd done at the pool, he would have already swept her off to his bed. She resolutely forced down her elation, then said softly, "Thank you, milord. You are most kind. I am truly tired, and I beg your leave to retire."

Justin stood and helped her to her feet. "Of

course, Jillian, and I look forward to the days ahead, when we will get to know each other better."

Jillian nodded, then veritably fled his presence, before he could change his mind.

# SIX

Jillian had barely quit the banquet hall before she raised her skirts and ran with a rustle of satin to the domed foyer where the curving stairs led to her bedchamber. She rounded the steps at a run, not daring to slacken her pace until she reached the sanctuary of her room where she leaned breathlessly against the closed door.

It took her a moment to steady herself, then she moved across the rose-patterned carpet, pulling the veil free, inordinately pleased at the course of events. A low knock behind her sent her whirling in panic, but only Mauve's face appeared at the portal.

"Will he come to you?" Mauve whispered, her voice worried, and Jillian tossed the veil upon the bed as she walked to the fire. "Nay, I am safe. He said he will come to me only when I am ready."

Mauve's eyes widened with surprise. "Does he speak the truth?"

Jillian turned her wrist up and began to release the tiny buttons on the tight sleeve. "I believe him. I could see no guile in his eyes."

"So he is an honorable man, after all,"

Mauve mused aloud, and Jillian's answer was steeped in sarcasm.

"Do not be taken in by his kindness. 'Tis the ugliness of this mask that makes him so honorable."

Mauve only smiled. "But now you are safe from him, and that is what matters to me."

"I am safe for the present. He wants to get to know me first, which means he eventually intends to demand his rights as a husband. We can only hope that King James will make his move before that happens."

Mauve helped her with the pearls securing the back of her gown, then unlaced the tight stomacher and laid it aside. She picked up the fine satin nightgown and held it as Jillian slipped her slender arms into the wide, flowing sleeves.

"Perhaps this Justin Spenser is different, Jillian. He spoke most regretfully when he thought he'd been responsible for the drowning. Perhaps he is kinder than you think."

"Kind men do not molest women at their whim."

"He is an English earl and no doubt used to taking what he wants. The English nobility are given liberties with the serving classes, just as they are here in Ulster."

"Aye," Jillian replied, "as Sean Flanagan would have taken with my poor mother if my father had not saved her."

"Justin Spenser did not harm you as Sean would have my cousin, Maire," Mauve pointed out to her.

"He did not have a chance to dishonor me, but who can say what would have happened if I had not gotten away when I did."

Mauve could not answer, but she was very pleased that they had gotten away with their deception. She hugged Jillian's slender shoulders and smiled. "Regardless of that, you are safe from him tonight, and I am relieved. I will go now and see to the servants. Most have left the banquet hall now and dance and sing at the fires."

Jillian watched her friend leave, then walked to the window and looked through the panes. Bonfires glittered in the dark night like fairy lanterns held aloft, and she could hear the faint strains of faraway fiddles. She leaned her forehead against the cold glass, pain clenching like a tight band around her heart. The dancing figures against the glow of the fires celebrated her own marriage, and yet she stood alone in her room, wed to a stranger, a man who did not love her as she did not love him and never could. It was unfair. Fate had pinched her life with cruel fingers, twisting and turning it until nothing was left.

She closed her eyes, wishing she knew where Brian was and if he were well. He was all she had left now, for although she did not like to admit it, it was likely that Pierce had perished at sea. The thought of never again seeing her happy-go-lucky brother tore at her heart. She had been very close to Pierce, and they had been inseparable throughout their childhood. She adored Brian as well, but he was so much older, he rarely joined in their games.

She raised her hand to where the mask touched her hairline, wishing she could remove it. It had grown uncomfortably hot, scratchy, and tight. She sighed, staring dully at the nearest fire, her eyes narrowing as she recognized the tall, broad-shouldered frame of her new husband standing among the merrymakers.

Her mouth hardened as she watched Justin lift a bottle and drink. So he celebrated, she thought bitterly, no doubt looking for a pretty wench to share his bed while she stood alone and miserable, a prisoner in her own house. She turned away, angrily pacing across the room.

If only things were the way they used to be before her father died. They had been so happy then, with her brothers at home, laughing and teasing her. Tears burned deep behind her eyes as pain knifed deeper into her heart. She had lost everything. Everything she loved.

She bit her lip, sinking dejectedly to the stool before her mirror. The hideous mask looked back at her, warm tears tracking down the pock-marked skin, loosening bits of gray matter. Frustrated at her helplessness, she grasped the edge of the mask with her fingernails and pulled it away, angrily stripping it from her face until all of it was gone. She hated it! She hated having to marry the Englishman! She hated her whole life!

She had not wept openly since the day she learned of her father's death, but now, in utter despair, all the tears and loneliness that had been locked behind a proud will of iron came bursting forth. She laid her head in her arms, and great agonizing sobs of wretchedness shook her slender shoulders as her torrent of tears soaked her white satin sleeves.

From where Justin leaned against a tree he could see Ryan at the fire, drinking with Philip Hammond and some of their men. As he watched, two young women caught Ryan's arms and drew him with them into the circle of dancers.

Justin lifted the bottle and drank deeply, not wishing to join in the celebration. He had nothing to celebrate, and he wanted to be alone with his thoughts. It was very late, and he realized, rather indifferently, that he was slightly drunk. But he had a right to get drunk, he decided, especially after his poor bride had scurried off alone to her bed.

He had lost the most beautiful woman he had ever seen and gained an ugly bride who cringed away from his touch—all on the same day. He gave a deep sigh, placing the bottom of the bottle on his bent knee as he stared broodingly into the distant fire. Visions of the woman at the spring with her turquoise eyes and satin-soft skin rose to dance within the leaping flames. To his disappointment her image began to fade, and another replaced it, a face hideously pock-marked, devoid of beauty.

Justin leaned back his head and wearily closed his eyes. Sleep was what he needed, hours of dark, dreamless oblivion in which to submerge his mind and body. Whispering voices intruded into his daze, and he turned his head to find a couple just yards from him. They did not see him, and the man laughed softly as he drew the woman into his arms. She willingly met his embrace, and as Justin stared despondently at their entwined limbs silhouetted against the orange glow of the fire, elusive memories of full, red lips parting beneath his mouth tortured him. He gave a low groan, then tipped the bottle to his lips again. He was startled when the girl suddenly cried out in fear, and he swung his eyes back to her.

The couple no longer touched but stood apart, and Justin squinted blearily, trying to see what held their gaze as the woman crossed herself and took one step backward.

" 'Tis the witch, Jillian," she breathed, her voice trembling with fear, and Justin frowned as he discerned a small, dark shadow low against the ground. He did not comprehend what it was until it moved forward in a slow, graceful walk. The woman shrieked and fled at once, and the man backed slowly away as if he expected to be attacked. When he turned and lit out after the woman, Justin threw his head back and gave a hearty laugh.

"A bloody cat," he muttered to himself. "Scaring the wits from them."

The sound of his voice caused Ebony to stop in a low crouch, then slowly turn her head toward Justin until the firelight glinted against her eyes with a pure turquoise glow. Justin's mocking grin faded abruptly, and a cold chill feathered quickly up his spine to raise the hair at his nape. The cat remained motionless, and he froze in an unnamed dread until the animal darted off again to be swallowed by shadows. Justin stared after it, then looked slowly down at the bottle in his hand.

"I am drunker than I thought," he grunted hoarsely, then took the bottle by the neck and sent it spiraling upward in a high arc. It smashed to the ground a good distance away, and Justin got unsteadily to his feet, breathing deeply in the cold night air. He'd had enough talk of witchcraft and black cats and drowned maidens and ugly brides. All he wanted was to sink into a deep black hole where he could forget it all.

He started toward the manor, glancing to the fire. Ryan was gone, no doubt with one of the Irish beauties, he decided, or, knowing his brother, with both of them.

The manor was very quiet when Justin entered through the dark, deserted kitchens. He took one of the candles that burned in the recessed brick niches in the wide corridor, then made his way to the front of the house. He paused before the curving stairway, raising his eyes to the darkness above, then changed his direction toward the drawing room. He passed through the doors and went directly to the portrait, holding his candle up to it until the flame leapt, casting a flickering yellow glow on the age-darkened oil canvas.

He stared hard into the lovely face. The turquoise eyes seemed to look down into his own eyes. *Was* the girl he'd seen at the pool a phantom, he wondered, a figment of his imagination? But how could he have imagined her, when he looked at her now. He gazed at the woman above him for a long time. Was he bewitched? Had she been a spirit?

"No!" he whispered firmly, clenching his jaw. "You were real."

He turned quickly and left the room, only stopping when he reached the landing at the top of the staircase. He leaned against the wall and shut his eyes, a little dizzy. A low sound came to him, and he cocked his head to listen. It took him a moment to realize that it was weeping, and he frowned slightly as he moved down the dark hall.

The muffled sobs were heartbroken and pitiable, and he knew instinctively that it was Jillian. She is miserable, he thought, miserable and alone. The poor child was only eighteen, younger than his sister, Catherine. She needed someone to comfort her, and he was her husband; it was his duty to help her. The doorknob turned easily, and he pushed open Jillian's door, peering into the darkness for his poor bride.

She lay in her bed, her face buried in the

soft satin pillows. She still wept softly, but she stiffened and raised her head when a sound came to her.

"Jillian?"

The deep masculine voice was instantly recognizable and sent her into utter panic. She snatched the veil from the table beside the bed, backing quickly into the shadows formed by the velvet bed hangings.

The fire had burned low, and Justin moved across the shadowy room, finally discerning the small huddle pressed into one corner of the bed.

"Don't be afraid, Jillian. I heard you crying, and I want to help you. . . ."

He rounded the foot of the bed, his hand on the post, and Jillian shrank farther into the darkness of the headboard.

"Go away," she said hoarsely from the shadows, her heart thundering against her breast.

"I won't hurt you," he said thickly, close enough now for her to smell the ale upon his breath. He reached out to touch her, and Jillian darted away, scrambling frantically across the bed.

"Wait," he cried, and she gasped as he caught her arm and turned her to face him, his other hand grasping the edge of her veil. It slipped away before she could catch it, and they stood face-to-face, the full glow of the fire on her beautiful features.

She stared up into his face, her turquoise eyes wide with fear as Justin stood like stone, the silken veil sliding forgotten from his fingers. His mouth dropped open in astonishment, and he took one step backward.

"What sort of witchcraft is this?" he muttered thickly, then crossed his hand over his eyes as if he doubted what he saw.

Jillian was incapable of movement, her heart still frozen in midbeat, but she read the sudden fear in his eyes, and her mind raced, knowing she must take advantage of it.

"Does this witchcraft not please you then, milord?" she murmured softly, curving her lips in a slow smile. "Or perhaps you prefer the face I must hide behind my veil?"

He took another step back, and Jillian waited, expecting him to flee the room in terror, but Justin did not move. He stared at her face, then let his eyes drop briefly to the full curve of her breasts beneath the smooth satin gown. His fear dissolved as a streak of raw desire set fire to his soul.

Before Jillian could move, he had her in his grip, one hand at her waist as strong fingers grasped the nape of her neck.

"Oh, yes, witch," he breathed, holding her head still as his eyes glowed as hot as molten silver. "You please me."

Jillian gasped as his mouth found the graceful curve of her throat, and she began to struggle against his hold, but his long, tanned fingers were threading their way beneath the raven silkiness of her flowing hair, his palm molding the satiny curve of her hip. Then his lips were upon hers, hard, insistent, demanding, until her good sense began to leave her in a long, spiraling, downward slide to incoherence. She hung limply against him as his lips burned into her cheeks, her neck, then took her mouth again. Before she realized what he was about, she was swept against his hard chest, and a moment later, she lay upon the bed, his hands entangled in the heavy fall of her hair as he lay half across her.

He stared down into the pure blue of her eyes, unable to think of anything but the sweet fragrance of her silky hair, the incredible velvet softness of her skin as he slid one palm up the fragile column of her throat to gently cup her jaw.

"You are real, you are real," he muttered hoarsely, burying his face against her neck, and she moaned weakly as hot male lips moved along the sensitive cord of her throat. Her pulse raced, her body flaming higher as his mouth inched a fiery path over her cheek. He sought her parted lips and found them, tasting a sweetness that brought forth his own muffled groan. His mouth subjugated her very will with a twisting, demanding, breathless excitement, until she lost all grasp on reality, completely enslaved by the new stirrings of her body.

When his mouth finally left hers again, she felt weak and hot, and her long lashes fluttered open to find his warm, silvery gaze caressing her face. He brought one hand to her cheek then, running gentle fingers in a tender caress down her soft skin, and Jillian could only gaze up at him, her eyes clouded with bewildered wonder.

"You are real, and you are mine," he breathed.

She was very still as he lay his head upon her heaving breast; her body still pulsated from his touch, and it took several moments for her to realize that he had fallen into a besotted sleep. Against her will she lifted one hand and slipped her fingers beneath his thick black hair. It felt soft and clean, and when the riot in her blood finally faded, she swallowed hard, realizing how foolish she had been.

After all the lengths she'd gone through to keep Justin Spenser from her bed, she now lay willingly in his arms. When he touched her and kissed her, she lost all control over herself. It was frightening, and she shivered with reaction to her own weakness. She pushed against him, twisting from beneath his heavy limbs, and he mumbled a complaint, then lay still, his hair dark and tousled against the white satin pillow. Jillian found that she was shaking uncontrollably, and she clasped her trembling hands together as she knelt beside him, staring down at his large frame sprawled across her bed.

What had she done? she thought, her eyes wide and frightened. And what would happen on the morrow when he awoke in her bed?

# SEVEN

Justin struggled out of a deep black hole, his brain not quite functioning. After some effort he opened bleary eyes to stare at a rich canopy of crimson velvet. He could not think where he was, and his head felt bloated and heavy. He groaned as he sat up, then dropped his head into his hands as a sharp pain pierced his temples. His tongue felt thick and furry, his mouth sour, and he muttered a low oath as he clutched the bedpost with one hand and pulled himself to his feet.

His bloodshot eyes swept the room without recognition, a deep frown drawing his eyebrows together as confusing memories began to crowd into his mind. His Irish wife, Jillian, had been weeping, he thought, or had it been her? Visions of a more beautiful face intruded, blurry images of his touching her and kissing her. He passed his hand over his face, then almost warily turned his eyes to the bed.

Jillian Devlin lay half-hidden by the shadows of the bedhangings, but even in the misty light, Justin could see the terrible scars upon her face. He stared at her in stunned dismay, his eyes on her bare shoulder above the satin coverlet. He couldn't remember what had happened between them. He tried to concentrate but only succeeded in conjuring up the feel of silky black hair slipping through his fingers. He swallowed hard, sharp spurs of shame digging into him as he realized that he'd forced himself on his young bride, drunkenly taking her in place of the beautiful peasant girl. Sickened by his own actions, he moved slowly to the door, knowing Jillian Devlin would surely despise him. He had dishonored himself as well as her, and he was filled with self-disgust.

Jillian did not move for several moments after the door clicked behind the Englishman, then her lips curled in a wicked smile. He obviously suffered, both from drink and remorse, and she derived the greatest satisfaction from it. A low chuckle sounded from deep within her throat as she swung slim legs over the side of the bed. He was ashamed of his actions; it had been written all over his handsome face. Neither she nor Mauve had been sure he would be fooled when they reapplied the mask, but now that he wrestled with guilt, she might be able to keep him from her indefinitely.

"So Lord Spenser has been tricked again," Mauve said, smiling as she stepped from the tapestry that led to the secret passage.

"Aye, Mauve, his face turned the white of a winter's moon. He will scourge himself soundly for so cruelly robbing his innocent wife of her maidenhood."

They were still laughing together when Bridgit entered with water for her bath, and Jillian sank into the softly scented water, feeling quite secure again. She closed her eyes and heaved a deep sigh of satisfaction.

Justin did not fare nearly so well, and his face bore ravaging signs of the vast quantities of ale he'd downed the night before as he entered the luxuriously appointed dining room. He had bathed and shaved, but his stomach was unsettled, and the breakfast aromas emanating from the silver dishes upon the sideboard did not help.

"There are potato pancakes for our morning fare, brother," Ryan said cheerfully, filling his plate with healthy gusto. "It seems the Irish eat little else. But I must admit that Ulster agrees with me. The local wenches have made me feel most welcome." He grinned as he carried his plate to the long table covered with a white cloth of the finest linen.

"I'm glad you like it here," Justin muttered sourly as he sat down at the head of the table, making a determined effort not to look at Ryan's food.

Ryan glanced at him as he spread fresh-churned butter upon a crust of wheat bread. "You must strive for a more pleasant attitude, Justin, or it might be said that marriage does not agree with you."

Justin didn't answer, looking away as Ryan bit into a poached egg. He took a deep breath, cursing the very existence of Irish ale. In the past it had been rare indeed for him to overindulge, and he swore total abstinence for the future.

"Has the Lady Jillian arisen for the day?" he asked Ryan, and his brother lifted one shoulder in a small shrug.

A moment passed, then Justin spoke, his voice low. "I am afraid I have given my bride reason to hate me."

Ryan jerked surprised eyes to him as he lifted his tankard to drink, and Justin looked away. "I awoke in her bed this morning with no sure memory of what passed between us."

Ryan choked on a mouthful of milk, and Justin looked at the marble fireplace across the room. Ryan wiped his mouth with the back of his hand, staring at his brother.

"Good God, Justin, did you not promise her you'd wait?"

Justin's dark frown verified it, and Ryan shook his head. "What did she do?"

"She was asleep when I left her, but I fear I have ruined any opportunity to gain her affection." He stood suddenly, his own words chafing his conscience. He felt like an utter fool and, disturbed with himself, paced to the window to look out on the verdant lawns that stretched in a velvety carpet to a thick deer park. His mind taunted him with clouded pictures he could not explain, but as if in a dream, he could see Jillian's veil slip away to reveal wide turquoise eyes. He shook his head impatiently as tales of Jillian Devlin's witchcraft drifted uneasily into his mind. It had been nothing but a drunken dream, he told himself firmly, a hideous nightmare he'd inflicted upon his young wife. He had no one to blame but himself.

Jillian paused at the double doors of the dining hall, nervously smoothing the silk folds of her skirt. The bodice and waistline were padded quite thick with linen, and she had intentionally dressed entirely in black. It was fitting for the occasion of her deflowering, she thought with a smug smile as she adjusted the black veil that revealed only a vague outline of her masked features. Her gaze touched briefly on the Englishman named Ryan, where he sat at the table, then moved to the broad back of her husband. His wide shoulders were fitted in dark blue silk, the wide cuffs of the well-tailored coat embroidered with silver thread. He stood ramrod-straight, his legs looking long and muscular in high, black boots. His stiffly held posture indicated a brooding disposition, which met with her approval.

Ryan looked up when he heard the soft rustle of silk, quickly glancing at Justin as he rose to greet her. He smiled at the darkly veiled woman, bowing from the waist. He had felt sorry for Jillian Devlin from the moment he'd learned of her disfigurement, and now she was even more to be pitied.

"Good morning, Lady Jillian," he said, gallantly holding her chair as she sat, and Jillian murmured a low reply, well aware that the man at the window had turned and was coming toward them. She sat very still as

Justin stared down at her. He frowned, suddenly at a complete loss for words, and Jillian waited, hoping that he was as uncomfortable as he looked. As the silence lengthened Ryan looked down in embarrassment, and Justin's square jaw tightened. He felt like a villain with his own wife, and he did not like it.

"Good morning," he said finally, his voice slightly gruff. "May I offer you a bite to break your fast?"

Jillian smiled, lowering her head to affect embarrassed injury. "Nay, milord, I fear I cannot stomach food this day."

Justin frowned at her answer, then glared at Ryan until his brother received his message. With not a little relief he folded his napkin and stood. "I beg your leave, Lady Jillian, but I have duties elsewhere this morn."

Jillian inclined her head without answering, and Ryan strode quickly across the expensive Oriental carpet to the door, distinctly happy to escape.

"Since you do not have an appetite, madame, perhaps you will join me before the fire?"

Justin's smile was forced, and Jillian nodded, though she was more than reluctant to put her hand upon the arm he proffered. Gritting her teeth, she placed her fingers very lightly on his forearm. Her distaste was obvious to Justin, and Jillian felt his muscles flex hard beneath the smooth blue silk. She chastised herself as she remembered with a wave of heat how those muscular arms had locked her tightly against his hard chest.

Justin led her to a carved chair with an embroidered cushion of gold-and-black brocade, and she sank gracefully upon it, careful to hide her slender ankles in the voluminous black silk skirt. Their slim proportions did not match the heftiness at the waist, and she had no doubt that the Englishman would note the discrepancy, for she was quite sure that he had much experience beneath a woman's skirts.

She watched him move to the fireplace and clasp big brown hands tightly behind his back. He stared down at the smoldering rods of turf, his profile as straight and finely chiseled as the marble busts of Greek gods lining the Devlin gallery. Against her will her gaze dropped to the compressed lines of his lips that had moved over her flesh like a red-hot iron. She was not unaffected by the notion, and she shivered as he turned abruptly, subjecting her to a steady silver scrutiny that gave no hint of his thoughts.

"I offer you my sincere apology for my insensitive behavior." His words were low but clearly stated. "It was inexcusable. Undoubtedly the ale I consumed was the cause; that and the fact that"—he faltered momentarily, thinking again of an exquisitely beautiful face—"strange dreams of magic and witchcraft plagued my sleep."

Jillian wanted to laugh but debated instead whether or not to dissolve into hysterical tears. His next words, uttered matter-of-factly, negated the idea.

"But it is hardly a tragedy that I came to you as a husband, for the consummation of our vows was inevitable. I can only hope that I was not unfeeling toward your"—a slight embarrassed hesitation punctuated his speech— "innocent state."

So the besotted cad did not remember a thing, Jillian thought, gloating with inner elation. Well, she would let him flounder about in his own guilt, let him wonder what he'd done in his drunken stupor, and it would be good enough for him! She did not answer, only bowed her head. His dark brows slanted together, and wicked delight bubbled irresistibly inside her.

"I would know if I hurt you, Jillian."

His words were stern and brooked no refusal, and although his tone told Jillian that he was accustomed to absolute authority and obedience, she refused to be intimidated. She allowed the silence to stretch out interminably before she answered.

"Aye, you hurt me, but 'twas not more than I could bear." Her voice trembled pitiably, and she delighted at her ability to bait him under the guise of innocence.

Justin stared at her, overwhelmed with regret and compassion. After all, Jillian Devlin was but a sweet, innocent child.

"That is the way it is the first time, Jillian," he told her gently. "But it will be easier for you when next we lie together."

For the first time alarm filled Jillian's eyes, and she jerked her face toward him. Justin could not miss the tensing of her narrow shoulders, and her fear annoyed him, but he knew it was the expected response under the circumstances.

"Do not fear me, Jillian. It will be as I said to you at the banquet. I will gladly give us time to know one another before I come to you again. You must forget last night so that we can start our marriage anew."

His arrogance infuriated Jillian, as if she would be willing to forget his abominable behavior if he had truly used her in the way he thought he had. Anger flickered alive, and it took a good amount of restraint to control her voice.

"I do not think I will ever forget last night," she whispered, triumphant as his bronzed jaw grew hard.

Justin inclined his head in a stiff adieu and left the room with long, angry strides. Jillian leaned back and smiled, more than gratified, for she did not think he would enter her bedchamber again, and that was all she wanted from Justin Spenser, the mighty Earl of Wellingford.

# EIGHT

The fragrance of summer roses wafted in the air, and Jillian breathed in the sweetness with appreciation. She sat alone on a stone bench, half-hidden in the shade of a small arbor whose arched walls hung with glossy green leaves and white roses. The rose garden was her favorite hideaway with its tall red-brick walls and winding walkways. In the fortnight since the English lord had been at Devlin Manor, it had afforded her a peaceful solitude she could not find elsewhere.

She frowned as she thought of the Englishmen, lifting her veil slightly outward so that the cool breeze could reach her face. To her surprise the Spensers had not treated the Devlin household with the haughty superiority she'd expected but with the utmost kindness and respect. When she allowed herself to admit it, she rather liked Ryan Spenser. He often made an attempt to converse with her, and although she said little at such times, she listened attentively to his stories of his sister and other brother in England.

She lifted a rose from the basket in her lap, staring at its fragile petals. Unlike his brother, Justin Spenser rarely spoke to her at all. Since the morning he'd apologized to her, he'd spent most of his days riding with his men to inspect the vast Devlin holdings.

Her fine brow creased again, angry that he now claimed them. Only at night, after their evening repast, would he join Mauve and her in the drawing room, and only then could Jillian observe him at length while he worked at her father's desk. Her interest was well hidden by her veil, but despite her dislike of him, she had to admit that he was a very attractive man, tall and strong and handsome. He had not come near her or acted as if he wanted to; instead he seemed preoccupied with matters of the estates and the Devlin enterprises in Belfast. His disinterest heartened her, and his habitual absences throughout the day had given her the confidence to leave off the stifling herbal mask until she dressed for the evening meal.

She did not wear it now, and she longed to snatch off the scarf she wore as well and lift her bare face to the warm summer sun. She did not dare, for Mauve already had scolded her soundly for leaving off the dreadful disguise, even if it was only in the Englishman's absence.

Masculine voices drifted to her from the carriage road on the other side of the wall, and Jillian frowned, recognizing Ryan Spenser's voice.

"I have seen her enter here, Justin. Perhaps she wiles away her time in the rose garden. I will check the walks through the hedge maze."

Jillian grimaced as Justin's lean frame entered the gate at the far end of the garden. His great height made it necessary for him to stoop to enter the archway, and his presence set her nerves jangling. Her disquiet increased as his silvery eyes found her place in the shade.

"Good day, milord," she murmured, watching warily as he stopped in front of her, leaning one shoulder against the stone arbor. He was dressed casually in riding clothes, his thighs molded by fawn breeches above dark brown boots. His white linen shirt was untied at the throat, giving Jillian a glimpse of black chest hair, and she quickly averted her gaze.

Justin looked down at her, then away, wishing she'd quit wearing black mourning clothes all the time. Her father had been dead for three years, and so had her brother. She looked like a bloody crow flitting around the hallways of the manor, her black cat on her heels.

"It is a nice day for a ride," he said, smiling into the opaque shroud of her veil. "I would be pleased if you joined me."

"I thank you, milord, but I do not think so."

She had refused his every overture or attempt to be civil since he arrived in Ulster, and Justin suddenly grew tired of her reticence. "I insist."

His words amounted to little other than a command, and Jillian's teeth came together.

"Very well," she said stiffly, rising, "but I beg leave to change into my riding habit."

"We have no time for that. Our ride will be short; your mare is saddled and ready. Come, Ryan awaits us."

Jillian barely reached his shoulder as he led her from the garden, and they found perhaps a score of the Spenser retainers at the side portico. Jillian held her breath as Justin's strong, brown fingers closed around her thick waist, lifting her effortlessly to her sidesaddle. Her pulse reacted as he boldly positioned her knee into place, smiling briefly up at her. She placed unsteady hands upon her reins as he stepped to his white Arabian stallion and swung easily into his saddle.

Jillian took her place between Ryan and Justin at the head of the column, and the retinue fell in behind them in pairs. Her composure was dangerously frayed as they walked their horses down the entrance road. The cool wind that flapped gently against Jillian's veil gave her more cause for apprehension, but the day was clear and bright, and despite her vulnerability without the mask, it felt wonderful again to be atop her small chestnut mare, Jewel. Her brother Brian had taught her to ride at a very early age, and it had been many a week since she had ridden across the green hills and wooded valleys of her lands. She began to enjoy herself, keeping a firm hold on her scarf as Ryan asked her questions about the villages they passed. She answered him dutifully but in low tones, knowing that Justin listened carefully to each word she spoke, though he contributed little to the conversation.

Justin rode in silence, trying to control his increasing impatience with the Devlin girl. She was too meek to suit his taste, trembling like a leaf if he even looked at her. He wished she would show some spirit, even if it were anger. He glanced at her, his gaze going to her waistline. It seemed even thicker and more unappealing in the dreary black linen dress, although she had not felt unduly heavy when he'd lifted her into her saddle. He turned his regard to the road ahead, wondering if his seed had found fertile ground on their unhappy wedding night. Even if it had, her plump figure would hide it in the months to come, and he certainly could not ask her.

His sigh was heavy enough to gain Jillian's attention, but he didn't care, his thoughts wandering over skin as soft as velvet and hair as black as midnight. His vivid dreams had continued each night, and he scowled darkly, a prisoner of his own obsession. They neared the Enchanted Pool where the maiden had drowned, and hoping that another sight of it might rid him of her, he reined his mount to enter the thicket that led to the spring.

Ryan and Jillian followed. Slanted shafts of smoky sunlight penetrated the dense forest tangled above, forcing them to proceed single file to the edge of the pool.

"We will stop here for a time," Justin said, swinging off his horse and striding away, leaving Ryan to help Jillian dismount. She placed her palms on Ryan's shoulders as he lifted her to the ground, then sat upon the mantle he spread upon the grass.

The men had dismounted as well, and Ryan took a place beside Jillian, both watching as Justin walked a good distance down the side of the spring. He stopped where a tree bent close upon the water. He leaned one elbow against a large branch, staring impassively toward the boulder near the center of the pool.

Jillian watched him, wondering if he thought of the day he had caught her there. She hoped that he did, for she was certainly plagued by the memory. Even now, her face grew very warm just thinking about it. She was glad when Ryan spoke.

"Are the peasants truly afraid of this place as Mauve once told us?"

"Aye, they believe it haunted by spirits."

"But there are no such things," Ryan returned with a smile.

"Spirits inhabit all things around us. Trees, water, stones, all have spirits just as people do."

Ryan frowned at his own insensitivity as she lowered her head, remembering that they sat in the very place where her mother had perished.

"Forgive me, Jillian, I had forgotten that

this place harbors painful memories for you. Justin should not have brought you here."

Jillian darted a look at him, thinking he somehow knew her secret, but his amber-brown eyes were dark with compassion, and it was only then that she remembered Mauve's fabricated tale of her mother's drowning. For the first time a slight twinge of guilt pricked her conscience. The web of lies she had woven around the Englishmen grew more intricate every day, but she had no choice. Her brothers meant everything to her. They were all she had, and she must protect their inheritance as long as she could. She looked out over the calm blue water without answering, and while she watched, Justin suddenly threw down a stick and came back toward them, his footsteps long and agitated. There was no trace of anger in his voice, however, when he stopped before them.

"We have yet to explore the far woods," he said to her, pointing to the trees on the other side of the spring. "Do my lands end near here?"

His casual, proprietary tone sent Jillian's body rigid with resentment. "The *Devlin* lands extend to the edge of yonder copse. The trail across the way leads to a creek that marks our boundary with Sean Flanagan."

Surprised, Justin looked down at her. Her bitter tone was at direct odds with the subservient mien she usually presented, and he found himself perversely pleased at the spark of spirit she had shown. He grinned at her.

"Then come, you can show it to me."

Justin reached down and caught her hand before she could protest, then lifted her into her saddle without asking her permission. He spoke to Ryan as he mounted Caesar. "We will ride ahead. Mount the men and follow us."

He guided his stallion down a footpath choked with heavy undergrowth that ran along the side of the pool, and Jillian carefully maneuvered Jewel around the low-hanging branches and tall bushes that plagued their way. She drew back sharply on her reins as she moved past a thornbush, halting the mare as her scarf became hung upon a sticker. Her horse neighed and moved sideways, causing Justin to turn, but Jillian held her reins firmly, trying desperately to disentangle the veil.

If the woman would take off the damned thing, Justin thought irritably, such things wouldn't happen. His patience was wearing dangerously thin, especially with his plans to return to England in the next few weeks. It rankled him to have to leave without having seen his wife's face. Probably years from now, after many sons and daughters had been born to them, she would still cover her face and hide from her own husband.

"Please allow me," he said as Jillian continued to try to loosen the scarf from the long barbs.

Jillian held her breath, still clutching the edge of her veil as Justin urged his horse next to hers. His proximity affected her heart as she picked up his pleasant, manly scent of horses and leather. If he could not get the veil loose, if it should fall free and he saw her face . . .

She let out her breath as he succeeded in his task and looked at her.

"There, Jillian, you are free again. If you will tuck it in your neckline, perhaps it will not be quite so worrisome."

Jillian caught the hint of impatience in his voice, and she hastily took his suggestion.

They rode on, Jillian making a mental vow that if she made it safely through this day without her mask, she would heed Mauve's warnings and never take it off again. They stepped their horses around a vine-draped log, then Justin held Caesar back as Jillian turned her mare and preceded him through a field of high grass that led to the creek bed.

Once there, Jillian carefully guided her horse down a gentle slope where the water was shallow, rippling over moss-covered rocks, interspersed with rocky patches that were completely dry. She allowed Jewel to drink, and Justin drew up beside her, admiring the beauty of the place. He glanced at his veiled wife, who had not spoken a word since they'd left the others.

Jillian watched him warily from beneath the veil. She was very uncomfortable alone with him. Not since the wedding night had they been alone, and a sensual shiver rippled down her back at the memory of their embrace upon her bed. She frowned as he dismounted and looked up at her.

"Why don't we sit here a time while we await Ryan and the men? This is a lovely place."

Jillian grimaced as he lifted her down, quickly moving away from him as he set her on her feet. A fallen tree lay nearby in a deep, cool shade, and Jillian perched there nervously as Justin tied their horses to a branch. To her dismay he walked straight to where she sat and leaned back indolently on the tree trunk beside her.

He glanced at her, noting her tightly clasped hands. He smiled slightly.

"Are you afraid of me, Jillian? Is that why you never converse with me as you do with Ryan?"

His blunt question caught Jillian off guard, and she shook her head, looking longingly for Ryan in the direction from which they had come. She did not want to talk to Justin Spenser. He was much too near, and they were much too isolated. She inched away from him, her eyes on the rippling current. He wiped sweat from his brow with the back of his hand in frustration, unsure of how to handle the situation with Jillian Devlin. But the fact remained that she was his wife and would remain his wife forever. Furthermore, it did not help his guilty conscience to know that her reticence toward him had more to do with his treatment of her on their wedding night than it did with her blemished appearance.

He looked at her, trying to see through the blasted veil. It was a hot day, and the scarf must be stifling. It was a shame for such a young girl to hide from the world in such a way, but he well knew that her self-consciousness was justified; just his brief glimpses of her ravaged face had shown him that much. But if she were ever to lead a normal life, she would have to eventually accept her fate, and perhaps he could help her to understand that.

Jillian gasped aloud as he reached out, his fingers grasping the edge of her scarf.

"It is warm today, Jillian. Will you not remove your veil for a time here in the shade? We are alone, and I have seen your face before, have I not?"

One slight tug and her deceit would be discovered; never had Jillian felt such fear. Her heart felt paralyzed, and fright quivered in her voice.

"Please, milord, please do not take it from me! I cannot bear for you to look upon me in the full light of day!"

She trembled all over with a most genuine fear, and her distress stayed Justin's hand. He was truly appalled at her reaction to his request, and he took both her hands between his. His eyes were earnest.

"Do you think me so cruel that I would take it from you against your wishes? You need never fear me, Jillian. You are my wife, and I only wish to be your friend. I will never take your veil from you, I promise you that, not until you feel ready to remove it."

Jillian stared into his handsome face, wondering if he could really be so kind. His silvery eyes were sincere, and she found that she wanted to believe him. She wet dry lips, trying to formulate an answer, but before she could speak, the splashing of horses in the creek sent Justin to his feet. Jillian whirled around, stifling a cry at the sight that met her eyes.

A small band of men approached them, the scarlet-and-green banners of the Flanagan clan fluttering in the wind. Jillian's eyes locked with dread upon the man who led them. He was large and brawny with shoulder-length hair, its coarse red color streaked liberally with gray, but Jillian stared in horror at the thick white scar that split his cheek. Sean Flanagan!

A freezing fear slid over her, and her eyes flickered to the other Flanagan men. She recognized Patrick Flanagan behind his father, although she had not seen her childhood friend for nearly five years. He had grown into a tall and handsome man with a closely trimmed red beard.

"Who trespasses on Flanagan lands?" Sean Flanagan bellowed, drawing his sword, and Jillian gasped as Justin's fingers closed over her shoulder and thrust her behind him. He drew his sword with a scrape of metal, and it winked ominously in the sun as he turned hostile eyes on Sean Flanagan.

"I am Justin Spenser, Earl of Wellingford, and the Devlin lands are now mine, granted by King William of England. If anyone trespasses here, it is the Flanagans."

"I have heard an Englishman rules at Devlin Manor with a Devlin bride who hides her ugliness behind a veil," Sean returned, his dark eyes briefly settling on Jillian. She tensed at the hatred she could read in them.

"And you are welcome to Hugh Devlin's lands," he continued, his gaze hard on Justin's face. " 'Tis only Devlins with whom I feud. The daughter is the only Devlin left in Ulster. Hand her over to me, and the two of us can live peacefully as neighbors."

Jillian bridled with outrage, but before she could speak, Justin's deep voice rang out.

"Listen well, Sean Flanagan," he said, each word laced in steel. "The Devlin lands are now Spenser lands, and the Lady Jillian is a Spenser. Be warned, I hold and protect what is mine. Do not think to harm her."

"Do you think a lone swordsman frightens me?" Sean roared in fury, and at his signal, his men unsheathed their weapons.

"Run to your horse, Jillian," Justin said softly.

"But I cannot—"

"Now!" Justin gritted, and Jillian obeyed.

Before she reached it, a shot reverberated from upstream, and one of the Flanagans screamed and clutched his wounded shoulder as he fell from his horse.

Sean reined up, his eyes upstream where

Ryan now splashed through the shallows with the larger force of Spenser men. His look was ugly as he sought Justin again.

"You have chosen war, Englishman," Sean growled harshly, his black eyes glittering with hostility, "for I will not rest until every Devlin rots in his grave."

Justin held his place as Sean wheeled his horse, watching as the enemy clan retrieved their wounded comrade and splashed down the creek. After the last of them had disappeared from sight he slowly sheathed his sword. He turned serious eyes on Jillian. He could see that she was still frightened, and he walked over to her and drew her against his chest. She did not pull away. His whispered words were reassuring. "Do not be afraid of him, Jillian. You are my wife, and I will protect you."

She leaned weakly against him, and for the briefest of moments, she almost believed that he really might care about her. His presence and his words somehow gave her comfort.

# NINE

Jillian leaned close to her mirror, putting the finishing touches on her face. Since Mauve had left earlier in the day for the village of Lybowdin, she had the task of fashioning the mask herself. She scooped up a fingerful of the grotesque substance and smoothed it over the bridge of her nose, rather pleased with her first attempt. It looked nearly as ugly as it did when Mauve applied it, and she smiled, feeling very powerful over her success at duping her English husband. She had just learned from a traveling poet that King James had joined a French invasion force at La Hogue just that past April, which meant it might not be long before Brian returned home to claim his lands. She would be rid of the mask for good then—and Justin Spenser.

Her face sobered momentarily as she remembered his kindness about the veil, and the courage he had shown by confronting the Flanagans the week before. He was a very brave man, she could not deny that, but nevertheless, he deserved what she was doing to him. She frowned. Did he not consider her just another piece of Devlin chattel, like the cattle or her father's ships? Did he not try to seduce her at the spring and had he not come to the marriage bed in a drunken stupor? Even so, she could not help but wonder about him, and more than once she'd been troubled by dreams of warm, silvery eyes and strong arms that held her captive. She sighed, and for the first time, she let herself wonder what might have happened if things had been different between them. If perhaps he'd been an Irishman who had come to visit her brother Brian and found her company pleasant. She smiled dreamily over these impossible imaginings for a time, her chin braced in her palms, then released another heavy sigh.

She looked with distaste at the black silk dress that Bridgit had hung on the armoire for her to wear for the evening meal. She was tired of wearing the ugly black gowns, and she was sick to death of the uncomfortable mask and hot veil. If there were another way to protect Brian's interests, she would surely use it, but until then, she would have to put up with the discomfort.

She dressed quickly, stopping before the mirror to arrange the silken veil, then made her way slowly downstairs to the dining room. Both men stood immediately when she entered, and Justin came forward to meet her. She had grown much more comfortable with him since their confrontation with Sean Flanagan, and her heart skipped a beat as he took her hand and led her to her chair. He was dressed formally in a dark green coat and tan breeches, and she chastised herself for the pleasure she felt when he smiled warmly into her veiled face.

"Mauve begs you to excuse her this night, milord. She has gone to help in the confinement of her cousin's niece."

"Then Mauve is also a midwife?" Justin asked as Ryan sat across from Jillian.

"She is well versed in that as well as many other healing arts. As am I."

"With the threat of the Flanagans it was most unwise for her to travel alone. I trust she had a proper escort."

"Only Donal goes with her on such errands."

"It would have been an easy task to send a pair of my men along with them," Justin offered, and Jillian was surprised that he seemed so concerned for Mauve's safety.

"Donal is enough."

"Donal is a sturdy lad, I agree, but I caution you against similar such travels. Sean Flanagan's threat against you was not an idle one."

The horribly scarred visage of her red-bearded enemy caused a shiver to rise on Jillian's arms, and her reaction was well noted by Justin. He put one hand over hers where it lay on the carved arm of her chair.

"You must not fear him, Jillian, for I intend to keep you safely with me."

His fingers tightened over hers, and Jillian's shaky reaction had little to do with her fear of the Flanagans. She was distinctly glad when George moved between them to serve succulent roasted mutton from a silver tray, and Justin was forced to remove his hand.

"Perhaps your expertise with medicines is why many of the peasants believe you and Mauve to be witches," Ryan commented, and Jillian saw Justin give a warning frown to his brother. Her lips curved wickedly as she remembered Justin Spenser's doubts concerning witchcraft on their wedding night.

"Perhaps you are right, but many of the peasants think I am a sorceress because they have seen me work magic."

Ryan grinned, and Justin frowned as he lifted his glass, the delicate crystal goblet looking lost in his large tanned hand.

"Such talk is dangerous, Jillian. There are some less educated men who still believe in witchcraft and black magic. Not long ago women were hanged in England for spouting such nonsense."

"But it wasn't witchcraft I mentioned, milord," Jillian protested sweetly. "It is sorcery I am talking about, and that is not the same."

"How is it different?" Ryan asked, leaning forward, truly fascinated with the subject.

"Sorcery is the knowledge of potions and is magical indeed," Jillian told him, aware that Justin's smile was one of tolerant amusement. "The sorceress uses her skills for her own benefit, but witches serve Satan and are evil with their spells. My faith lies solely with God in heaven, and my powers I use to serve good."

Justin shook his head, muttering something unintelligible under his breath as Ryan persisted.

"A peasant once told us that you could turn yourself into a cat. Can you truly do such things with your sorcery?"

"I have the ability to do many things," Jillian answered, thoroughly enjoying herself, "but I dare not tell you my secrets, for I may have use for them one day."

"If you indeed possess such magical powers," Justin suddenly interjected, emphasizing the last with obvious skepticism, "perhaps you will allow us to observe such a miraculous transformation when next you attempt one."

His words were more than a little mocking, and Jillian turned her eyes to him.

"Aye, milord, perhaps I will assume the shape of my cat, Ebony, just for your amusement."

Ryan laughed, but Justin had heard enough of the nonsensical conversation, and he pushed back his chair.

"Come, I believe we are finished here. Let us go to the drawing room."

He took Jillian's arm, and Ryan followed them across the marbled foyer, then took a place near Jillian once she had settled upon a small velvet settee near the hearth. Justin stood with his back to the fire.

"Tell me, Jillian," Ryan asked a moment later. "What pastimes do Ulster men embrace to while away long June evenings? At home in Kent we often use playing cards or listen to my sister, Catherine, as she plays the harpsichord."

"We share much the same pleasures, it would seem," Jillian answered softly, "except it is yonder lap harp and fiddle we enjoy." She raised one small gloved hand in a gesture toward a finely crafted walnut cabinet that sat before a beautiful gold tapestry.

Ryan followed her direction as Jillian looked back into her lap. Her next words were so sorrowful that Justin's brows dented into a frown.

"It has been many a month since such happy sounds were heard in this house."

Ryan exchanged a look with Justin, then stood.

"Then you must play for us now," he said, walking to the case where several instruments were encased. Jillian watched as he pulled open the glass doors.

"Do you play the fiddle or the harp, Jillian?" he asked.

"I am versed in both," she replied, and he took them from their places.

"And what is this?" he inquired, touching a large, drumlike instrument.

"That is the bodhraun that my brother Pierce used to play. My older brother, Brian, played the uellean, which you English call elbow pipes."

"I am no piper," Ryan said, smiling as he lifted down the bodhraun. "But I dare say I can beat on a drum. We will play a tune together. A lively one that will chase the gloom from this room."

He grinned engagingly as he moved back to her, and Jillian had to smile at his attempts to charm her. She took the harp from him, running slender fingers lovingly over the smooth wood intricately carved with shamrocks inlaid with gold. Her father had loved to hear her play, for it had reminded him of her mother, who had also been accomplished upon the harp. Sadness touched her heart as she brushed supple fingers down the strings.

Justin stared openly at his wife as low and haunting music filled the quiet room, and Ryan eagerly pulled a footstool close against her wide skirts. Jillian bent forward to show him how to hold the drum, and Justin watched them, glad that she seemed to get on well with his brother. In truth Ryan was much closer to her age than he, and Justin's own drunken actions had robbed him of her trust. He was somewhat heartened however, since Jillian seemed more friendly and open toward him lately. Perhaps someday she would forgive his unfortunate behavior on their wedding night and they could enjoy some kind of marriage.

Jillian laid the harp aside and took the small fiddle to her chin. A lively tune followed, and Ryan joined in with the bodhraun, but after a time both players dissolved into laughter because Ryan's drum playing was most decidedly off beat. Justin grinned himself when he heard Jillian's soft laughter, and he stared at her darkly veiled figure as Ryan again urged the harp upon her. He was suddenly curious as to what sort of girl she had been before the ravaging illness had forced her to hide herself from the world.

"Now the harp, if you please," Ryan was insisting, "and sing for us, for I know your voice will be as sweet as the angels'."

Jillian took it, glancing at Justin. He was smiling at her in a most pleasant way, his silvery eyes quite warm, and she quickly looked back to Ryan.

"I will play a tune for your pleasure, a Gaelic ballad of olden days that tells the legend of Cuchulainn and the Cooley Cattle Raid."

Her fingers rippled fluidly across the strings for a moment before she began. Justin listened in awe to a voice that caressed his mind like the softest velvet. His heart tightened with pity for her, a child so ugly she must hide her face, but whose song could mesmerize and hold the listener spellbound. Her hauntingly beautiful song filled the room, and almost against his will, his eyes strayed to the portrait upon the far wall. He stared at lovely turquoise eyes, so like the girl's at the pool, and his heart twisted with regret. She still invaded his thoughts, no matter how hard he tried to put her from him.

When the last note dwindled into silence, Jillian hazarded a sidelong look at Justin to find him staring at her mother's portrait. She smiled slightly, somehow pleased.

"That was truly lovely, milady," Ryan said with genuine admiration. "But I fear I must leave you now, since I sail for Belfast on the morrow."

"You are leaving Devlin Manor?" Jillian asked in surprise, then looked at Justin, wondering if both Englishmen were going.

"I am sending him to look into the Devlin enterprises there," Justin explained. "I had planned to go as well, but after meeting the Flanagans, I do not think it wise to leave you here unprotected."

Jillian looked back to Ryan as he lifted her hand with the utmost chivalry.

"I bid you good-bye then, milady, for I ride for Lough Swilly before the sun rises."

"Good night. I wish you a safe voyage."

He bowed and left, closing the doors quietly behind him, and Jillian laid her harp aside.

"I beg your leave to retire as well, milord," she said, still uneasy whenever she was alone with her husband.

"Please do me the honor of staying a bit longer, Jillian," Justin said, then smiled. "And I think that it would now be acceptable for you to call me Justin."

"As you wish," she murmured, settling back gracefully on the settee.

They lapsed into silence for a time, Jillian watching as Justin moved restlessly around the room before he stopped in front of the portrait of Maire Devlin.

She wondered at his thoughts, glancing away from him to watch her black cat appear from beneath the draperies, then pad silently behind Justin to leap atop a chair in a shadowy corner.

"Do you truly believe in magic and spirits?" Justin asked suddenly, and Jillian jerked her eyes back to him.

"Aye, milord, I do."

Justin shook his head. "I do not mean to insult you, Jillian, but such heathen beliefs are ridiculous. I must insist that you avoid such talk in the future."

Jillian looked at his broad back as he turned to the picture, and his superior attitude suddenly made her furious. Heathen beliefs, is it? she thought angrily. He probably considered everything about Ulster heathen! How dare he tell her what to believe in! What did he know of such things! Perhaps the insufferable buffoon should be taught a lesson in magic, she decided with clamped teeth. She moved to a small chest of drawers beside the fire where Mauve kept many of her powders. She slid open a drawer and gathered a pinch of yellow powder.

"Perhaps if you saw my power over fire, you would not be a disbeliever," she said softly, and Justin turned in surprise.

He smiled. "I think that would be most interesting to witness."

Jillian turned to the fire, then stared into the flames for a moment before raising her arms. Justin was startled as her voice came eerily in a low-pitched chant.

"Fire, obey me and dance with anger," she

cried, sending the powder onto the low blaze with a flick of her fingers. The fire immediately leapt as if in answer to her words, yellow smoke billowing up the chimney. Jillian turned, eager to see Justin's reaction. To her shock he laughed out loud.

"Good God, girl, no wonder the peasants fear you. That is quite an effect."

Jillian's mouth fell open in astonishment at his lack of fear, for never had her flaming powders worked better. When she remained speechless, Justin shook his head.

"Have you forgotten, Jillian, that I have been all over the world in my travels? I have seen such powders on the streets of Cathay and in the temples of Arabia. They are used in those countries for street celebrations, and their properties are well known by even the peasants."

He smiled again, and Jillian was very glad for her veil and mask, for her face burned with humiliation.

Justin chuckled as he moved to the cabinet where the wine was kept.

"Really, Jillian, I must insist that you stop this playacting of yours, for it could possibly have dangerous consequences if seen or heard by the more superstitious."

Jillian's fists tightened until her nails drove into her palms, and she looked around furiously, her eyes alighting on Ebony curled up on the obscured chair. An idea born of revenge for his ridicule occurred to her. Justin's back was still turned, and she smiled wickedly, keeping her eyes on him as she put Ebony on her chair. Still watching Justin, she ducked silently into the secret passage behind a tapestry, and after the door had slid into place behind her, she put her eye to the peephole. She waited, a smug smile on her face.

Justin was still amused at Jillian's attempt to trick him. The girl was obviously much more spirited than he had thought, and that was good. He poured a second goblet of wine, then replaced the top of the crystal decanter before he turned. His amused expression dropped like a weighted stone.

The black cat, sitting on the chair where Jillian should have been, did not move but returned his openmouthed stare, its turquoise eyes glittering in the candlelight. Hairs rose on the nape of Justin's neck, and he stood frozen as Jillian's low, mocking laugh broke into the silence of the room.

She watched his astonishment with a great deal of glee behind the safety of the wall, but her heart stopped as he looked first at the closed door beside him, then began a slow and thorough search of the room. She tensed with dread as he began to knock upon the walls, obviously suspecting a secret panel, then went limp with relief when he passed over the wooden rosette that triggered the hidden door. She did not breathe fully until he gave up his search and, after one long, frowning look at the cat, left the room without a word.

Jillian hurried up the hidden staircase to

her bedchamber, smiling in triumph as she bolted her door. Perhaps now the sneering Englishman would take her magic a bit more seriously, she thought, then laughed at the memory of his stunned expression.

# TEN

In the days that followed, Jillian was surprised when Justin Spenser refrained from mentioning her trick with her cat. He treated her with polite respect as if nothing had happened, but to her endless amusement, she had often caught his wary eyes on both her and Ebony. With Ryan and Mauve gone they had gradually settled into a daily routine in which Jillian saw little of her English husband. Sean Flanagan had begun raids upon the Devlin villages, burning the crofters' huts and stealing their cattle, and Justin had spent most of his time leading armed patrols in an attempt to capture them in their cowardly acts.

More often than not he would return in time to join Jillian for the evening meal, and she had found him to be a complex man of varying moods. Sometimes he was most agreeable, relating entertaining stories of his sea voyages to the Far East or the Americas, but on other evenings he would remain withdrawn throughout the meal and their time afterward, staring introspectively into the fire while she stitched upon her sampler. But there were some nights when she would lift her eyes to find his silvery gaze upon her veiled face with the most unsettling look, and her pulse would race as she remembered the heat of his mouth upon her naked shoulder. Afraid that he harbored the intention of sharing her bed, she would hurriedly excuse herself on those occasions, but true to his word, Justin Spenser had not touched her.

She would lie safely in her bed, wondering perversely if he had found a willing servant girl with whom to vent the passionate nature that she knew him to possess. Thoughts of her dark and handsome English husband in bed with another did not give her pleasure, nor peace, and her own contradictory feelings about him began to show in the shadowy, violet smudges beneath her eyes.

During the days when Justin rode with his men, however, Jillian dwelled not so often on his amorous pastimes, for it was his masculine presence that disconcerted her. She worked diligently with her herb garden while he was gone, drying plants and crushing various flowers and roots into medicinal powders. She longed for Mauve's return, for her cousin had been gone a long time, and she missed her. She did not worry overmuch because Mauve's visits to Lybowdin were often lengthy. Her loneliness grew as the weeks passed into July, and it was to this that she attributed her growing eagerness each night for her husband's return.

It was no different one cool night as she entered the dining room where Justin was wont to await her. The empty room brought a slight frown to her brow. Justin had left with Philip Hammond and a contingent of soldiers before the sun had risen, having received word that the Flanagans intended to raid the village of Brendaghen. She had not heard their return, and when George entered to serve the meal, Jillian turned to him as he laid a silver tray on the sideboard.

"Has the English patrol returned to the manor?"

"Nay, milady," George answered, and Jillian remained quiet as he served her, contemplating the reason for Justin's tardiness. If they had clashed with the Flanagans, he could be wounded, or even dead, she realized, a sick feeling congealing in the pit of her stomach. The thought of his death no longer gave her the pleasure it once had, and she stared at the steaming bowl of stew before her. She laid down her spoon, unable to eat as Sean Flanagan's hideous face rose in her mind. He had vowed to kill her, and it could very well be he who next walked into the door.

She swallowed hard, knowing that the scarred enemy of her family would make no honorable promises to her as Justin Spenser had done. Fear shook her, and she dropped her linen napkin upon the table and hurried to the windows to peer anxiously into the darkness.

She began to prowl the floor restlessly as

the hours stretched out interminably with no sign of returning horsemen. When the candles burned low, she retired to her bedchamber, allowing Bridgit to help her into a soft blue nightdress. She sat in dread, her heart a hard lump of ice, as Bridgit brushed her heavy hair until it shone with ebony glints.

After the yawning chambermaid had left her, Jillian moved fitfully around the room, feeling very alone and vulnerable when she finally stopped at the window. A dark face loomed in the panes before her, its handsome features streaked with blood, and the pain that wrenched her heart was so intense that she was appalled, wondering with terrible foreboding if she could be growing to care for the tall Englishman who had forced his way into her life.

She stared dully into the dark fields for a long time, confused by her own feelings, until a faraway twinkling caught her eye. Hope blossomed as it moved nearer, and she leaned close against the cold glass. When she was finally able to discern the English retinue with Justin's white stallion in the lead, she hurriedly pulled on her heavy velvet robe and carefully arranged her veil before entering the secret passage and flying down the stairs to the drawing room. The deep tones of Justin's voice sounded, and as Philip Hammond answered him, Jillian put her eye to the peephole.

Both men stood near the door, soot and dirt streaking their clothes and faces. While Jillian watched, Philip helped Justin shrug out of his black leather vest, but it wasn't until he turned that Jillian saw the blackened burn across his chest. She sucked in a horrified breath, watching as he tugged off his gloves, his voice sounding very tired as he directed, "See to the others now, Philip. I will be all right."

The gray-haired sergeant hesitated, looking again at the angry-looking wound, then obeyed, and Jillian turned and moved silently back through the narrow passage, her candle sending flickering shadows up the dark walls behind her.

Inside the drawing room, Justin closed the door after Philip, then removed his sword and eased carefully into a cushioned chair beside the windows. He was dead-tired. He had been in the saddle for most of the day, and despite all the efforts to stop them, the Flanagans had managed to burn Brendaghen to the ground. He touched his side gingerly and grimaced in pain. He had been unable to wheel Caesar from a flaming rafter, and the stallion's leg had been burned. It would heal, given the time, thank God, and he supposed his injury would as well.

A silver tray with a decanter of wine sat on the polished table beside him, and he poured a liberal amount into a silver-stemmed goblet. He tossed it down quickly and refilled it, then leaned back, his eyes going wearily around the room as he thought of the night that Jillian Devlin had so effortlessly become a cat. He still had not figured out exactly how she'd done it, although he felt sure there was a secret tunnel of some sort in the room. He had searched for it more than once without success, and he briefly considered the possibility that his Irish wife did have some strange powers. The concept was so alien to his pragmatic nature that he laughed without humor. The sound faded as his eyes fell upon the portrait of the blue-eyed woman. Sadness touched him, and he closed his eyes to block the image from his sight. He had not had a minute's rest since setting eyes on the maiden at the spring. Never before had a woman controlled his mind in such a way, and he sighed heavily, wishing he could cleanse her from his thoughts. He had killed her that day as surely as if he had driven a knife in her heart, yet she lived still, forever tiptoeing down the dusky corridors of his mind.

His eyes flew open a moment later as something landed on his lap. His hand went instinctively to the dagger at his thigh, and Justin chided his own nerves as he met the slanted eyes of Jillian's black cat. He relaxed, his hand upon Ebony's silky coat as the cat rubbed sensuously against his legs. Her contented purring was loud in the silence, and Justin grinned.

"This is proof enough that you are not Jillian, for she has not willingly touched me since our wedding night," he muttered dryly, closing his eyes again as Ebony curled in a soft ball upon his lap.

"I have brought medicines for your burn, milord."

Justin jumped a foot at the soft voice, and Jillian smiled beneath her veil as his eyes darted in confusion to the closed door, then back to her.

He watched warily as she moved forward carrying a tray piled with strips of clean linen and various bottles and bowls.

"How did you know of my injury?" he asked as she knelt before him.

"I have ways," she answered cryptically as she set her tray upon the floor.

"I am finding that out," Justin said with a wry smile.

"You will need to remove your shirt," Jillian murmured quietly, and Justin's face creased with pain as he moved to obey.

"Perhaps you would be good enough to assist me?" he grunted, and heat flooded Jillian's face as she carefully lifted the singed fabric of his shirt from the damaged flesh, then gently guided the loose sleeves over the bulging muscles of his arms. She was not unaffected by the wide expanse of lightly furred chest that emerged from the tattered shirt, and her fingers shook slightly as she examined the burn, finding it less severe than she had first thought. Even so, it would fester if not cleaned and dressed.

Justin sat still, eyes on his small, veiled wife. She was such an enigma to him, and he found as time had passed that he had developed a certain fondness for her. She was being most kind now and very gentle. She sat between his knees, and as she leaned toward him, her breasts brushed his thigh. He frowned, thinking that she somehow looked smaller than usual, and when she moved to sprinkle a brown substance into a cup, a sweet perfume wafted from her veil, bringing vague recollections he could not place.

"What is this brew you prepare?" he asked as she stirred the powder into a tea with hot water from the kettle she'd brought with her.

Jillian handed him the cup. " 'Tis only a tea of hops and chamomile flowers that will relax you. I will use it on the bandage as well to deaden the pain."

Justin took an exploratory sip, finding it not unpalatable, as Jillian pressed the linen strips into a substance of beeswax and mutton that lay warming above a bowl of hot water.

"Your doctoring is different from our English physicians'," Justin observed as he drank again, watching her carefully stir the cloth until it was coated with the greasy mixture. "They rely on the leech to work most of their cures."

"Bloodsuckers sap the strength and only weaken the patient," Jillian replied quickly, then added vehemently, "I hate the leech. The very thought of one upon my skin makes me shudder with horror."

A delicate shiver coursed over her as she

dipped out a palmful of the warm concoction and began to spread it gently over his tender flesh. It soothed the sting of the burn, and Justin was half surprised by the pleasure he felt as her soft palms moved slowly and caressingly over his naked chest.

She marveled at the hardness of the muscles beneath his smooth, sun-bronzed skin as she put on the last of the salve and wiped her hands on a linen towel.

"You must lean forward now so that I can apply the bandage," she said softly, looking away from his silvery eyes.

Justin did as he was bade, and Jillian pressed one end against the ridged muscles of his stomach, holding it in place as she guided it carefully around his torso. The breadth of his chest was amazing in a man so lean, and it took the full extent of her arms to grasp the strip at his back.

Each time she leaned close, her breasts pressed against his chest, and by the time she knotted the last strip into place, her breath was ragged. She swallowed hard, hating her reaction to his body.

Justin looked at her curiously as she quickly gathered her medicines onto the tray, intending to escape. He stood and moved to the fire, his face serious as he ran careful fingers over his bandage; he was surprised to find his injury no longer painful.

"Please sit down for a moment, Jillian. There is a matter of some importance that I must discuss with you."

Jillian sat, fearful that he was about to demand his rights as a husband. The thought brought all kinds of contradictory responses from her, and she bit her lip with anxiety.

"I am afraid for your safety here in Ulster," Justin said, turning to face her, and Jillian could not help but let out a long breath of relief. "The Flanagan clan is stronger than we are at present," he went on, "and I feel certain that they will eventually attack the manor." He paused. "So when Ryan returns from Belfast, I intend to send him to England for reinforcements. I think it would be best if you go with him."

Jillian was so stunned for the first few moments that she could not move. It was the last thing she had expected him to say, and the idea was too horrible to even consider.

"My sister Catherine is there," Justin continued, "and I'm sure you would get on well with her, since she is about your age. My brother Aaron is there as well, and I would feel much better if I didn't have to worry about your safety."

With that Jillian found her tongue. "I will not go."

Justin jerked his head up at her flat refusal.

"I am sorry, Jillian, but I have already made up my mind on the matter."

"I will *never* go to England for any reason," she said firmly, and Justin frowned.

"I think, madame, that you forget to whom

you speak. I am your husband, and you will go to England if I decide it is best for you."

Jillian's teeth came together with fury, but she turned from Justin as the door opened behind them. She jumped to her feet at the sight of Donal in the doorway, his face bewhiskered and gray with fatigue.

"Donal! What has happened? Where is Mauve?"

Justin followed Jillian, watching as Donal tiredly gestured answers to Jillian's frightened questions.

"What is it?" he asked in concern at Jillian's distress.

"Plague and fever have struck the countryside. Mauve is very ill."

Justin's consternation increased as she turned back to Donal. "Come, Donal, I will get my apron and medicines; then we can go to her."

She started out the door, but Justin reached out and stopped her with a hand on her arm.

"No," he said softly.

Jillian tried to pull away from his grip. "I must go to Mauve! She needs me!"

"Donal can take the medicines to her." Justin's voice was firm, and Jillian tried to reason with him. "Please, milord, Mauve is like a mother to me. I cannot let her die."

"And I am sorry, but I cannot allow my wife to expose herself to the plague."

Donal gestured animatedly for several seconds, and when he finished, Jillian looked at Justin.

"They have barricaded the streets around the church to isolate the sickness. Donal escaped only because he subdued a guard."

"Then I will send my men with him, and he can bring Mauve home."

His face was set in inflexible lines, and Jillian clenched her fists in frustration, knowing that he would not change his mind.

"Then I beg your leave to take Donal to Mauve's room and show him what medicines he must have for her."

"Do you think I do not know that you intend to leave with Donal the moment my back is turned?" Justin asked gently. "I will come with you."

Jillian hid her dismay at his insight into her very thoughts, and she sought a way to change his mind as she led the way up the stairs. Justin followed his wife and Donal, genuinely sorry about Mauve, but nevertheless, Jillian Devlin was his wife, and her well-being was his primary concern.

One corner of Mauve's room had been made into a workplace where herbs and medicinal supplies were kept, and clumps of drying plants and flowers hung on wooden racks behind a long table. Small jars and bottles filled with various liquids and powders lined the top, and Justin watched Jillian take a jar with a peculiar green, ground mold and hand it to Donal.

"You must boil this into a broth, but it must be strained and fed to her morning and night. But be sparing with it, for too much will be fatal."

She took a handful of long sulfur candles from a drawer.

"Use these to fumigate the air, and she must be bathed constantly with cool water."

Donal's eyes widened somewhat as she lapsed into Gaelic for an instant.

"You must escape your English guards and meet me in the stables. Godspeed—"

"Speak in English, Jillian," Justin interrupted quietly, glancing at the big mute who stood without a hint of expression on his face.

"I wished him godspeed," Jillian said, already having decided how she would escape her husband's watchful eyes.

In the next hour Justin ordered six men to ready themselves for the journey while Donal rested and ate what he could. When he rode away in the midst of his escort, Jillian stood forlornly at her husband's side.

"Do not worry," Justin said consolingly. "Donal will bring Mauve home where she can be tended."

Jillian nodded but remained quiet as he led her back into the drawing room. Justin sat down beside her, his eyes concerned.

"I did not like refusing you tonight, Jillian, but it was a dangerous thing you considered. Do you bear me ill for it?"

"One must follow his heart in such matters," she answered quietly, "or one could surely not live with oneself." She paused and made her voice very pitiful. "I am very worried about my cousin, and I fear I shall lie awake all night if I do not take a glass of wine. Will you have one with me?"

Justin nodded, and Jillian moved to the tall cabinet across the room. Justin looked away as she poured the ruby-red liquid into two of the goblets, hoping she truly did not resent his refusal to let her go to Mauve. Both that and his insistence on her going to England for a visit were in her best interest. He did not see the white powder she had brought from Mauve's worktable, nor did he see her stir it into his glass.

Jillian handed him a goblet, then sat beside him, patiently waiting for him to finish his wine. The powder was very strong, and only minutes passed before he leaned his head back and closed his eyes, his glass still in his hand. She waited until his body had relaxed into a heavy, drugged sleep, then took his glass and set it on the table. She stared into his handsome face for a moment, thinking that he looked very different. She could not stay her hand, and she reached out to stroke a tender caress down his tanned cheek. She sighed and left him, hurrying up to her bedchamber where she dressed quickly in a dark gown and tied her herb apron around her waist.

Ebony mewed from her place upon a chair, and Jillian picked her up. The cat disappeared into the largest pocket of her apron where she often rode, and Jillian tiptoed down the stairs again. Once outside, she moved stealthily through the shadows near the house, and as she neared the stables, Donal stepped into sight, leading Jewel and his own horse.

"Did you have trouble?" she whispered as he lifted her into her saddle, and he shook his head, gesturing with hand signs that he had jumped from his horse and made his way back through the deer park.

"They will search for a time, but we must hurry before they return here."

She pulled her heavy Kerry cloak closer, raising the black hood as she galloped behind Donal toward the road which led to Lybowdin. The night was dark with only the pale white crescent of a quarter-moon piercing the starless sky, and the air was brisk and cold against their faces.

Neither spoke as they kept their fast pace, and Jillian refused to consider what would happen when her English husband awoke and realized what she had done to him. He would sleep deeply well into the following day with no harmful effects, but she had no illusions about the extent of his fury when the powder wore off. She shivered beneath her woolen cape, hoping he would not be able to find her.

They rode hard for hours without stopping, skirting small villages where pestilence fires burned a warning to travelers. Although the plague had not yet reached the Devlin boundaries, they found it rampant in the towns near the lough. An increasing sense of foreboding about Mauve crouched ominously in Jillian's mind.

When finally the tang of the sea touched her, she breathed easier, relieved that they were near Lough Swilly. She was tired from the unrelenting trek and felt dull from lack of sleep. A humpbacked bridge of gray stones led into Lybowdin, and they found the town silent and empty, dramshops and inns shuttered and bolted for the duration of the sickness. Donal preceded her through the narrow streets toward where the glow of a fire reflected on the tall spire of the Catholic church. They slowed their horses where bales of hay and wagons acted as a barrier to the isolated section of the village.

Jillian could see several men squatting nearby at one of the sentry fires, and a burly man with dark hair and a straggly beard rose and walked toward Jillian's horse. Jewel danced uneasily when he grabbed the reins, her hooves ringing on the cobblestones.

"Hold up, I tell ye," he warned, his small, dark eyes squinting up at her. "Unless ye want a look into the muzzle of me pistol."

Jillian removed her hood and veil to reveal her hideous mask, and the guard's jaw dropped as if unhinged.

" 'Od's blood," he muttered, a bit frightened by the ugliness of the woman before him, though her cloak and the fine trappings of her horse indicated that she was a lady of quality. "Ye canna be thinkin' to pass into the plague—" he began, but Jillian cut him off.

"I am Lady Jillian Devlin, wife of the English Earl of Wellingford. Move aside, for I bring medicines for the sick."

Two other men had sidled up beside the first, and one quickly crossed himself at the mention of her name. The leader stared up at the pocked and horrid face, a bead of sweat wetting his upper lip as stories of her witchcraft came back to him.

" 'T-tis rumored ye're the Devlin w-witch that caused this terrible pestilence to befall us," he stuttered, eyes afraid, and Jillian frowned, angered that his ignorant prattle wasted precious time.

"I warn you, step out of our way or witness my powers!"

The three men shifted heavy boots uneasily, but the whiskered man's hamlike hand stayed her horse, his eyes on her face.

Jillian muttered a low curse. "Is it my face that offends you then?" she cried shrilly. "Then I will remove it for you!"

The peasants watched in astonishment as she raised her hands, her nails raking down both her cheeks. Great hunks of gray, scarred skin came off on her fingers, and eyes bulging with fright, the man holding her bridle let out a bloodcurdling howl of fear. The others scattered in different directions, and Jillian wasted no time but leapt her horse over the barricade with Donal close behind her.

Unlike the outer streets of Lybowdin, the

thoroughfares within the boundaries were crowded with families bearing their dead and afflicted, their wailing and weeping filling the air. Jillian cringed away as a man in the keening throng grabbed at her cloak. As she desperately tried to control Jewel, Donal thrust him away with one swing of his arm.

Jillian looked around in horror, never before having seen a town overcome with plague. The cases she had known had been isolated, and under Mauve's careful tending with her molds and teas the victims had usually survived the illness. But the scene they entered was like a nightmare of hell with its long, twisting shadows lunging up the walls painted with the orange glow of fires while shrill shrieks of agony and grief rent the night.

Open bonfires burned at each corner, and nearly every portal they passed was painted with a rough cross and the inscription LORD HAVE MERCY ON US. Jillian shuddered as a creaking death wagon rumbled past them, filled high with its grisly cargo.

At the churchyard other wagons unloaded bodies stiffened by death to be burned upon a huge bonfire. Jillian turned her eyes from the horrendous sight, holding her cloak tight against her nose to block out the acrid smell of burning human flesh. Donal opened the iron gate for her, and she hurried up the stone steps. When they reached the immense iron-hinged doors, Donal shouldered them open, and the fetid stench that met them made

Jillian want to retch. She braced herself, her stomach rolling in revulsion, picking her way among dozens of plague victims lying upon the cold stone floor. Several open fires in the nave gave off a smoky pallor that hung in a haze against heavy rafters far above.

Donal pointed to an alcove to the left of the altar where candles burned, and Jillian hurried forward, fear for Mauve clutching her heart. She could not stifle her cry when she saw her dear friend lying on a dirty pallet below a narrow window set with stained glass. She dropped to her knees at Mauve's side and took her limp hand in hers as Donal knelt across from her, his stricken eyes on his mother's face covered with the open, red sores of the plague.

"We are here to help you, Mauve," Jillian whispered, tears flowing down her cheeks. "I have brought your medicines."

Mauve looked at her out of dull eyes, and Jillian pulled off her Kerry cloak and tucked it around Mauve's thin body.

"I must have a brazier with hot coals and a cooking pot to heat water, Donal, and quickly," Jillian instructed, knowing that Mauve's condition was very bad. "And open every window and door in the church to clear out the air."

Donal hurried off to do her bidding, and Jillian placed Ebony on the floor, then lit several sulfur candles around Mauve's pallet. Ebony watched as she lifted Mauve's shoulders and carefully fed her a sip of the wine she had brought. Her neck was so swollen that she could barely swallow. Jillian let her rest and quickly stripped off the residue of her mask, which hung in uncomfortable shreds.

Donal returned not long afterward, and Jillian boiled a handful of the mold in the water, then strained off the broth. She fed a spoonful to Mauve, then afterward sat huddled over the sick woman, bathing her with cool water.

It was several hours before Donal took her place and Jillian was able to lean back exhaustedly against the wall. Her eyes fell on another pallet a few feet away where a little girl with blond pigtails lay writhing, her small face flushed and delirious. Jillian's heart tightened with pity, and she arose to dip out a cup of the warm broth. She knelt beside the child's mother, who wept quietly as she held her daughter's hand.

"I have medicine that might help her to live," Jillian told her tiredly, giving her the bowl, and the woman kissed her hand, her speech broken with grief.

"Oh, thank ye, milady, she is all that is left to me. My husband, my sons, all dead and burned."

Jillian nodded, hoping it wasn't too late to save the child as she looked around at the mass of suffering humanity. Children, men, old women, all dying, and she stood, knowing that she had to help those she could. She moved among the victims and their weeping kin, giving away broth to people whose eyes were bleak with hopelessness and faces hollow with resignation. She kept the brew boiling, freely giving it to anyone who asked, her eyes ever going back to where Mauve lay suffering. It was not until late the next morning when her limbs felt like lead and her brain could no longer function that she curled upon the floor beside Mauve and, with Ebony curled in her arms, fell into an exhausted sleep.

# ELEVEN

"Good grief, Justin, you look terrible!"

Justin whirled from his agitated strides toward the stables to find Ryan grinning at him.

"Ryan! Where the bloody hell have you been?"

"And I'm happy to see you too," Ryan said mockingly, as he hurried to catch up to his brother. "I've been in Belfast as well you know."

Justin resumed his walking, restlessly slapping his leather gloves against his open palm.

"What did you find out? Are the Devlin accounts in order?" Justin asked impatiently as they reached the open stable doors.

"Aye, their merchant fleet still lies anchored in the harbor. All except the one ship that Brian Devlin sailed to France, and I hired an English solicitor, as you told me, to supervise the books and channel the monies home to Aaron."

Justin took Caesar's bridle from a hook and led the stallion out of his stall, and Ryan frowned at Justin's heavily whiskered jaw. It had obviously been days since he shaved, which was a radical departure from his usual immaculate grooming.

"I take it things aren't going too well around here," he ventured, and Justin gave a humorless laugh.

"I'd say not," Justin muttered darkly. "Sean Flanagan has not stopped his damnable attacks for days now, and I've just had word that Philip's patrol is pinned down in an ambush. And as if that were not enough, Jillian Devlin's gone."

Ryan frowned. "Jillian's gone? But where?"

Justin pulled the saddle blanket off the shelf and threw it onto Caesar's back. "She left twelve days ago with medicines for Mauve Hennessey, and I know not where she went."

"Why in God's name did you let her go? Haven't you heard that plague and fever have overrun the countryside?"

Justin's fingers tightened dangerously around the pommel as he swung the saddle atop the horse. "I did not *let* her. Mauve is ill with the plague. I refused her request to go to her, so she put a sleeping potion in my wine."

"She drugged you?" Ryan asked incredulously, then went on hesitantly as Justin's jaw locked in hard lines.

"No one knows her whereabouts? Not even the servants?"

"No one knows anything, damn the girl!"

Justin rammed a doubled fist angrily into his palm, his face dark.

Ryan did not speak, and Justin looked at him out of tired eyes.

"I have inquired after her in villages where we've ridden patrol," Justin said, sighing out, "but no one has seen her. There is little else I can do now with the war with the Flanagans growing worse each day. I ride now to help Philip's patrol, but since you're here, you can take your men and search for her."

"Did she give you no hint of where she meant to go?" Ryan asked, and Justin shook his head.

"Only that it was the village of Mauve's relations, and I've found from the servants that Mauve has kin in hamlets for miles around. And most are overrun by the plague. The only thing that Donal said that might help is that the streets around the church have been cordoned off. That is all I know."

Ryan jerked his eyes back to him. "The church at Lybowdin is cordoned in such a way. We rode upon the hills behind the town and could see the barricades."

Justin swung into his saddle and took his reins.

"Then take your men to Lybowdin and see if Jillian is there. If you do find her, I want you to take the vixen to the ship before you return here. Put her in the care of Hutchings for the voyage to England, and make sure he knows that Aaron is to send back enough men to help us win this fight with Flanagan."

Justin turned his horse and yelled for his men to mount, leaving Ryan to stare after him. He watched as Justin barked commands impatiently. His men scurried to obey, and within minutes, the patrol had galloped away in a thunder of hooves.

An hour later Ryan himself was in the saddle with a ten-man retinue behind him. Jillian's maid, Bridgit, rode with them as well, and Ryan had instructed her to pack enough of Jillian's clothes for the voyage. He could only hope that they were right about Jillian's whereabouts. He pressed hard, afraid even to hope that he would find his sister-in-law well after such a long time among victims of the plague.

It was long past nightfall when he led his men in a clatter over the cobblestoned streets to the sealed section of Lybowdin. His stomach knotted with fear at what he might find if indeed Jillian were inside, and he reined his horse as a sentry yelled at them.

"Halt, no one passes. . . ."

Ryan frowned at the delay, then swept his sword from his scabbard, pressing the honed point against the guard's bobbing Adam's apple.

"I look for the Lady Jillian Devlin. Has she passed into the plague?"

The man could barely nod, his eyes wide with fright as the razor-edged blade pinned him against the wagon like a butterfly to a board. He lifted a trembling finger to point mutely at the church spire.

Ryan issued a sharp order for two of his men to follow him. His face grew rigid, and his mouth compressed as they traversed streets rank with the sickening odor of death. Peasants backed away from the armed horsemen as they rode through their midst on their way to the churchyard.

When they reached it, Ryan dismounted and took the stone steps three at a time in his haste, thrusting open the doors to stare upon rows of writhing bodies. Horror rose inside him as he pushed through them, his eyes desperately scanning the pathetic faces of the moaning victims. A pile of blanket-draped corpses lay in wait of the fire, and Ryan looked away, reluctant to search for Justin's wife there.

His grim eyes were on the altar at the front of the church as he passed a mother crooning and hugging a smiling little girl with flaxen braids. A blanket hung over a recessed alcove beside the altar, and Ryan jerked it down. Donal sat propped against the wall with Ebony in his arms. His eyes were bloodshot and exhausted, and a great dread flooded Ryan as his gaze went to the small figure beside him.

"Jillian," he grunted hoarsely, going to one knee beside her.

Jillian sat shivering in the shadows, her face hidden in her dark cloak. She roused at the sound of the English voice, and her eyes opened, bright with fever. She pulled her hood closer around her face.

"Justin?"

"No, Jillian, it is Ryan. Justin has sent me to take you out of here."

"Nay, I am stricken with fever," Jillian whispered. "You must not touch me. Let Donal help me."

Ryan frowned in concern. "Where is Mauve? I will carry her."

Jillian began to cry as Donal lifted her slight weight and held her securely against his chest. "We were too late to save her. Mauve is dead. They burned her. . . ."

Jillian then laid her head feebly against Donal's strong shoulder, barely hearing Ryan's voice as he picked up Ebony and bid Donal to follow him quickly.

Her mind began to slip away as the hot mists that had endlessly tortured her closed upon her once again in swirling, dark clouds. She was only vaguely aware of being lifted to the saddle and cradled gently in Donal's arms as he spurred his horse and followed the armed Englishmen toward the lough.

For days Jillian lived in a lilting, swaying netherworld of dreams and darkness, drifting aimlessly within a misty fog where Justin's handsome face haunted her. He would hover over her, a wavery image with warm, silvery eyes that blurred eventually into angry condemnation. She would groan as he faded away, struggling desperately to open her eyes.

At other times low voices would soothe her, eerily reverberating in echoes around her while cool hands tenderly touched the terrible fire that burned her brow. The moments of comfort were always fleeting, and ghastly nightmares took their place where gruesome apparitions of her brother Pierce appeared in her feverish mind, his face white and skeletal in the dark depths of the ocean, while Brian cursed her for marrying an Englishman, his clear blue eyes full of hatred.

She would sob out her torment as the accusing faces closed around her, and many days passed before a midnight-blue wave rose at the edge of her mind, rolling over her dreams to drown her in a dark and peaceful sleep.

When she awoke she was lucid. She opened her eyes, then squinted them shut against the unaccustomed brightness. A moment later she tried again and was startled to find a small heart-shaped face leaning over her.

"So there you are at last," a feminine voice said, and Jillian stared into darkly fringed sea-green eyes.

Confused, she tried to think where she was, who the lovely young woman was, but it was difficult to think clearly. She lay still as the woman spoke again.

"Aaron will be as pleased as I am to hear that you are finally awake. We have all been mad with worry these past weeks."

She smiled, and Jillian licked dry lips but found her throat too parched to speak. The woman perceived her want and took a glass from the table beside her.

"Here, I will help you drink," she said,

lifting Jillian's head. "You will be very weak for a time, I'd imagine. You have been delirious for nearly three weeks now."

"Where am I?" Jillian rasped out, and the woman's smile was friendly.

"Why, in England, of course. I am Justin's sister, Catherine."

Shocked, Jillian stared at Catherine as she busied herself with plumping the pillows. She was too weak to show how appalled she was. To her surprise Bridgit loomed behind Catherine with Ebony in her arms, her chubby face wreathed in smiles. Jillian smiled in pleasure as Ebony leapt gracefully on the bed, purring contentedly as she pressed her soft back against Jillian's hand.

"Bridgit, run fetch Aaron. He's in the stables, I believe."

The maid hurried away, and Catherine carefully propped a pillow behind Jillian's back, then sat on the edge of the bed beside her. She picked up a white bowl, and Jillian obediently sipped the warm chicken broth that Catherine fed her from a silver spoon. The soup heated a warm path into her empty stomach, and with each spoonful, she felt a little better.

Justin's sister dipped the spoon into the broth, and Jillian's eyes roamed wonderingly over the Englishwoman's clothes. She was dressed like a boy in black breeches and a white linen shirt with billowy sleeves; Jillian had never before seen such a thing.

"Bridgit helped me care for you," Catherine said as she carefully guided the spoon to Jillian's mouth. "And Aaron even sat with you at times because you had such terrible dreams. Do you remember them?"

She barely gave Jillian time to nod before going on. "I have been very worried about you, especially when Bridgit insisted on doctoring you with some kind of terrible, moldy brew that someone named Donal gave her." She shivered with distaste, then smiled. "But it seems to have worked, because you are better now, and the fever was very bad."

She leaned forward to dab at the corner of Jillian's mouth with a linen napkin. "Aaron sent for the queen's own physician to tend you." She leaned back her head, and a delighted laugh bubbled over. "But when the poor man made to attach a leech upon your breast, Bridgit went into hysterics, saying you hated bloodsuckers, so Aaron would not let him. He frowns upon bloodletting, anyway."

Catherine shook her black curls in amusement.

"And if that were not enough, Dr. Radcliffe insisted that your hair be cropped, as if that would make you better. He is surely a quack; even the queen is rumored to be losing confidence in him."

Suddenly concerned for her hair, Jillian lifted her hand to the back of her head.

"Do not worry, Jillian, I would not let anyone cut it," Catherine soothed, lifting the heavy black plait from Jillian's shoulder. "Bridgit has kept it clean and braided."

She smiled at Jillian's relieved expression, then frowned slightly at the sickly pallor of Jillian's skin and the dusky circles beneath her eyes.

"Perhaps we might have time to brush your hair a bit and make you presentable before Aaron comes. He is only out back in the stables, but Bridgit will no doubt tarry to flirt with the groom who has been courting her since she came."

She had been carefully unbraiding Jillian's hair as she spoke, combing through the silky, dark locks with her fingers before she picked up a silver-backed brush.

"Your hair is so beautiful," she murmured, stroking the brush to the end of a thick strand, then carefully fashioning it into a fat curl. "I envy such waves, for these wretched curls of mine are nothing but a nuisance."

Jillian looked at the wispy, black tendrils that softly framed Catherine's face, thinking the ringlets most becoming, but before she could say as much, a man's voice interrupted from the door.

"So our patient is awake. And it is certainly time."

He approached the bed, and Jillian knew at once that he was Aaron. The resemblance to his brothers was most apparent. He was as tall as Ryan, and lean, but his hair was not as black as Justin's and much longer, tied neatly at his nape.

He stopped beside the bed, his black eyes friendly, and Jillian could not help but think that the Spensers were indeed a handsome family.

"You'd best be glad that Justin isn't here to see you in those breeches, sister; you know he does not like you to wear them."

Catherine shrugged carelessly as Aaron moved to the other side of the bed. Jillian shyly returned his smile as Catherine continued to fuss with her hair, arranging silken waves over the plain high-necked white bed gown.

"You had us all most concerned, Jillian. Do you feel better?"

"Aye, but I am very weak."

"Then we will take care to make you stronger."

His smile was warm and welcoming. "Your beauty is a welcome addition to this house. It is certainly our gain to have you here, and Justin's loss."

Catherine shook her head. "I still can't imagine how Justin could send such a beautiful bride away as he did, and I said as much to him in the letter I posted last week. It is incomprehensible, especially when you were so ill."

Jillian paled at the thought of Justin reading such a letter, and Aaron noted her white face and mistook the reason for it. He patted Jillian's hand.

"Justin is embroiled in strife with a neighboring clan; is that not right, Jillian? He no doubt feared for your safety there in Ulster."

He frowned at Catherine. "Come, Catherine, we are tiring Jillian."

"But I want to talk to her," Catherine argued, until Aaron took her elbow.

"Later, sister. Bridgit will stay with her while she rests."

They left, and when the door shut softly after them, Bridgit glided to the bed from where she hovered near the door.

"I am so glad you are better," she whispered. "I prayed mightily while we were at sea that you would recover."

Jillian smiled, happy to have a friend from Ulster with her. "Thank you, Bridgit, but there is so much I do not understand. How did you get here? I remember nothing except Ryan Spenser coming to the church."

Talking exhausted her, and Jillian closed her eyes as Bridgit answered her questions.

"Master Ryan brought me with him to find you. He was very worried, and so was Lord Spenser, but he fought the Flanagans nearly every day you were gone."

Jillian opened her eyes in sudden concern. "Did Ryan see me without my mask?"

"Nay, milady, Donal and I shielded you from him."

A great fear welled inside Jillian about her cousin. "And what of Donal?" she whispered. "Is he well?"

Bridgit smiled. "Aye, he was only tired when he carried you to the ship's cabin. But he refused to sail to England with us. He returned to Devlin Manor with Master Ryan."

Jillian lay still for a moment as Bridgit quietly stroked Ebony's fur.

"What is it like here in England?" she asked after a time, and Bridgit bubbled with enthusiasm.

" 'Tis a grand place here and only a short ride from Londontown, and I have heard Lady Catherine speak of another even larger Spenser estate in the country."

"Have they been kind to you?"

"Very kind, milady, and very concerned about you."

Jillian closed her eyes again, contemplating all that had happened to her. Tears welled in her eyes as she thought of Mauve and the terrible days they had spent in Lybowdin. She was too weak even to grieve for her cousin, and as her mind slowly gave way to slumber, her last image was of Justin Spenser's face as he read Catherine's letter.

It took several days for Jillian to regain enough strength to sit, and both the Spensers were very kind, one or the other visiting with her most of the day while she recuperated. Two weeks passed with the warm days of mid-August, and Jillian gradually grew to like Catherine and her constant chatter, and the good-natured teasing between Aaron and Catherine reminded Jillian, with some pain, of her relationship with her brother Pierce.

The day came when Jillian had fully recovered and began to take her meals with the family. She found the huge beige-bricked mansion very beautiful and told Catherine as much one warm afternoon as they strolled through the formal gardens.

"This house belonged to my mother's family. The Wavertons have been successful merchants for many years. Now Justin owns everything, but Aaron says that now that Justin is married to you, he'll probably settle at Spenser Court. Is that true?"

Jillian thought that very unlikely since she meant to return to Ulster, but her answer was noncommittal.

"My husband has not discussed that with me. Are those the new water gardens you are having built?"

"Yes. Come, and we'll walk there. They are coming along nicely now."

Jillian followed her to where a walk graveled with white shells encircled a small man-made lake that lay glittering in the sun. Carpenters still worked on a lattice gazebo on an island in its center, and the sound of their hammers punctuated the afternoon quiet. Jillian listened as Catherine pointed out different hedges and flowering shrubs being planted, but her thoughts were on Justin Spenser. Ever since she learned of Catherine's letter to him, Jillian had lived in dread of her husband's arrival at Waverton Hall. She had not yet summoned the courage to tell either Catherine or Aaron about how she had deceived their brother, since they had been so kind to her. They welcomed her as a beloved sister-in-law without question or qualification, and now that her ruse would surely be found out, she felt guilty accepting their lavish hospitality.

She worried the most that they would hate her for what she had done to their brother, because they all seemed very fond of one another. Both Catherine and Aaron had intimated their eagerness to have Justin and Ryan home again, and although it was very difficult for Jillian to admit it, she missed them, too, especially Justin. She thought of him often, more than she ever considered possible, and worried about his fight with the Flanagans, hoping that the men Aaron had sent to Ulster had ended the warfare.

She sighed, turning her attention back to her sister-in-law. Catherine wore a summer dress of the softest white lawn, trimmed with blue silk ribbons, and looked quite lovely with her curly black hair and sparkling green eyes. She was always so animated and friendly, and she had given Jillian a whole armload of her summer dresses since the weather had grown so warm. The mint-green organdy gown that Jillian now wore was lovely and cool in the hot August sun.

"I am very pleased with the progress, and I so want it to be finished by the garden party that Aaron and I have planned for the first of September," Catherine was saying. "Did I tell you that Christopher Wren himself laid out this design for me? I was surprised he could take time from St. Paul's and all his other royal endeavors, but it will be magnificent when it is completed!"

Jillian followed her down one of the walkways that led across the small lake to the gazebo.

"It's in the shape of a wheel, you see," Catherine explained excitedly. "The gazebo there is the hub, and the spokes will be the six walks like this one leading out to it. Aaron has promised to purchase white swans for me, and the lake is big enough for rowboats."

"It will be most beautiful," Jillian said admiringly, looking out over the water to where a thick deer park stretched along a grassy field.

"Are there many plants and wildflowers in yonder forest?" she asked.

Catherine glanced absently toward the far trees. "I suppose so. Why?"

"It would be a likely place to gather herbs and flowers. Do you think Aaron would mind my going there?"

"Of course he wouldn't. There is a path there near the huge oak tree. Do you see it?"

Jillian picked it out and nodded, and Catherine went on. "It leads to an old caretaker's hut, and it would be safe for you to walk there, but do not go much farther. At least that is what Justin has always told me." She shook her curls. "But for the life of me, Jillian, I cannot understand why you worry about picking flowers and such when there is an apothecary shop not far from here."

"I prefer to make my own remedies."

"Well, that horrid moldy tea certainly worked. You do not look the least as if you've just recovered from fever. Aaron stares at you all the time, and I am sure Justin would be terribly jealous if he were here to see it." She laughed. "But that would do him good. He has always been far too arrogant with his women."

They walked for a time around the lake, Catherine giving detailed instructions to each workman, and it was teatime by the time they reached the house.

Jillian admired Waverton Hall as they approached the south wing that faced the gardens. Catherine had told her it was relatively new, built by her grandfather after the Great London Fire in 1660. It was modeled after the ancient Scottish castles with crow-stepped gables and distinctive corner turrets, but Jillian especially liked the huge windows mullioned in the shape of a cross that made the interior rooms so bright and airy.

They entered through the long gallery, Jillian looking with appreciation at the blue velvet chairs and pink wallcovering with its gilt moldings. It was a peaceful place, and she spent many hours in the warm squares of sunlight that spilled through the high windows.

As they made their way toward the front of the house, intending to take tea upstairs in Jillian's sitting room, Aaron stepped out of the red drawing room near the massive front staircase.

"There you are. I would like to speak with both of you for a moment, if I may."

He stood back and allowed them to precede him into the magnificent room, its walls hung with red Spitalfields silk, the high ceiling gaily patterned with octagons enclosing colored circles.

"Please sit down."

The women obeyed, and Aaron walked to a table where he picked up a sheet of folded parchment. He frowned as he looked down at it, then moved to stand before the marble fireplace.

"I have just received a letter from Justin," he said, looking at Jillian, and she dropped her eyes in dismay. Her heart skipped a beat.

"And I'm afraid I do not understand most of it," he admitted, causing Catherine to laugh.

"Surely Justin's spelling is not that bad, Aaron."

Jillian did not smile, and Catherine sobered somewhat at the way her brother watched Jillian.

"Well, what did he say, then?" she prodded him.

"He first says that he is glad Jillian is so much better; then he chastises you, Catherine, for your reference to Jillian's beauty with the warning that you are not to make unkind jests about his wife."

"What?" Catherine exclaimed, her brow

wrinkling with confusion. "I don't understand, either."

"He goes on to say that Jillian is most sensitive about her disfigurement and that we should use tact and allow her to wear her veil without comment."

Jillian's face flamed as Catherine looked blankly at her, then back to her brother.

"I do believe poor Justin must have suffered a head injury in battle," she began slowly, but Jillian's low voice stopped her.

"Nay, Catherine, he believes me to be quite ugly."

Both Spensers stared at her without speaking.

"That cannot be," Catherine finally said. "If anyone knows a beautiful woman when he sees one, it is Justin."

Aaron was watching Jillian closely, and he spoke quietly. "Perhaps Jillian can explain why he thinks her ugly."

Jillian took a deep breath, knowing she must tell them the truth. She began, afraid it could not help but alienate her new friends.

" 'Tis a most difficult story to relate." She hesitated, still loath to tell them. "And I hope you will not despise me for what I have done to your brother."

Catherine sat straighter with renewed interest as Jillian continued. "You see, I feel very strongly that my brothers are the rightful owners of my family's lands, and when King William gave them over to Justin, I was very angry."

"That is understandable, Jillian," Aaron said softly. "Anyone would have felt that way."

Catherine nodded agreement, and Jillian went on, her eyes downcast. "I decided that if he thought me to be very ugly, he would not wish to"—she paused with embarrassment—"consummate the marriage, so I"—her voice lowered—"told him I had been disfigured by the pox and wore a veil to hide my face."

She stopped and glanced at them to find them both staring at her in openmouthed astonishment.

"And Justin took your word on such a thing without seeing you for himself?" Aaron asked incredulously.

"Nay, my cousin made a concoction to apply to my face to give the effect of the disease."

She stared down at her hands in shame as they looked at one another but jerked her eyes up as Catherine's delighted laugh spilled forth. Aaron was grinning as well and shaking his head, and Jillian stared at them in amazement.

"That is the most ingenious trick I have ever heard!" Catherine cried, clapping her hands. "How I wish I had been there to see it!"

"You are not angry?" Jillian breathed, and Catherine giggled again.

"I think it is wonderful! Did Ryan know?"

Jillian shook her head.

"I have to admit that I find the whole thing

rather amusing myself," Aaron said, still smiling, "but I daresay Justin might feel differently when I explain it to him."

"Oh, please, Aaron, do not tell him," Jillian entreated, her eyes huge and fearful.

Aaron grew solemn at her obvious distress. "But, Jillian, you cannot keep it from him now. He says that he and Ryan are coming home shortly now that your enemies in Ulster have been beaten back."

"I would like to tell him myself," Jillian said, her eyes going from one to the other. "Please allow me that."

Aaron hesitated. "I am not sure that is the best way. Perhaps a letter from me would prepare him and give him time to cool down a bit. I daresay it will be quite a shock for him."

After a good deal of persuasion Jillian finally agreed, and Aaron grinned to himself as he looked at his brother's letter. Justin had been subjected to quite an elaborate hoax, and he could not help but think Jillian very resourceful to have pulled it off as well as she had. Justin had always had a keen sense of humor, and perhaps after his initial rage was over, he would see the humor and be in a forgiving mood by the time he got home.

"Tell me more about it, Jillian," Catherine interjected gleefully. "Every detail."

Jillian told her some of it but could not bring herself to mention the fact that Justin thought her to have drowned in the spring, nor the fact that she'd drugged him. The mild reaction from Catherine and Aaron about her deception did not lessen the heaviness of her heart. It was over now, and her brother would surely lose his inheritance forever when Justin Spenser arrived in England.

# TWELVE

"Did Justin really believe you turned yourself into a cat?"

Catherine's voice was threaded with amusement, and Jillian looked up, her pestle still in her hand as she paused from grinding a dried marigold blossom.

"I am afraid so."

A bubble of laughter met her smile, and Catherine lifted Ebony closer against her cheek to feel the cat's velvety fur.

"It is just hard to imagine that Justin could be so easily tricked. He's always so level-headed."

Jillian only smiled, carefully pouring the marigold powder into one of the small pockets of her herb apron.

"It would be great fun to trick a man like that, I think," Catherine mused aloud, idly stroking Ebony's back. She grimaced. "But I am ever surrounded by brothers who watch my every move like hawks hunting a hare. It is a lucky thing for you that your brothers do not treat you so."

Jillian's fine brows creased in pain, and Catherine was immediately contrite, having forgotten for a moment the unhappy fate of the Devlin brothers.

"Forgive me, I beg you, Jillian, I did not think. Justin has always scolded me for speaking out of turn, and I fear he's often right."

Jillian dropped her eyes to the small tray of herbs on the table in front of her.

"I know you meant no harm. I understand your plight full well, for my older brother, Brian, has a tendency to treat me like a child even now that I am grown."

Jillian went back to her work, but her chest was heavy with regret as it always was when she spoke of her brothers.

"Do you miss them awfully?" Catherine asked gently.

Jillian tried to smile. "Aye, we were very close. I pray daily that Pierce is still alive somewhere. Sometimes I feel very alone now that Mauve is gone and Donal is far away in Ulster."

"Justin will come soon, and perhaps you'll be happy with him once he forgives your trick."

"Since he has not answered Aaron's letter, I fear he must hate me for my deceit," Jillian replied, and Catherine frowned.

"Perhaps you should cast another spell on him," she suggested with a devilish smile. "And make him do whatever you want."

Jillian didn't answer, thinking she had no more tricks to use against Justin. All was lost, and she was helpless now to save Brian's inheritance.

Catherine sat up suddenly, her eyes alight. "Show me how you pretended to turn yourself into a cat. Is it truly magic you use?"

Jillian had to laugh at the excitement in Catherine's green eyes.

" 'Twas but an illusion I created. There are many hidden passages in my house in Ulster, and I only ducked into one and left Ebony in my stead."

Catherine giggled with enjoyment.

"How delicious! Do it for me, please, Jillian."

Jillian hesitated. "Your brothers might be angry with me if I put such devious ideas into your head."

"Oh, hang my brothers. All three of them certainly do whatever they please. Is not Aaron hunting at Windsor while we sit at home bored to death? Show me, I pray, it will be fun!"

Jillian smiled, for Catherine's exuberance had a way of becoming contagious. "My tricks are few, really. I use only illusion and certain powders for effect. 'Tis Ebony that makes it possible to frighten people, because her eyes resemble mine."

Catherine held up the small cat and cooed into its face. "Pray tell how such a sweet little pussycat could scare even a mouse."

Jillian watched, her lips curved in a knowing smile.

"Come," she said sharply in Gaelic.

Catherine gasped as the cat leapt from her lap and ran to her mistress, and Jillian scooped Ebony into her arms and carried her to the fire.

"See, I have taught her to obey many commands. Watch."

Jillian reached into the apron pocket containing the yellow powder, then muttered a low Gaelic chant as she flung it into the fire, her fingers outspread ominously. As she expected, Catherine stared wide-eyed at the flames and clouds of yellow smoke, giving her time to drop Ebony and step behind the drapery.

"This is magical indeed!" Catherine cried, delighted by the spectacular sight at the hearth, but her expression changed when she turned to find Jillian completely vanished.

Jillian peeked from behind the curtain to find Catherine looking at Ebony in astonishment. She laughed as she stepped from her hiding place.

"There, you see, 'tis but a simple trick but effective, if one is unprepared for it."

"It is no wonder that Justin was tricked," Catherine murmured, very impressed. "How did you make such strange smoke?"

Jillian retrieved more of the powder from her apron and held it in her cupped palm.

" 'Tis only a powder that gives off yellow smoke."

Catherine chuckled and came toward her. "Let me try your trick with Ebony. Perhaps I will use it to frighten the next libertine who tries to maul my bosom."

Jillian laughed as she brushed the powder into Catherine's hand, but both turned as a quiet voice broke into their conversation.

"Pardon, Lady Catherine, but there is a visitor in the entry foyer."

It was Geoffrey, the tall Negro butler who had been with the Spensers for many years. His gaunt, cadaverous features gave him an ominous look that belied his kind and gentle disposition. His wide lips curled with distaste as he named the one who waited outside.

"Lady Eleanor Marlowe requests that you receive her since Lord Spenser is not in residence."

Jillian looked curiously at Catherine and found the other girl's nose wrinkled with disgust.

"Tell her we're all dead and gone to heaven," Catherine said. "For, in truth, she could never gain entrance there."

Jillian stared at her as Geoffrey hid his amusement behind his hand.

"I am sorry to say, milady, that she is most insistent."

Catherine sighed heavily, the most put-upon sound imaginable. "Then send her in, and I will get rid of her myself."

Geoffrey nodded, and Catherine turned to Jillian.

"Eleanor is the most despicable woman I have ever met. It is said her mother died insane, and I do believe Eleanor shares that same affliction. She has chased Justin like a common trollop ever since she laid eyes on him years ago, and she is most adept at hiding her true colors from him although everyone else can see how wicked she is. I cannot believe Justin ever truly cared for her. She is too selfish and hateful for anyone to love. Except perhaps her groom. They say he strokes her flanks much more often than those of any mare in the Marlowe stables."

Jillian gasped at Catherine's outrageous remark but quickly hid her grin as a woman swept into the room without seeing Jillian where she stood beside the door. Eleanor Marlowe was tall and slim, her pale blond hair curving back in smooth wings at her temples to a neatly braided coil atop her head. She was dressed splendidly in a black velvet riding habit with scarlet lace at her wrists and throat.

"When will Justin return from Ireland?" she demanded sharply of Catherine. "I need to see him."

Catherine stared at Eleanor with open contempt, for she knew full well what Eleanor needed from Justin. She needed to resume their affair.

"Justin is married now, and I am sure your needs can be taken care of elsewhere, as they were in his absences."

Eleanor gave her a frigid smile. "But what of his needs, Catherine? His marriage is but a farce, and all of London knows it. He married the Irish estates, not the Devlin wench."

"And it could be that you are jealous of her wealth, since the stipulations of your father's will are common knowledge."

Eleanor's eyes iced over as Catherine hit a nerve. Since her father had died a year ago, she had been on a ridiculously small allowance and would be until she reached the age of four and twenty, the following May. She had depended on Justin to ease her finances since he had always been free with his gifts in the past, despite his indifference about their affair. He might very well be married, but she meant to see that he did not forget her.

"My beauty attracts Justin to me, not my money, and that will never change, especially since his bride is an ugly witch who hides her face beneath a veil. I have heard as much from sailors aboard the ship that brought her here."

Catherine laughed in her face. "See her ugliness for yourself, Eleanor, for she stands directly behind you."

Eleanor spun around, her large brown eyes so cold as to send chills down Jillian's back. Eleanor stared at the small woman before her, inwardly chagrined by her delicate beauty. The gossips were obviously mistaken, and her hopes to ensnare Justin for herself rapidly dwindled. Her face tightened as she looked at the woman whose title she had coveted for so long, and her words oozed with bitterness.

"Justin is mine, and your heathen witchcraft will not keep him from my bed. No other woman has been able to satisfy him as long as I have, and neither will you."

Fury surged hot in Jillian, but before she could respond, Catherine moved in front of Eleanor, green eyes blazing.

"How dare you come here and say such things to Justin's wife!"

Jillian spoke up, her Irish brogue floating melodically over the angry words of the Englishwomen.

"Not many in Ulster would risk a witch's wrath with such insults," she warned, her blue eyes delving into Eleanor's with a look that made the blond woman squirm.

"Beware," Catherine interjected, catching Jillian's intention at once. She squeezed the yellow powder tightly into Jillian's palm. "Jillian will surely put a spell upon you if you anger her further."

Eleanor's contemptuous laugh cut into the air. "Do not try to frighten me with tales of sorcery. I am not an ignorant sailor, nor a love-struck suitor. You are but a conniving woman out to win Justin's love with tricks and lies."

"I can easily demonstrate my powers," Jillian answered calmly. "If you are not frightened to witness them."

A chink in Eleanor's brown eyes bespoke hesitation, and Jillian noted it with satisfaction. Out of the corner of her eye Jillian saw Ebony before the hearth, watching them.

"Hide," she ordered the cat in Gaelic, smiling as Ebony obediently disappeared behind the drapery.

Eleanor looked at her strangely, not understanding her word, and Catherine smiled in anticipation as she moved into her position by the fire. Jillian gestured at Catherine, then raised both hands, fingers apart.

"Fire, jump high and dance with smoke."

The flames seemed to obey her cry as Catherine cast the powder upon the logs, and Eleanor's jaw dropped as yellow clouds billowed into the room. Catherine ducked out of sight, and Jillian's next words came low.

"Catherine be gone to live forever as a cat."

Eleanor's eyes bulged as the haze dispersed enough to reveal the black cat where Catherine had been only seconds earlier. She froze, fear squeezing her breath from her. She stepped back, one well-manicured hand pressed over her mouth. While she stared at Ebony Jillian issued another Gaelic command, and the cat stood upon its back legs. Catherine's low laugh sounded eerily.

Eleanor backed away, horrified eyes on Jillian's composed face. She knocked into a table in her haste, heedless of the vase that splintered upon the floor in a tinkling of china as Jillian's cry sounded in shrill warning.

"Be gone or taste my powers!"

Jillian lifted her arms high over her head as if to rain magic upon the hapless woman, and Eleanor shrieked in terror and fled the room. She scrambled past the shocked Geoffrey, clawing at the front doorknob in a frenzied attempt to escape. The door opened, and she took the steps at a run, completely oblivious in her panic to the peals of laughter that had followed her out of the drawing room door.

# THIRTEEN

Justin was glad when they left the narrow, twisting streets of London and set out for Waverton Hall. The city was teeming with activity on the first day of September, and they had dodged horse-drawn drays and wagons, as well as elaborate carriages of the nobility as they fought their way through the cobblestoned thoroughfares from the Pool of London where their ship was anchored amidst a myriad of others.

Despite the screams of dirty street urchins and the shrill cries of vendors, the ever-ringing bells of London were a welcome sound after the quiet countryside of Ulster. It was a mild and sunny day, and Justin spurred his horse, eager to reach the comfort of Waverton Hall. At the moment a hot bath and a hearty meal sounded like the greatest of luxuries, especially since rough summer squalls had delayed their arrival by several days. The foul weather aboard ship had only deepened Justin's mood over the letter he'd received from Aaron. It was still hard for him to accept the fact that the little vixen had managed such a hoax, and he had been furious that first day when he read of it, crumpling Aaron's letter and hurling it into the fire. Ryan's jests about the matter and the amused smirk he wore for days afterward had not helped, but the fight with the Flanagans had been Justin's first priority at the time.

Now that he had arrived in England, he found his disposition toward his wily Irish wife to have calmed somewhat, and the more he thought of Catherine's allusions to her beauty, the more eager he was to see her unveiled. After all, he was already fond of the girl, even with her attempts to frighten him with her magic, and if she really was fair to look upon, it would certainly make his marriage easier to bear. He had wondered endlessly what she might look like, but regardless of her true features, anything would surpass the scarred visage he thought her to possess. He thrust such ponderings from his mind, deciding that it was useless to dwell upon it when they would reach Waverton within the hour and he would see Jillian Devlin Spenser for himself.

The coach road they traversed was fairly well maintained and not nearly so rutted as those in Ulster, and the traffic was light for such a pleasant day. The ride was a short one, and both men grinned with anticipation as they passed the last farm before the Waverton estate. They drew up when it came into sight, and Ryan stood in his stirrups, pointing his crop to the distant house.

"I've never been so glad to get home, for I am sick to death of chasing Flanagans!"

Justin laughed as Ryan kicked his horse into a gallop, then followed at a slower pace. He, too, had grown tired of the raids and fighting, and he was thankful that Aaron's reinforcements had allowed them to put an end to much of Sean Flanagan's mischief. He had left Philip Hammond to command the patrols that were constantly riding the perimeters of Devlin land, so that Justin could return home to see his family and conduct his business, as well as collect his wayward wife.

Ryan had pulled up to await him at the bricked gateway arch, and both eyed the long line of carriages and coaches in the circular drive with less than enthusiasm.

"It seems Catherine is hostessing another of her parties," Ryan remarked as they walked their mounts past the grooms and footmen lounging around the finely appointed conveyances.

"I suppose we should dismount at the stables and clean up a bit before we show ourselves," Justin suggested, and Ryan nodded as they proceeded around the side of the house.

A young stableboy caught sight of them and came running, a wide smile on his face, and Justin ruffled his dark hair, then walked with Ryan through a high box hedge that led to the rear entrance of the long gallery. They stopped there, dismayed to find the rear gardens full of elegantly dressed ladies and gentlemen.

"It looks like a garden party, Ryan, so brush some of the dirt off your coat or Catherine will scold us for embarrassing her in front of her guests," Justin said, smiling as several of the people nearby greeted him. They wended their way toward the house, stopping as one old drinking friend from Whitehall came up with a grin and slapped Justin on the back.

"Congratulations, you devil, what a woman you've married. It's hard to believe that she's an heiress, too, but you always were the lucky one!"

Justin looked at him, then at Ryan, who wriggled his eyebrows suggestively. Similar comments were heard as they neared the doors of the long gallery, and Justin began to look for his unseen bride with new interest.

"There's Catherine and Aaron by the pillars, and there's a woman with them," Ryan said, and Justin turned his eyes to follow his pointing finger. He stared at the small woman beside his sister, wondering if it was his wife. She was dressed in yellow, but her back was to him and she wore a large hat. He frowned, thinking that she looked much smaller than he remembered.

"Come on, Ryan, I think it's time I met my bride face-to-face."

Across the way Catherine stood beside Aaron, looking around, most pleased with the success of the party. Everyone seemed to be having a wonderful time. She had expected her water gardens to be the focus of attention, but Jillian had outshone even Christopher Wren's work. Even now, several handsome young gentlemen were striving for Jillian's attention. She smiled fondly at her Irish sister-in-law, pleased with her popularity. Her happy expression dwindled to shock as she caught sight of Justin and Ryan heading straight for them. Justin's eyes were on Jillian, and Catherine grabbed Aaron's arm.

"Look, Aaron, there's Justin! You'd better go head him off in case he's still angry!"

Aaron sought out his brothers in the crowd, then smiled. "He doesn't look out of sorts, but maybe you should warn Jillian. You know how she's dreaded this."

He moved to meet his brothers, truly glad to see them home and well. He grinned when he reached them, shaking Justin's hand.

"It's really good to see you two! Why didn't you send word that you were coming today?"

"Is that Jillian?" Justin demanded abruptly, frowning as one of the men with the woman in yellow bowed low before her as he kissed her hand.

"Aye, but she's rather nervous about this meeting, you know," Aaron began, then hurried after him as Justin started toward Jillian.

Catherine pushed her way between two of Jillian's admirers, her whisper urgent next to Jillian's ear.

"Jillian, Jillian, Justin's here!"

Jillian's smile disintegrated; her heart

skidded to a stop. She turned slowly, blanching as her eyes collided with curious silver ones just yards away. She could not move, and Aaron and Ryan both bumped into Justin's back as he stopped in midstride.

Justin's face went white, his jaw dropping a degree as he looked into wide turquoise eyes. He could not believe what he saw at first, thinking it was one of the visions that haunted his mind.

"It cannot be," he muttered hoarsely. "She is dead, drowned."

He stared at her equally shocked face until he saw fear rise in the blue depths of her eyes. In that moment events began to fall into place like pieces of a puzzle. She had not drowned that day but escaped, letting him suffer the endless guilt and regret for months while she continued to play her little games with him! His square jaw hardened, the full comprehension of what she had done darkening his eyes with fury. He took a step toward her, shaking off Aaron's restraining hand, and Jillian waited no longer but fled toward the house, oblivious to the curious stares of those around them.

Catherine looked once at Justin's outraged face, distinctly glad to see Aaron and Ryan holding him back, before she lifted her skirts and followed Jillian. She ran up the steps to the portico, then took the back stairs to Jillian's bedchamber. The door was locked, and she knocked softly.

"It is only me, Jillian, let me in."

Jillian opened the door warily, her face very pale, and Catherine entered quickly and closed it behind her.

"You cannot lock the door against him, Jillian, that will only make matters worse."

Jillian began to pace back and forth, wringing her hands, and Catherine stifled her own panicky feelings as she pulled her friend to a chair.

"Sit down and calm yourself, Jillian. There is no need to be so terrified. Justin will not hurt you."

"But he looked so furious," Jillian said, her voice quivering.

"I thought he looked more stunned than angry, but, anyway, Aaron and Ryan are talking to him. They'll pour some brandy down him until he calms down and acts rationally. I cannot imagine him still being so angry. He received Aaron's letter weeks ago."

Jillian looked at her, knowing exactly why he was so angry. Her nerves were drawn as tight as a bowstring, and she put her hand to her mouth, her eyes on the door. Catherine again tried to soothe her.

"Now, really, Jillian, do not take on so. Justin is not one to lose his temper. I can never remember him going into a rage, although he has been most upset at times with my behavior. He will not yell at you, either; he's always deadly calm when he's angry. Maybe he will find the whole thing amusing once Aaron talks to him. Yes, I am sure he will."

They both gasped as the door was suddenly thrown wide. It banged hard on the wall behind it, and Jillian stared at Justin where he loomed in the threshold, his face working with contained fury, his fists clenched hard at his sides.

"Then again, maybe he won't find it so amusing," Catherine breathed, her eyes wide as Justin turned his dark glare upon her.

"See to your guests, Catherine," he gritted, and Catherine stood quickly, looking sympathetically at Jillian.

"Justin, you'd better not hurt Jillian; she—"

"Out!" Justin barked harshly, and Catherine skirted his imposing frame and scurried out the door without another word.

Justin slid the bolt into place after her with a most final sound, and now that Jillian finally faced his wrath, her pride did not desert her. She raised her chin defiantly, vowing never to show him that she was afraid of him. She returned his glower with as much courage as she could muster, but the steel-gray anger in Justin's eyes won the battle. Jillian's gaze dropped away, and she stood and moved to the window. Justin stared at her slender back, trying very hard to master the rage he felt. He did not like to lose his temper, and never could he remember a woman goading him into it. But this was too much.

Jillian kept her eyes on the fields below but could not help the chill that raced up her spine as his voice came, low and deadly.

"Why did you play me for a fool?"

Jillian turned to place cold azure eyes upon his hard and handsome face.

"Because the mood struck me," she uttered with such haughty scorn that a stronger wave of fury went surging through Justin's blood. "Beat me if you will," she continued airily, turning away from him, "but do not expect me to beg for mercy—"

Her words were stopped short as air waved close behind her and hard fingers closed over her shoulders, turning her with one angry jerk. She caught only a glimpse of blazing silver eyes before she was drawn against his chest, his mouth hard upon hers. Jillian could not move as he lifted her off the floor, one arm like a steel band behind her waist, the other snarled in her hair. She tried to struggle but found herself completely impotent against his lean strength as he continued with his brutal kisses, removing his hand from the silkiness of her hair to slide it down to cup her hip.

Jillian's resistance renewed, she was horrified at the sensations he was able to awaken in her. Fingers of fire raced to her core as his hard lips left her mouth to scorch into her throat. She moaned helplessly, and as suddenly as she had been seized, he thrust her from him. Jillian fell back upon the bed, breathless and humiliated at the response wrenched so unfeelingly from her.

"How dare you do that to me?" she spat at him, her fingers on her lips, and Justin gave a cold laugh.

"I dare because the mood struck me," he mocked, a muscle flexing hard in his tanned cheek.

Jillian stared up at him, suddenly realizing her own danger. He had it in his power to do to her as he would, and his eyes still burned like molten silver. She moved back against the carved headboard, fear surfacing in her eyes.

Justin saw it and turned away, running impatient fingers through his hair as he sought to control his anger. Jillian watched warily until he looked back at her, his angry eyes pinning her to the bed.

"I will have an answer," he said, growling, the threat in his tone readily apparent as he finished tersely, "Why did you use me for a fool?"

Jillian's own rage erupted then, and she forgot to be afraid, rising on her knees, her lovely face flushed high with color. Her turquoise eyes blazed with indignant rage.

"Is it so hard to figure out, *milord?*" She emphasized his title sarcastically. "I hate you! You fought with the English troops who killed my father at the Boyne; your friend, the king, exiled my brother Brian! English ships sank Pierce's ship until I know not whether he lives or dies! And if that is not enough, my family's lands were stolen from me and given to you, a swaggering, rutting English dog who attacked the first innocent Irish maiden he set his eyes upon!"

Justin stared at the beautiful woman before him. Her long, silky black hair swung over her shoulders in glorious disarray, and her pure blue eyes glinted unmitigated hatred. His eyes dropped to her small fists, clenched at her sides, then to her full breasts, heaving the bodice of her gown. His anger faded away as a streak of raw desire staggered his control. He had wanted her since the first moment he had seen her and in all the days of regret when he'd thought her dead. And now to discover that she was his wife to have as he would!

Justin smiled suddenly, causing Jillian to stiffen distrustfully. His eyes moved at will over her body, making her feel naked, and she crossed her arms over her chest, her eyes cold enough to freeze.

"Your life has harbored many changes. I will agree with that, but as a woman, you must learn to accept your fate without complaint. Or trickery." An arrogant smile accompanied his admonition, and Jillian grew rigid.

"A woman I am, and I have no recourse from it, but 'tis a sad lot for all of my gender to be used and commanded by men without regard for our feelings."

"I am most happy with your gender, my sweet Jillian, and the fact that you are my legal wife is a happenstance I find much to my liking, despite your devious ways."

His silvery eyes raked over her with open desire, and Jillian met his insulting appraisal with pure contempt.

" 'Tis not to my liking, and you will soon find it less so, for I will never willingly submit to you, husband or not. For if I do, my brothers will lose their birthright, and I will not be a willing party to such injustice."

Her words rubbed at Justin's simmering temper as did the stubborn slant of her fragile jaw.

"You go too far, madame. A wife's place is in her husband's bed, and there you will find yourself this very night. You will be wise to resign yourself to the fact that you are mine and have no say in the matter."

Jillian's eyes remained hard, as she vowed never, never to succumb to the arrogance of this Englishman who treated his wife as a slave made only to do his bidding.

"And what if a similar fate befell Catherine?" she asked quietly, her eyes searching his face. "She is near my age with only brothers to protect her. What if you were exiled, the others killed? Would you tell her to submit to the foreigner who stole your own lands and inheritance? Would you call it her fate as a woman and have her spread herself willingly upon the bed of the man who plunders her family of everything precious to her?"

Justin frowned darkly, as Jillian's words gave him pause. He would certainly not want Catherine so used.

"My sister is not the issue here," he said finally, "but my wife." He smiled, a slow, insolent grin that flooded warmth into Jillian's cheeks. "You are legally bound to me, and your lies and deceit have already cheated me of many nights of pleasure." He looked at her closely. "Except for one drunken tumble into your bed, which now I readily suspect was all it was."

"Aye, that indeed was all, thank my spirit for protecting me." She stared into his eyes, their wills clashing. "You are stronger than I, Englishman, and can force me to your will, but I will never yield. I will lie like stone beneath you, abhorring your every touch as if it were vermin that crawled upon my flesh."

Justin's face blackened. She was his wife, dammit, and she would learn to obey him.

"No, my love," he gritted out furiously. "I will not force you. I have never yet forced a woman once she lay in my bed, and I doubt if you will be of a different mold. But we will see this very night, because, my little beauty, your deception is at an end. You will lie with me from this day on, as long as I want you there." He stopped, his lips curving into a cold smile. "And if a wager were made, one day hence I daresay you will welcome me with open arms and use your womanly wiles to entice me to stay in your bed instead of seeking less wily company elsewhere."

Jillian's teeth clamped, amazed at his strutting masculine confidence. "Do not lay gold upon such a thought, milord," she answered tightly. "For I would sooner bed Sean Flanagan and his entire band of filthy ruffians than to lie for one moment beneath your weight."

To her astonishment Justin threw back his head and gave a hearty laugh. "You might have had that honor, my sweet, if I had not spent the last months fighting your enemies for you while you whiled away your time at garden parties here on English soil."

Jillian's face flamed with outrage, and unheeding of any recourse he might employ against her, she snatched up the pitcher beside her and sent it hurling, water and all, toward his head.

Justin ducked it easily, watching as it crashed in streaming rivulets upon the wall beside him. "Until tonight, my love, when I shall show you how soft and willing stone can become beneath the right hand."

He smiled again and left her looking for something else to throw at him.

From a recessed doorway down the hall Bridgit watched Justin Spenser leave Jillian's room. She had waited and worried as they quarreled, and she wrung her hands with helplessness as Justin paused just outside. A tinkling crash sounded in the room behind him, along with muffled Gaelic curses, and Bridgit heard his low laugh before he strode off toward the other end of the wing.

She waited another moment to make sure he did not return, then glided down the hall to her mistress's door. She knocked softly, then entered. Her eyes widened, and she held up both palms in defense as Jillian made to throw a heavy silver candlestick at her.

" 'Tis only me, milady," she cried, and Jillian lowered her weapon to the dresser, her face flushed with fury. She began to pace, angrily tearing off the yellow gown she wore.

"He is an arrogant, insufferable monster! I despise him! I detest him!" she cried, moving agitatedly around the room. "I will leave this place forever before submitting to him! I will go home to Ulster this very night!"

"But how, milady? Ulster is far across the sea."

Jillian did not answer at once, staring stonily into the cold grate, and Bridgit's voice was hesitant. "I fear there is nowhere that he could not find us, milady."

Jillian looked away, unwilling to admit to Bridgit her own humiliating response to the detestable Englishman. His touch inflamed her, and she cursed her own betraying body.

"I will never let him touch me," she said stubbornly.

"Will he punish you for your tricks against him?" Bridgit asked, remembering with a shiver the rage on his face when he passed her on the way to Jillian's room. "Will he beat you?"

"Is not being forced into his bed the worst punishment I could ever endure?" Jillian said, hopelessness welling up in her voice, but she lifted her chin suddenly, making up her mind.

"We will go to London tonight and book passage for Ulster, but you must help me, Bridgit, and do exactly what I tell you. For no matter what else happens, Justin Spenser must never find us."

# FOURTEEN

It was suppertime when Ryan Spenser descended to the entrance hall in search of his eldest brother. He paused at the bottom of the steps, more than curious about what had happened when Justin had confronted his Irish wife. Ryan had only stared into Jillian Devlin's eyes for a moment, but even so, he knew she had to be the beautiful peasant girl from the Enchanted Pool who had caused Justin so much grief. He had told Catherine and Aaron as much, and he grinned, wondering how she accomplished such a thing.

He was still smiling when he entered the dining room and found Catherine and Aaron sitting silently before the fireplace.

"Where's Justin?"

"He's in the drawing room acting like a boor," Catherine answered in disgust. "You would think Jillian tried to kill him or something equally horrible."

Ryan recrossed the hall and found Justin standing motionlessly before the windows, his arms akimbo. He wisely suppressed his growing amusement over Justin's predicament. He took a chair near him.

"Well, brother, did you settle matters with your bride?"

Justin spun, not having heard Ryan enter, then frowned at the glint of humor in his brother's eyes. "We discussed it," he said stiffly, and Ryan couldn't help but laugh at his expression.

"By the look on your face when you went after her, I assumed that you would either shake her senseless or tumble her into your bed without pause."

"I assure you that both occurred to me," Justin admitted as he sat down opposite Ryan. "But I did neither. Yet," he added with a hint of a smile.

Ryan grinned. "So your anger is already spent. The Lady Jillian must have pleaded prettily for such mercy."

Justin gave a derisive snort. "Plead? Jillian? I do not think she would beg for anything, especially from me."

"So the lady has a proud streak."

"That is a mild way to state it. But the deed is done and finished, and little good will it do me to punish her for her deceptions. The marriage is off to a bad beginning as it is."

"Could her beauty have anything to do with such generosity from you? I only glimpsed her face, but I saw eyes as pure and blue as sapphires." Ryan smiled, stretching out his legs to cross his booted feet. "It seems to me you are most fortunate. Not only is your bride rich, she's beautiful. What more could you want?"

Justin sighed and leaned back his head. "A wife less eaten with hatred, for one."

Ryan's surprise faded into a thoughtful smile. "The Battle of the Boyne has soured her against you, I suspect."

"Aye, and that is only a part of it. It is not just my part in it that she loathes, but I play the villain in her eyes for the death of her father and perhaps of her brother as well, plus the loss of her lands and every other misfortune that has ever beset the bloody isle of Ireland."

Ryan chuckled at his brother's grim face. "Come now, Justin, you are well known at Whitehall for your charm with the ladies. They seek you out even when you stand aloof and scorn the gentle wooings of other men."

"Jillian is not so disposed. In truth, I wonder if she'll even condescend to dine with us this night." He glanced at the mantel clock and frowned. "It is past time."

"Perhaps she only readies herself for her husband. I cannot see her able to summon the courage to disobey you after the events of the afternoon."

"And you have not seen the extent of my bride's pride. She bears little resemblance to the plump and docile maid in Ulster who hid from us beneath a veil."

"And if she does not come, what then?"

"She will come," Justin gritted out with hard purpose. "If I have to carry her down bodily and hold her on my lap for every bite of the meal."

"That will not be necessary, milord. I have come as you bade me."

Both men jerked their faces around at the soft, smooth voice, and Justin's breath was snatched from him as he saw Jillian in the doorway. She was dressed in a gown of fine satin, the shimmering fabric matching her lovely turquoise eyes. His eyes moved over her petite form appreciatively, lingering on the soft white curves above the low, square-cut neckline where a heavy blue stone hung on a long golden chain. A silky mass of black waves cascaded softly to her waist, tempting a man to gather the lustrous tresses in both hands.

She smiled, a warm and open smile that Justin had never seen before. Although it enhanced her beauty, it served to make Justin wary. He glanced at Ryan to find the young man's mouth slightly ajar, amber eyes glued to the diminutive vision of beauty before them. Irked by his brother's response, Justin frowned at Jillian as Ryan moved to her, taking her small hand as he bent in a bow.

"Your beauty is blinding," he murmured truthfully, looking deep into her eyes before his lips brushed the back of her hand.

"Thank you, milord," Jillian returned evenly, aware of the dark scowl that overtook Justin's features as Ryan continued to smile at her.

"Come, your tardiness has delayed our meal," Justin said brusquely, moving forward to take Jillian's arm. Ryan was left to stare after them.

Jillian walked obediently beside Justin, very aware of the long, brown fingers pressing into her bare arm. She forced a warm smile, determined to work her charm upon the egotistical English cur until he drooled helplessly at her feet. Then, when he was satisfied that she accepted her fate, she would flee his house forever.

She was surprised when he led her past the chair at the foot of the table, which was her customary place, to seat her on his right. She spread her skirts carefully upon the chair as Ryan took a chair across from her. Catherine and Aaron took their places, and Jillian returned their friendly smiles with a lovely one of her own. She dropped her eyes as she met Justin's unreadable silver stare.

"We are going to a masque later this evening, Jillian," Catherine said, trying to break the stilted silence. "You and Justin must come with us. It is said to be most enjoyable."

Everyone looked at Justin, but he did not speak, his eyes roaming freely over Jillian's exquisitely chiseled face until the flawless white skin eventually became tinged with warm pink. Jillian bore his rude scrutiny with inner chagrin as they were served duck and chicken with side platters of shrimp pie and venison pastry. None of the diners showed much interest in the delicious fare, but Jillian strove for an animated smile as the dining-room maids efficiently met their needs. She conversed freely with the others, while Justin said little, wondering at his bride's charming deportment, so very different from the spitting she-cat he had done battle with only hours before. Her changeability disturbed him, but he found his mind more often on the satiny swells revealed so temptingly above her gown. His attention perked when Ryan broached the subject of her ruse.

"Come, Jillian, tell us how you escaped," Ryan asked, smiling across at her. "The pool is very small, yet you disappeared without a trace."

"Perhaps she turned herself into a fish and swam about as you searched," Catherine suggested, giving a wicked sidelong look at Justin.

Everyone laughed except Justin, and Jillian felt his eyes burning into her face.

"Nay, there is an underwater passage that leads to a cave. I but swam through it to safety."

Justin was not even listening to her answer; his eyes were on her red lips as she spoke. They looked moist and soft, and he could almost taste them. He wet his lips as a tingle of desire stirred his loins. Tonight he would hold her and touch her as a wife, and he grew increasingly impatient for the evening to end.

Ryan and the others continued to ply her with questions about the tricks she had played, and Justin's face gradually grew hard at their obvious enjoyment at his expense. He added nothing to the conversation, and when their repast was done, he watched with sardonic eyes as Jillian swept gracefully before him into the drawing room.

Catherine quickly drew Jillian and Aaron to a small card table near the fire for a game of basset, and as Ryan pulled a chair close to Jillian, Justin frowned darkly before moving to a desk across the room where he was assured a clear view of his wife's position.

Annoyed by her familiarity with his brother, Justin grumbled irritably under his breath as he picked up a quill pen. He needed to write instructions to Philip Hammond in Ulster, and he drew a piece of fine parchment in front of him and dipped the pen into a silver inkwell, trying to ignore the fascination Jillian Devlin seemed to have for his brother's every word.

"I fear I am not very good at this game," Jillian finally protested after Catherine had won consistently. "Perhaps you should take my hand, Ryan, and let me watch."

"I would love to take your hand, my fair lady," Ryan said with exaggerated gallantry, going to one knee beside her as he lifted her fingertips to his lips. Jillian and Catherine laughed at his silliness, but across the way, the scratching of the quill stopped.

Justin stared at his wife, at where the firelight gleamed against the satin luster of her black hair and tinted her skin to pale gold. His jaw hardened when she laughed again, this time at a jest of Aaron's, and he became irritated with all of them, feeling like an outsider with his own family. He muttered an inward oath, then determinedly renewed his efforts at letter writing.

"Catherine has won again," Ryan said, groaning as the last trick fell against him.

"Because I paid attention to my cards, Ryan. You looked at Jillian more than your hand."

"But can you blame me with such beauty at my side?"

Justin gritted his teeth at the sound of their gay banter, and when Jillian glanced at him, she was startled to find a black scowl on his face. She smiled to herself, pleased that her merrymaking irked him.

"Come, Jillian, play me," Aaron said. "Since you are new at the game, perhaps I might have a chance to win."

Jillian sat across from him, and Ryan leaned close over her, helping her to choose the correct cards to beat his brother.

They all laughed when Aaron threw down his cards in disgust, and when Ryan gave Jillian a winner's hug, it proved to be the last straw for the man simmering across the room.

Red-faced, Justin dropped his pen and brought down both palms hard upon the desk top. The loud noise brought four startled faces to him.

"Leave my wife to me, brothers," he gritted out. His square jaw tensed, and both Ryan and Aaron stared at him, amazed by his uncharacteristic outburst and the jealous flush upon their older brother's face. Justin was not a jealous man.

"Come now, Justin, Ryan was only—" Catherine protested, but Justin cut her short.

"Leave us, I say, and go to your masque," he intoned sternly, gray eyes intense, and Catherine shook her head in exasperation. Ryan and Aaron exchanged a knowing look, then Ryan smiled at Jillian.

"It seems my brother would like to have you to himself," he said, kissing her hand again despite Justin's frown of disapproval. "And little can we blame him for that pleasure."

He ignored Justin's glower as he crossed the room, pulling Catherine with him, but his amused chuckle floated back as Aaron closed the door after them.

Jillian turned mildly inquiring eyes on the darkly flushed face of her English husband.

"Perhaps you will explain your behavior with my brothers," Justin demanded tightly. "After this spectacle I am afraid even to contemplate what passed between you and Aaron while I fought your battles for you in Ulster."

Righteous indignation flared inside Jillian at his insulting accusation.

"I fear you base other's actions upon your own propensities," she replied icily. "Your brothers and Catherine sought only to entertain me tonight in otherwise dreary company."

Justin stiffened, and Jillian arose and gave him a frigid look before she turned to leave. Justin's voice stopped her. "I trust you have resigned yourself to your wifely duties and will await my pleasure upstairs."

It was not really a question but a command, and fury smoldered in a fiery glow within her. She turned steadfast eyes on him, wishing she could see his face when he found her gone.

"Aye, milord, 'tis my fate, I know, though a most repugnant one. I only pray that you are gentleman enough to allow me to prepare myself for bed."

She left him without another word, and Justin stared after her for a moment, then paced restlessly to the windows. He frowned into the night, angry at himself for his treatment of her, angry at his inability even to carry on a rational conversation with the girl. Ryan and Aaron certainly had no trouble charming her, but there was icy hatred in her turquoise eyes when she looked upon her own husband.

Furthermore, her resignation to the marriage bed did not parallel her display of pride during their heated quarrel, and as the minutes ticked by, doubts began to nag him. What if she planned to leave Waverton? Would she have the courage for such a dangerous flight? Visions of her galloping down the dark road into London soon became vivid enough to send him racing across the drawing room toward the door.

He rounded the curved stairs in haste and ran down the upstairs hall to her room, teeth clamped as he cursed himself for trusting her.

He was furious as he thrust open her bedchamber door, completely convinced that she would be gone.

Jillian whirled from where she stood before her dressing table. She crossed her arms over her breasts, staring in fear at Justin where he stood in the portal, his handsome face flushed and angry. He had come much too soon, hardly given her time to undress, much less flee to London. Now what would she do? She watched with hammering heart as he slid the bolt.

Justin looked at Jillian, silvery fires darkening his eyes, and she braced a hand on the dressing table as he came slowly toward her. She forced herself to stand very still as his eyes scorched into her chemise of ivory satin edged with delicate crocheted lace. He lowered his eyes to her bare flesh above the gown, his gaze seeming to penetrate the fabric to burn her skin.

Justin's whole body pulsated with the need to touch her. Her flesh was as white and smooth as the satin she wore, and his breath stood still in his throat at the way the thin fabric clung provocatively to her breasts, swirls of delicate lace teasing his eyes with tantalizing glimpses of pink crests. His swallow was convulsive, and he stepped closer, lifting the heavy blue stone that nestled in the shadowed softness of her breasts.

"What is this stone you wear?" he asked gruffly, his eyes on the moist lips so very close to his mouth.

Jillian's pulse leapt as he raised his eyes to hold her in their unbreakable silver spell. He towered over her now, very close, forcing her to bend her neck to look at him.

"'Tis my birthing stone, which was put upon my neck when I was born. I am protected from harm by its magic," she said, half surprised by the breathless quality of her voice.

Justin smiled as she nervously moistened her lips.

"You no longer need such magic," he murmured, reaching out to lift a lock of soft black hair. He caressed its silky texture between his thumb and forefinger. "I am the only protector you will need."

To Jillian his words seemed possessive, as if she were an object, not a person, and she fought the overwhelming urge to slap his handsome face.

"Then I will have use of it to keep me safe from my protector," she said, but Justin only smiled, running one knuckle down the satiny softness of her cheek.

"And mayhap you will not desire such protection after this night."

Jillian stared up at him, incredulous at his arrogance. As if a night in his bed would make her crawl on her knees begging for more, the swaggering jackanapes! He would soon find out just how much his charms meant to her!

She jerked slightly as his hands settled on her shoulders, his eyes holding hers as he slid his palms down her arms. The narrow straps fell with them, leaving her shoulders bare, and she gasped weakly as his head dropped forward, his mouth, hot and moist, burning into her naked shoulder. An unwanted response swirled into existence, and Jillian resisted it, furious with herself.

Justin was totally inflamed by the sweet fragrance of her skin and hair, but as he felt her tense, he sought to get a grip on his control.

"Do not be afraid," he muttered hoarsely into her ear, drawing her closer until their bodies touched, his hands sliding over the lush curves beneath the satin. "I will not hurt you."

"W-wait, please . . ." Jillian stammered, pushing her small palms against the hard muscles of his chest as he started to slip the gown lower.

Through extreme force of will Justin released her, and Jillian lowered long, black lashes.

"I have not known a man, milord. Please allow me my modesty this first time. I wish to bathe and prepare myself."

Justin gazed down at her small, beautiful face, aware of how very young she was, how innocent, and he grappled with his thundering passion for her. He wanted her with every fiber of his being, but she was his wife, and he would treat her with the respect she deserved.

"Do not take long, my love, for I have waited long for this night."

# FIFTEEN

Justin walked quickly to his bedchamber down the hall, where he paced the length of his room and back again. He stopped and shut his eyes, smiling as he visualized Jillian awaiting him, her raven hair shimmering over the white satin pillows, her lips parted and moist. He entered the misty edges of his own fantasy, going to her, lying with her, sliding his hand down the slender column of her throat to the upper swell of her breast.

He groaned aloud, running frustrated fingers through his dark hair. His agitation sent him to the outside balcony, and he moved to the parapet, bracing his hands on the cold stone as he breathed in the cool night air. He stared into the gardens below, wondering how long he should give her. He wouldn't last much longer; his loins ached with his desire to go to her.

A movement caught his eye below, and he sharpened his gaze as a woman ran past one of the lighted windows. She clutched a bundle in one hand, and it took Justin only a moment to realize that she carried a cat in her other arm.

"Damn her bloody tricks!" he ground out, and wasted no more time heading downstairs to cut off her path to the stables.

Jillian hurried through the gardens, avoiding the intermittent lamplight. She had very little time to reach the stables where Bridgit awaited with their horses. Her only hope was that he would be considerate enough this time to allow her to bathe. Once in London she would be safe. He would never find her in the throngs of people.

She stopped behind a hedge as several of the servants appeared in her path, stopping near her to talk. She anxiously bit her lip as they laughed together and took turns drinking from a wine bottle. She clutched the small bag tightly, knowing that the emerald pin Catherine had given her was her only way to buy passage to Ulster.

She panicked as she heard Justin yell her name from not far away. She jumped up, dropping her bundle, her only thought to escape him. She ran blindly toward the water gardens with Ebony clutched tight against her, then flew down the wide, graveled walk. She could hear Justin's footsteps crunching on the loose gravel in the darkness behind her, and as she reached the lake, she ducked behind one of the azalea bushes planted near the water's edge, panting with exertion.

She held her breath as Justin rounded the hedgerow after her, slowing as he lost sight of her. He paused beside her hiding place, and she groaned aloud as Ebony mewled and tried to escape her grip.

"Come out of there, Jillian," Justin said through set teeth. Jillian did not move. He stood at the edge of the water now, very close, and Jillian's eyes went to the dark water for an instant, and hope returned.

She moved forward quickly, pushing against his chest with all her strength. Justin's arms flailed as he stepped off the bank behind him, and he made a valiant attempt to regain his balance but was too far gone. He cursed as he disappeared beneath the water with a huge splash, but Jillian didn't stay to watch; she headed at a run for the stables.

She had barely reached the end of the graveled walk when Justin grabbed her by the arms. He jerked her around, snarling in fury, and Jillian fought him desperately until he shook her with enough force to set her head to spinning. He scooped her up in steel-thewed arms and stalked furiously back to the lake, still churning with anger from his plunge. Before Jillian knew what he was about, he heaved her into it, and Jillian screamed in outrage as she hit the muddy water.

She struggled furiously back to the top, screaming every Gaelic curse she knew, when she felt a very large palm against the top of her head. She had time only to gulp a breath of air before he mercilessly ducked her under again. She surfaced to Justin's mocking laughter.

She splashed furiously to the side to pull herself out, but to no avail; Justin's hands captured her again. He lifted her bodily from the water with no show of effort, and Jillian cursed him venomously as he swung her over one broad shoulder.

She had never felt so humiliated as he carried her dripping wet and dirty toward the house.

Justin stomped up one of the back staircases, ignoring Jillian's jerking as he strove for a hold on his raging temper. Never had anyone, not even Catherine with her headstrong antics, gotten him as angry as the tiny bundle on his shoulder. His patience was worn threadbare by her constant treachery, and he was determined that there would be no more tricks, no more lies, no more of her making a fool out of him. He had her where he wanted her at last, and there she was going to stay.

He took the corridor to his own bedchamber with long, purposeful strides. He flung open the door, and Jillian's shrieks, along with the sudden intrusion of two bedraggled, filthy apparitions, sent Catherine's maid, Milly, running for safety from the center of the room where she prepared a bath for Justin.

Justin didn't give the maid a glance, carrying his squirming burden to his bed where he spilled her without a whit of ceremony. He glared down at her, his hands on his hips.

"It is over now, Jillian Devlin Spenser, you have nowhere to hide."

"Aye, 'tis over," Jillian screamed, scrambling to her knees. "I will never stay here with you! If it takes me forever, I will escape!"

Justin frowned blackly at her threat.

"You will not escape me again," he roared, and Jillian watched with defiant eyes as his long, brown fingers worked to loosen his belt. He jerked it off and started toward her. Jillian forced herself not to cringe back in terror of the beating he was obviously about to give her.

Justin saw the fear in her eyes, and his own anger abated as he realized what she thought he was about to do. It had not even occurred to him, though well she deserved it. He smiled grimly as he buckled the leather strap around her dainty wrists and secured it to the bedpost.

"I intend to bathe now, my love, and since I cannot seem to keep you with me any other way, I will bind you to me."

Jillian presented him with a scathing glare. Justin watched her slide off the bed as he shrugged out of his vest. He grinned as he pulled the grimy shirt over his head, and Jillian's eyes slid away from the bronzed muscles of his chest. When he started to unfasten his breeches, Jillian looked back at him, her voice dripping ice.

"Have you no decency? Forcing a woman to watch you undress?"

Justin lifted one dark brow, and his teeth flashed white in his begrimed face. "I am not forcing you to watch me, Jillian. I only secured your arms to the post. It is certainly in your power to look elsewhere."

A surge of color stained Jillian's high cheekbones at the truth of his observation, and she whirled away from him. He laughed and stepped out of his pants, and she stood stiffly erect until a splash told her he had settled into the hip bath. She muttered a whole string of low Gaelic curses as she endeavored to pull her wrists free.

"Easy now, my sweet," he said lazily from behind her. "I will not be long. Perhaps if I released you, you could make yourself useful and scrub my back."

Jillian's answer seethed with contempt. "And perhaps you could make yourself useful and drown in your bathwater."

To her shock Justin laughed, and she plopped angrily on the bed, facing away from him. She stared at her reflection in the mirror upon the wall, hardly recognizing herself beneath the grime and muck. She fumed there, her hands clenched together, until Justin rose from the bath, his reflection appearing in the mirror. Her eyes went to his lightly furred chest and flat belly.

A low laugh brought her gaze to meet his eyes in the mirror. Her face flamed as he caught her looking at his body. She stared at her hands after that as he moved around the room, shaving and dressing without haste. She did not look up as he removed the belt from her hands and tossed it on the bed.

"You mean, I am to be allowed to walk without a leash?" she taunted bitterly, and Justin lifted one shoulder carelessly.

"If you learn to behave."

She raised an obstinate chin as strong fingers encircled her wrist, and she was again pulled behind him down the corridor.

In Jillian's chamber Bridgit stood by the fire, wringing her hands with worry over her mistress and the big Englishman, when to her utter dismay, the frightening twosome burst through the door. She emitted a strangled squeak, then made to escape, but Justin's voice rang out in command.

"Stay! The Lady Jillian wishes to bathe and dress for bed."

He released Jillian, and she held her aching wrists as he lounged down in a chair near the hip bath Milly had just filled.

"Do you mean to watch my toilette?" she asked coldly.

Justin smiled. "Alas, I've learned I must be ever vigilant to keep my lovely wife at my side."

"I will not bathe with you here."

"You will."

Their eyes clashed, and Bridgit fidgeted nervously with the ruffled pocket of her apron, looking longingly at the door, until Jillian turned from the Englishman and spoke to her.

"Fetch a blanket to shield me while I disrobe."

She gave Justin a challenging look, daring him to object, but he only smiled, steepling his fingers and watching her over them. Jillian's teeth clamped together until she thought they would surely break. As Bridgit held the blanket in place, Jillian quickly slipped out of the wet, muddy gown and sank into the tub.

"Go now," Justin said in sharp dismissal to Bridgit, and the nervous girl looked helplessly at her mistress, then dropped the blanket and fled.

Jillian sat self-consciously in the hip bath before swiveling her head to address him, her words brittle.

"How, pray tell, am I supposed to wash my hair without Bridgit? I cannot lift the bucket alone."

Justin's eyes went to the bucket of warm water beside the tub.

"Do not fret, love, I can think of nothing that would give me greater pleasure than dumping yonder bucket over your head."

"Oh, you . . ." Jillian began, then, as he laughed, she decided to ignore him. She picked up the cloth and began to scrub the horrid silt where it had dried on her face.

Justin still smiled, his eyes following the cloth in her hand over one slender, bare shoulder to the soft mounds of her breasts swelling above the scented water. Her fragile jaw remained stiff with anger, and as Justin stared at her breathtakingly lovely face, framed now with filthy strands of hair, a surge of unfamiliar emotion mushroomed inside his chest.

In that moment he realized that he did not want to fight her, did not want to force her, nor break her indomitable spirit. She was stubborn and headstrong and beautiful, but he found that he admired in her the very traits that had goaded him beyond belief. Here was no simpering, weeping woman who would bore him with her silly chatter. Jillian was different, strong, loyal, lovely, and he wanted her willing response in his arms, wanted her eyes to look upon him with warmth and welcome and love.

A lump rose in his throat, for never in his life had he wanted anything or anyone with such devastating passion. He also knew he could easily force her to his will. Now, at this very moment, he had every right to lift her from the water and have her on the bed as he had dreamed of doing since the first day at the Enchanted Pool.

But he knew only too well that if he did, Jillian would fight him tooth and nail, or worse, lie like a victim beneath him. He stared at her, overwhelmed by his own realizations. He admired her courage in eluding him for so long back in Ulster, admired her strength, her loyalty to her brothers. He had been a fool to think she would ever yield to force. She would only give her love and loyalty freely to those she cared about.

All his anger fled him forever, and he looked at the wife he hardly knew through different eyes.

Jillian refused to look at the despicable Englishman as she lathered her hair, aware that his silver-gray eyes never left her. She tensed as he rose and came forward, fully expecting him to swing the bucket high and heartlessly drench her but was surprised when instead he poured it carefully over her soapy hair, then afterward turned away to stare out the window. She took advantage of his unexpected gentlemanly behavior, hastily wrapping a linen towel around her hair and reaching for her robe.

Justin intentionally gave her time to don her dressing gown, and when he did turn, she was watching him warily, fingers clutching her garment together at the neck.

"If you will listen, I would like to talk to you," he said. Jillian didn't answer, not trusting him. "Sit down, please."

She started to perch on the edge of the bed, then thought better of it and crossed to a small chair against the far wall.

Justin stood very straight, his hands clasped behind his back. "I have given much thought to your behavior since we met, and I think I can understand why you've done the things you have."

Jillian's eyes widened as he continued. "But since we're already legally married, it is futile to carry on with it any longer."

Justin's eyes dropped, against his will, to where one shapely, white thigh parted her gown and found he could not look away. Jillian noted his interest and hastily covered herself, and Justin went on.

"It was wrong of you to deceive me as you did, but I was at fault to make demands of you in anger. I assure you, I have never forced a woman into my bed, and despite the fact that you are my wife, I swear to you that I will not touch you again unless you wish me to."

Jillian's shock parted her lips, and she could only stare at him.

"But since we are married, it would please me greatly if you would grace my table as a wife, then perhaps afterward join me in the drawing room for a short time. Otherwise I will make no demands on your time, and you will be free to follow your own desires. Do you think you could agree to that?"

Incredulous at his abrupt turnabout, Jillian grew suspicious.

"And why this sudden change toward me?"

Justin's eyes seemed to look into her very soul. "Because you are my wife, and I am tired of lies and deceit."

"Do you give me your word upon these things?" she demanded with more boldness than she felt.

Justin nodded. "Gladly, if you will swear upon the grave of your father that you will not leave this place as you threatened."

Jillian hid her relief at the mildness of his one demand and nodded quickly in agreement, and Justin smiled, equally relieved.

"Then we are agreed. I will send Bridgit to help you dress for bed."

He strode out, leaving Jillian staring after him and contemplating what guardian angel had come to her rescue and gentled the Englishman's anger.

# SIXTEEN

As dusk settled slowly into night Jillian descended the main staircase, one slender hand gliding along the polished banister. She hesitated before the dining room doors, pulling nervously at the lace-edged ivory flounces at her elbow. The dress she had chosen was a deep wine-red, and she patted the heavy velvet skirt where it lay over her wide hoop. The hemline was lavishly embroidered with black satin, the swirling motif also emblazoning the tightly cinched bodice. She had been careful that the décolletage was modest, protecting her shoulders from Justin Spenser's view. She was determined to do nothing to tempt him. She'd been unable to fathom the reason behind his change of heart several nights ago, for she could not deny that the tricks she had played upon him would have enraged any man. She shivered to think how either of her brothers would have reacted to such duplicity in a wife.

She looked around the wide hall, wondering where Catherine was. Since her husband had arrived at Waverton Hall, she'd been careful to keep one of the others with her at all times. No one was in sight, and she took a deep, fortifying breath to bolster her courage, feeling like a lamb seeking out a lion as she stepped through the portal.

Justin stood motionlessly near the fireplace, his hands clasped loosely behind his back. Jillian could not stop the thrill that shot through her at the sight of his lean and virile appearance. He was clad formally but with the subdued elegance she had grown to expect from him. His coat was a soft dove-gray with a black silk waistcoat, and gray breeches of a darker hue encased long, hard-muscled legs. He did not see her, his dark head bent as he contemplated the dancing flames.

Jillian moved forward, her satin underskirts rustling prettily, and he turned at once, silver eyes glowing with the warmth of diamonds. She stopped uncertainly and watched him come to her until she was dwarfed beside his great height. He smiled as he lifted her hand to press it to his mouth, his eyes holding hers relentlessly.

"You are most lovely tonight, Jillian."

His words came softly, uttered like a silken caress, and she withdrew her fingers quickly, obediently taking the chair he held for her.

"Will the others not be joining us?" she asked timidly, and Justin shook his head as he took his place at her side.

"They are spending the evening in London with our aunt."

Jillian frowned slightly. "I am surprised

that Catherine did not mention such a visit to me this afternoon," she said, causing Justin to smile.

"Catherine did not know then that I wished time alone with my wife."

Jillian dropped her eyes but became increasingly unsettled as he kept his warm, admiring gaze upon her for the length of time it took the servants to serve a juicy roast of sirloin prepared with crusty slices of fried potatoes. Justin poured the rich, red Madeira himself as the servants backed a respectful distance away.

An uncomfortable silence descended upon them as Jillian found she had nothing to say to him, nor was the food appetizing with her stomach tightly knotted with nerves. She lifted her goblet of wine instead, a surreptitious glance from beneath her long lashes assuring her that the Englishman's enjoyment of the meal was not hampered in the least.

In truth Justin was more content with the state of his marriage than he had been in many days. He was enjoying the fine food and the presence of his most beautiful wife. Their truce was a welcome change from bitter anger and harsh words, and his sole intent was to make Jillian see him as a man who cared about her, not some monster to despise.

"It seems your appetite is lacking this evening," he commented when the servants removed her untouched plate, and Jillian nodded slightly and looked away.

"Perhaps some fruit and sweet bread then, my love?"

His casual endearment brought wary blue eyes back to him, but he met them with a smile, raising his hand for the maid to bring the dessert platter forward.

Justin leaned back as she was served, his eyes touching the fine, delicately chiseled profile and the skin as clear and flawless as the purest of alabaster. Her black lashes formed a thick crescent against her cheeks as she looked at her plate.

Liquid fire shot into his very core as she lifted a juicy purple plum and bit into it, his eyes fascinated by soft red lips moistened by its nectar. When she traced her mouth with the tip of her tongue to catch the sweet droplets, he shifted uncomfortably in his chair.

"Tell me about your brothers," he said abruptly, wanting to think about anything but the torturous course his mind had taken. He berated himself for the gruffness of his voice, dragging his attention off her lips to meet her eyes.

"They are lost from me forever, and now you have taken their inheritance. What else is there to tell?"

Her words were not sharp, only sad, and Justin persisted, wanting to know more of her past, her family, wanting to know everything about her.

"And you have no other kin?"

"Only Donal, now that Mauve is gone."

"You have family now, Jillian. I want you to consider my family as your own."

They looked at each other, Jillian confused at his new gentleness and the kindness of his words, and Justin fighting his desire to crush her in his arms. Her nearness made his blood boil, but he had struck a bargain with her, and he meant to see it through.

"Perhaps you will honor me with your presence in the drawing room," he said, and Jillian hesitated, much preferring to escape upstairs. But he was being most pleasant and agreeable, and she did not wish to make him angry.

A fire crackled and snapped a cheery welcome in the drawing room, and Jillian sat on a small silk divan that faced the hearth as Justin pulled the doors closed behind them. She watched as he walked across the room and took something from a cabinet. Her eyes widened when she saw that it was her lap harp.

"I brought this to you when I came from Ireland, but I have not had the opportunity to give it to you until now."

"That was most thoughtful," Jillian murmured.

"Will you play for me? As you did in Ulster?" he asked, smiling as he sat beside her, and Jillian took the harp from him, settling it in her lap.

"Is there something special you wish to hear?"

She gave him a tentative smile, still uncomfortable with the unfamiliar cordiality between them.

"Whatever you wish, for it is your voice that I enjoy."

Jillian looked at the strings for a moment, then began to play. It was a Gaelic ballad of lost love, sad and sorrowful. It had been her father's favorite, and she could remember times when he had sat close beside her as the Englishman did now, his eyes wet and mournful as he grieved for his beloved Maire.

Justin watched her as the velvet of her soft voice caressed his mind. The firelight behind her cast a golden halo around her dark hair, and he knew her beauty had no rival in his heart. She stopped her song abruptly, averting her face, and Justin put a finger to her chin to turn her face to him.

One tear rolled upon the soft curve of her cheek, and Justin was startled by the emotion tugged from his own heart. He wanted to pull her into his arms but knew he did not dare.

"Why do you weep, Jillian?"

"The ballad was loved by my father," she murmured, and Justin tenderly wiped away her tears. His voice was gentle.

"He was the victim of war and the politics of kings, Jillian, as are we all. But no longer will you suffer hardship and grief. I give you my promise on that."

His words were sincere, and although Jillian was touched by his kindness, she could not look at him. Justin could not resist the staggering need to touch her again, and he traced the delicate line of her jaw so gently that it took Jillian's breath. She looked up at him, and they shared their first real smile since they'd met.

Neither spoke, and Justin was triumphant that she stayed with him longer of her own accord. They settled into a comfortable silence for a time, Justin content just to look at her. His day had been long, since he'd risen with the sun to oversee work in his London offices, and a yawn crept upon him. His eyes widened in surprise as Jillian raised her hand to cover his mouth.

"Evil spirits seek entrance to the body when one yawns," she said, her eyes serious, and Justin considered not her silly superstition but only her soft palm upon his mouth. He caught it tightly in place with his own hand, and their eyes fused. Jillian's lips parted in a gasp as his lips caressed her palm, then moved to the inside of her wrist where her pulse hammered beneath his mouth.

Jillian knew fear then, remembering her devastating weakness to his touch, and Justin easily read the uncertainty in her wide eyes. He forced himself to release her and stood to stoke the fire, striving the whole while to calm the riot she stirred in his blood. When he mastered his passion enough to turn, she was gone. He groaned aloud, slumping into a chair, his eyes grimly upon the fire.

* * *

In the next weeks Justin was most kind to Jillian, and when he and Aaron left to greet one of the Spenser ships that had arrived in Harwich from a voyage to the Orient, she could not explain the sadness that touched her heart. He had remained true to his promise, but even so, her pulse raced wildly whenever she felt hot, silvery eyes upon her.

The fact that she had not betrayed her brothers gave her some comfort, but the days Justin was gone seemed endless, and she found herself eagerly awaiting his return. She no longer thought of him as a libertine or an enemy, and every day her admiration and respect of his family grew because of their kindness and generosity toward her. Her will to reject Justin as her husband was slowly crumbling, and she was frightened by feelings she could no longer control.

On the night that Justin was expected to return she sat in her bedchamber with Catherine as Bridgit skillfully twisted her hair into soft ringlets, gathered to each side with pearl combs.

Justin had ordered her many new gowns since he had come to England, and this evening she wore a lovely purple silk with insets of cream organdy billowing from each slashed sleeve. The wide skirts were sewn with golden lace and ribbons, and the waistline had been cinched very small with a narrow gold stomacher.

Bridgit finished threading the purple satin ribbons through the softness of Jillian's hair, then stepped back to eye her creation with satisfaction.

"You look most lovely, milady," she said with a bright smile, and Catherine nodded agreement.

"Aye, and Justin will no doubt drool at the sight of you as he does each time he looks at you."

Jillian's face grew pink with embarrassment, but Bridgit laughed. They all turned at a knock, and when Justin entered, Catherine rose, her green eyes dancing at the way her brother stared at his wife. Catherine thought it most amusing in a man who had heretofore scorned men obsessed by a pretty woman.

"Come, Bridgit," she teased. "Before Justin orders us out. How I wish that I had a man who found my company so fascinating. But instead I am courted by fat and ugly merchants with white beards or country bumpkins who spend their courtship pawing at my skirts."

"Only the fact that you are overly particular, sister, keeps you unwed," Justin said, glancing briefly at her. "Instead of welcoming a gentleman's attention, you find fault with every man who asks my permission to court you."

Catherine gave a haughty sniff.

"I am not inclined to put myself in a state of matrimony with any male who shows an interest. I do not relish the thought of forced subservience to a husband. I would much prefer to remain a maid, even though it means a life being bossed about by three older brothers who think they know everything."

Justin frowned as the door closed upon Catherine's mutterings, then gave Jillian a rueful grin.

"At times I consider a nunnery the proper place for her. Perhaps her willful ways would cause me less grief if she were dressed in a habit."

His words were far from harsh, harboring instead the tolerant affection toward his sister that Jillian had seen in him in the last few weeks. She smiled, most glad to see him.

"Perhaps Catherine has not yet found the man who will make her eager to obey him," she murmured.

"And have you found such a man?" Justin asked, his eyes going to her lips.

Jillian's mouth went dry at the way he looked at her. When she did not answer, he only smiled as if he knew her thoughts.

"Come, the others await us downstairs."

When they entered the red drawing room, Ryan and Catherine were playing whist at an inlaid walnut table. They both smiled as Aaron came forward and lifted Jillian's fingers to his lips.

"Your beauty has grown since I left a week past. Justin is surely the luckiest man on earth."

Jillian's face grew hot under his flowery compliments, and Justin chafed inwardly as his brother continued to hold his wife's hand.

Ryan noted Justin's uncomfortable expression, not bothering to hide his grin.

"Do not hold her hand overly long, Aaron, or we will be sent off to another masque. You know as well as I that green has tinged our brother's coloring since he wed."

Aaron chuckled and released Jillian's hand, glancing at Justin, whose stiff smile lent credence to the truth in Ryan's admonition. Justin's ardor was well motivated, he decided, for such a bride was well worth such protective zeal. Even the fairest of Mary's Court could not compare to Jillian's loveliness, with her jet-black hair. But he could see that Jillian was uneasy under their teasing.

"You must forgive our jests, Jillian," he said, winking at her. "But we never thought to see such behavior from Justin, though many ladies have coveted the devotion from him that you hold so charmingly—"

"The queen has planned a ball for the twenty-ninth day of September," Justin interrupted, clearly attempting to change the subject. "She has requested all of us to attend."

The news brought an animated cry from Catherine.

"Jillian and I must have new gowns then, for it will be Jillian's first presentation at Court! And we must have matching cloaks as well, and jeweled fans!"

She looked excitedly at Justin, and when he nodded his permission, she beamed at Jillian.

"I will summon the dressmakers tomorrow morning when Ryan and Aaron take me into London for my stay with Aunt Agnes! And you both can escort me to the ball," Catherine said, looking at Ryan and Aaron. "So I can dance with whomever I please."

Aaron held up his hand and shook his head. "I will have to leave that honor to Ryan, for I return to Spenser Court within a week."

"I thought you planned to select bloodstock before you returned," Justin said in surprise, and Aaron nodded.

"I thought to, but it is the harvest season at home, and I have been at Waverton most of the summer. I am needed there, so I will leave the selection to you. Perhaps you could bring them along with you when you come to Kent for the Harvest Feast."

Throughout supper the family discussed the preparations for the annual feast celebration they planned for their workers at Spenser Court. After they retired to the drawing room Justin took a stance before the fireplace, gray eyes steady on the burning logs.

After a moment he turned his head slightly to look at Jillian. She sat quietly, hands folded serenely. While he watched, Ebony purred and rubbed against her ankles, and Jillian placed the small cat on the shimmering purple silk of her lap. His eyes swept the delicate curve of her jaw to linger on her soft lips, before dropping to the modest show of creamy flesh above the lace bodice. He knew her skin felt as soft as it looked, and suddenly he was almost able to taste it beneath his mouth. He tore his eyes away, half-disgusted at his driving need to hold her, to lie close against her soft warmth. She had been like a fire in his blood since the first day he had seen her, and now that they were on better terms, it was a torture devised in hell to be so very close to her and not be able to touch her.

"The Lady Eleanor Marlowe requests to see Lord Spenser," Geoffrey's deep voice spoke from the door. "Shall I show the lady in, milord?"

A heavy silence fell over the group, and Jillian looked from Catherine's conspiratorial grin to Justin, who now wore a dark frown.

"I will see her in the long gallery," he said, and Catherine waited for him to leave the room before she sat down beside Jillian.

"She is probably here to tell on us for our trick with Ebony," Catherine whispered. "She is very spiteful, but do not worry, for Ryan said that Justin has been most exasperated with her since she made a scene on his ship before they left for Ulster."

Relieved, Jillian nodded and made no comment, but she declined Ryan's invitation for a game of cards. When the others sat down at the table to play, she listened to their chatter without really hearing it. Her thoughts were on the beautiful Englishwoman now closeted with her husband. Eleanor Marlowe had obviously played a special role in Justin's life before he had come to Ulster. Jillian was appalled at the pain that knifed through her to think he might still care for the hateful Eleanor.

As time passed and Justin did not return, her distress mounted, and she rose quietly and slipped into the hall, wanting the solitude of her thoughts. The foyer was deserted, the French doors of the gallery closed, and she turned away, moving through the dining room, then out onto the stone balcony that led to the rear gardens.

She strolled through the flower-edged walks for a time, thankful to be alone in the darkness. She could not blame Justin if he found solace with an old lover, because she had made it clear that she did not want him in her bed. And if she were to give in to her own desires and lie with him, all was lost for Brian.

She swallowed hard and slowed her steps along the lake, remembering the night Justin had been furious enough with her to throw her into the water. Things were so different now. She sighed, walking down one of the paths that led across the water to the gazebo. Catherine had directed that candlesticks be affixed to the latticework for summer evenings, and Jillian lit a long white taper, then sat on a low bench nearby. She stared at the small flame, and tears burned her eyes. She blinked them back determinedly. If only she could leave this place and go home to Ulster, maybe then she could forget Justin and be true to her brothers. Maybe she could be happy again.

"May I join you?"

Justin's deep voice startled her, and she whirled to find him leaning a shoulder against the door.

"If you wish," she managed, standing to move nearer to the candle.

Justin watched her as she stood in profile, her black hair gleaming with silken splendor. She turned suddenly to look at him, and his breath caught as her eyes flashed with the beauty of sapphires.

"I am surprised that you are not still with your guest."

Justin grinned at her tone, wondering if he could possibly be lucky enough to incur her jealousy.

"I was fortunate enough to rid myself of her easily this time, though not as expeditiously as you and Catherine seemed to have done."

Jillian's eyes were wary. "She told you?"

"With heartfelt delight, I fear, and I must say that I am only sorry I was not there to witness the scene."

"You are not angry?" Jillian asked in some amazement, having expected that another demonstration of her magic would infuriate him.

Justin gave a low laugh.

"I daresay Eleanor deserved it. Catherine told me a moment ago what Eleanor said to you. I think the fact that Catherine told others of Eleanor's frightened reaction is what bothers the lady."

Jillian smiled, her voice low.

"I thought that perhaps since you and Eleanor were old friends, our behavior would have met with your disapproval."

"I had a relationship with Eleanor at one time, but it was over long before I met you. She means nothing to me, and she never has."

Jillian lowered her lashes, his words giving her pleasure, and Justin moved very close. Jillian's heart went wild, and she felt weak as his fingers slid into the flowing silk of her hair, gently pulling her head back until she was forced to meet his eyes.

"You are the one I care about, Jillian, can you really not know that yet?" he whispered, the warm silver of his eyes mesmerizing her, demanding her surrender. Jillian's lashes fell closed as his warm lips touched her forehead to feather soft kisses to each closed eyelid. Her lips parted breathlessly, only to be possessed by warm and eager male lips, twisting, probing, savoring, until pleasure washed over her in ever-increasing waves that disregarded all thoughts of caution. Her arms moved around his neck of their own accord, and she pressed her body eagerly against him.

Justin groaned over her mouth like a man starved, and he pulled her closer with one hand, heedless of anything as his mouth moved along the sensitive cord of her throat, the other hand sliding down her back.

Jillian floated for a time in dreamy contentment but gasped aloud as his hand found entrance beneath her skirts, his warm fingers touching the bare curve of her hip.

"Yield to me, my love, be my wife as I long for you to be," he breathed hoarsely, and as his words penetrated her fuzzy mind, she began to realize what was about to happen. She stiffened in his embrace. Her weakness for the Englishman was close to ruining all her hard-earned victories to protect her brothers. She knew only too well that her willing surrender to the English usurper would disgrace her far more than if she had been forced into his bed.

She began to struggle against his hold, and Justin muttered a gruff protest against her neck. It was several moments before he could let her go, and Jillian fled the gazebo as if pursued by the devil himself. Justin stared after her, his face stiff with frustration, cursing his fate to be obsessed with a beautiful wife who feared his very touch.

# SEVENTEEN

Heavy mists still clung to the emerald lawns of Waverton Hall when Jillian arose in the pink light of early dawn. She dressed quickly in a simple white gown, tightly lacing the front with a black silk stomacher, then donned her white herb apron with its pockets for storing her powders.

She loosely braided her hair into a long queue down her back before slipping silently into the hallway. She glanced fearfully toward Justin's bedchamber, then moved down the steps and out the long gallery. Not a servant was about, and once safely outside, she inhaled deeply in the crisp air.

The morning was still and very foggy, and Jillian set her course for the dense forest that lay on the far side of the water gardens. She felt slightly light-headed from lack of sleep since she had paced her room for hours after she left Justin in the gazebo. No matter how much she wanted to deny it, she had wanted him to hold her and kiss her. She had wanted him to take her into his bed and show her the ways of love. Now, after her eager response, he knew her feelings, and Jillian could not face him.

She hurried her step through the garden paths, then struck out across the grassy fields, her shoes becoming damp with dew. It had been a long time since she gathered healing plants and bark in the woods, but herb gathering was a task she enjoyed. It was peaceful and quiet in the forest, and she hoped the solitude would help her to sort out her troubled thoughts.

She could not understand how the Englishman could rob her very will from her, how his touch could make her forget her brothers and their stolen inheritance and the disgrace of her family at his hands. She was tormented by her own flaming desires.

Dense, leaf-covered limbs kept the gray light from filtering to the floor of the forest as she entered, and she walked through the dim and smoky silence, her thoughts as tangled as the boughs above. Her footsteps were muffled in dead leaves and twigs, but she was unafraid, for she followed the path that Catherine had pointed out. She would only go to the caretaker's hut, so she would not become lost. Only once when she was a small child had she lost her way in a forest. A shiver coursed down her spine at the horrible memory.

A storm had blown up that day long ago, filling the woods with crouching, dark shadows that had become threatening monsters to the small girl lost in its depths. Night had fallen before her father had found her in a terrified huddle at the base of a tree trunk. Thunder and lightning had never failed to frighten her since, and often Mauve had sat at her bedside if the weather became violent enough to cause her distress.

Jillian thrust such fears from her mind, following the narrow path, her eyes intent upon the ground. When she came upon a comfrey plant growing in the shade of an elder tree, she pulled it up with infinite care. The roots were good for the treatment of boils, and she tucked it carefully into one of her pockets.

As she moved along, stooping now and then to pick dandelions or wild marigolds, she began to feel more tranquil. The quiet woods were punctuated only by the twitterings of birds or the fleeting step of a deer. She hoped that this retreat into nature would help to strengthen her resolve and give her an inner peace that she had not felt since Justin Spenser had come into her life.

The sun was high, dappling intricate patterns of shade on her hair when she came upon the old hut. Its stone walls were crumbling and thick with ivy. A brook flowed to one side of it, cascading crystal-clear water over gray-speckled stones polished round and smooth. She knelt where soft green moss hung over the bank and dipped up a handful of cold water.

Her sleepless night and long walk caught up to her as she looked around the solitary glade. She covered a yawn and lay down upon the blanket of moss to rest. Tangled branches created a living canopy above her, the green, glossy leaves rustling and swaying gently in a soft breeze. She watched the woodland dance with heavy-lidded eyes until her lashes slowly drifted closed. Visions of hot, silver eyes slid through the corridors of her sleepy mind until all faded into gauzy gray. A sound awakened her, and she sat bolt-upright, afraid. She shivered as a cold wind hit her, and as thunder rumbled far away, she scrambled up in alarm. The air carried with it the damp smell of rain, and the treetops no longer swayed but tossed wildly in the brisk wind that always preceded storms.

She knew she had slept a very long time, and a deeper roll of thunder brought gooseflesh down both arms. She hurried back along the path to the Hall, afraid the storm would catch her alone in the dark. She made good time but was only halfway home when the first drops touched her hair.

The sky had darkened considerably, making it hard for her to see, and just as she reached the fields, it began to pour, drenching her clothes. Shivering with cold, she darted frantically toward the gardens, barely able to hear a voice over the rising wind.

"Jillian! Wait!"

Justin was coming toward her, and as he reached her, he jerked off the mantle he wore and wrapped it around her shoulders, then held her protectively against his side as he led her toward the gazebo.

Jillian was trembling uncontrollably in her wet gown. They had barely reached the shelter when Justin turned her around, his eyes like silver frost-fire. His fingers bit into her shoulders, his anger taking her totally by surprise.

"You swore to me that you would not leave," he ground out. "I only took a kiss from you last night, yet it sent you fleeing from me without a word!"

His dark hair was plastered over his forehead, and rivulets of rain streamed over his face. Jillian stared up into his angry face, slowly shaking her head.

"I was not fleeing you!" she cried, pulling away and thrusting her hand into her apron. She held up a handful of flowers and roots. "I went to gather herbs. And I have returned here, have I not?"

Rain drummed on the water behind them, and wind rattled the latticework, but Jillian, her wrath ignited by his accusations, gave no thought to the weather.

Justin was still infuriated by the recklessness of her actions, and he berated her harshly.

"It was foolish and irresponsible to enter the forest alone without telling anyone! You have never been there before! What if you had lost your way or a wild animal or robber had come upon you whilst you were alone and defenseless?"

Jillian met his glare with defiant eyes, calmly pulling the blue stone from the low neck of her bodice. She held it up, dangling it before his eyes. Her words were contemptuous.

"I am never defenseless. The spirit of my Birthing Stone keeps me from harm. I do not need any other protection."

Justin went livid as his suppressed anger and frustration rolled into a gushing river of pure rage. All he had heard since he'd met Jillian had been her absurd tales of witches and magic and spirits. He was tired of tolerating such ignorant superstitions. And now Jillian dared to flaunt some ridiculous stone in his face after he had spent the entire day worrying over her safety. Teeth gritted, he jerked the amulet from her, ignoring her cry of protest as he drew back his arm and hurled it furiously into the lake. He looked back at Jillian then, and his fury dissolved upon the sight of her ashen face.

She stared in stunned disbelief at the rippling waves where her Birthing Stone had disappeared, then slowly turned horrified eyes on his face, their turquoise depths desolate with despair.

"You have taken the very life from my body," she breathed brokenly, and the way her voice caught tore at Justin's heart. She backed away from him; already ashamed of his childish action, Justin took a step toward her.

"Wait, Jillian, please. I did not mean—"

"I hate you!" she said, groaning, and Justin watched helplessly as she burst into tears.

She ran into the rain, no longer aware of Justin's shouts from behind her, her only thought that he had taken her spirit from her. The consequences of such an action were too horrible to imagine.

When she reached the house, she ran to her room, oblivious to the concerned looks from the servants. In her bedchamber she slid the bolt against Justin, then flung herself facedown on her bed. She sobbed into her pillows, her heart bursting with pain at what Justin had done to her. She would surely die without the stone of her birth, and her shoulders shook with aching grief and fear. She wept for a long time, harsh, racking sobs, until there were no tears left, no feelings left. She felt weak and empty and drained.

It was only after her tears were spent and she lay quietly that the fury of the storm outside filtered into her abject misery. She raised her tear-streaked face as a great flash of lightning whitened the darkness of her room. She stifled her scream with the back of her hand as the ensuing crack of thunder rattled the windows. She scrambled off the bed, her eyes wide, clutching her shaking hands together, terrified to face the storm without the magic of her amulet.

She grabbed a blanket and wrapped herself tightly inside it, backing into the farthest corner of her room. She cowered there, her moans of mindless fear obliterated by the deafening booms of thunder and the angry slashing of rain and wind against her windows.

Justin stood alone in the shadowy confines of his room, one arm braced on the heavy oaken mantel. He absently rubbed his hair with a linen towel as he stared into the flickering blaze. He cursed himself bitterly for his own stupidity. Never in his life would he have imagined that a small Irish girl could weave such a web of enchantment around him that he would not have a rational thought in her presence. In one illogical burst of temper he had ruined all the days of gentle wooing that had brought Jillian's tender response just the night before. And now that his brothers and Catherine were in London for a time, giving him time alone with her, she again hated him.

"Damn," he muttered without much feeling, vowing to take his ship and sail away to Holland or the West Indies or anywhere and leave his Irish bride to her potions and charms and rantings of magic.

He sighed in defeat, knowing he would not. He would never leave Jillian again. As he pulled off his damp shirt his mind moved unwillingly to the sweet moment when he felt her surrender into his arms, when her lips parted eagerly beneath his mouth, and he grimaced, cursing the king for giving him over to such sweet hell.

A fierce crash of thunder broke into his gloomy ponderings, and Justin glanced absently at the windows, where rain sluiced in blurry torrents against the diamond-shaped panes. Lightning flared in a jagged streak across the stormy sky, giving a brief glimpse of treetops bent by driving wind. Thunder cracked again, very close, with such force as to make the very timbers cringe from its wrath, and Justin bleakly eyed the grate, thinking that the turbulent elements well matched his mood.

He started with surprise as his door was suddenly thrown wide, jerking around to stare in openmouthed astonishment at Jillian standing just inside the threshold. The glow of the fire barely illuminated her small face, but he could see the terror etched whitely across her beautiful features. A fraction of a moment passed before she could move lips stiff with fear.

"I am afraid. . . ."

Justin took a step toward her, but a harsh blast of thunder splintered what was left of Jillian's frayed nerves, and she leapt toward him, throwing herself into his waiting arms.

He could not suppress his sigh of relief and pleasure as she pressed her quivering body against him, her slender arms locking his neck in a tight stranglehold. He closed his eyes and held her securely, one arm snug around her tiny waist, the other palming the back of her head as she buried her face against his bare shoulder.

"It is all right, my love," he soothed as more thunder sent her clutching him desperately. She quivered uncontrollably in his arms, and he drew a warm, woolen blanket from the bed, then positioned her across his lap as he sat in a chair before the fire. He began to croon comforting words into her soft hair while he struggled against the shattering effect of her warm body pressed so intimately against his naked chest.

The tempest continued to bring low sounds of anxiety from deep within her throat, and Justin tightened his hold until he feared he would crush her. It was a long while before she lay more relaxed in his embrace, and Justin lifted his hand to gently brush a tear-dampened strand of black hair from her cheek. The blaze had dwindled considerably, casting only a reddish glimmer upon the entwined couple before it, while the walls behind them were steeped in heavy shadows. It occurred to Justin that he should rekindle the fire into a warming blaze, but he found himself loath to release Jillian, for fear she would not let him hold her again.

When she grew quiet, he shifted her carefully so that he could look into her face. Her eyes were closed, her long, dark lashes forming twin shadows across the pale ivory of her cheeks. She appeared to sleep, and as his eyes wandered freely over satiny skin and soft lips, he could not resist the temptation to press his mouth upon such an irresistible offering.

His kiss was infinitely tender, a gentle caress of her brow that came to a reluctant end at her temple. She stirred, her eyes fluttering, and Justin smiled down at her. She did not return it but slid one silken arm around his neck, drawing him down, and he murmured his pleasure as her lips touched the hard angle of his jaw.

She held tightly to him, grateful for his strength, and for his gentleness, as his hand slid down her bare arm to rest upon her thigh. The fire's glow dimly illuminated his dark face very close above hers, and in that moment, she craved more from him. She wanted his lips hard upon hers; she wanted his hands to touch her.

Justin instinctively divined her desire, and his heart reacted as he lowered his lips to taste the honey of her mouth. Her lips parted invitingly, and at her yielding, his body ignited into wildfire. His pulse pounded in his temples, his grip increased, and the heated path his mouth took along her cheekbone robbed her of will and reason. Her senses quivered as his palm smoothed over her skirt, raising it until he found bare skin.

His lips closed upon her ear at the same instant her gown slipped off one shoulder, giving him access to the vulnerable hollow of her collarbone.

"I want you. . . ." he muttered, his words gruff with feeling, and she could only whimper a weak protest as his long fingers worked upon the laces of her stomacher.

"My brothers . . . I cannot . . ."

His mouth muffled further argument, and

the fastenings gave way, freeing the lush swell of her breasts. Jillian gasped, disbelieving the breathless sensation of his hard, molded muscles against her naked flesh. She moaned inarticulately as his hands went to her hair, loosening the braid to comb long, brown fingers through silky locks until it swirled around her bare shoulders in soft, ebony waves. He gathered a gentle fistful at her nape, his breath husky.

"Let me love you, Jillian, let me show you . . ."

She could not think, much less answer, and her lack of resistance was all that Justin needed. He stood, holding her half-draped body in the steel cradle of his arms, then carried her to his bed, only pausing to sweep her dress away. He lay her down gently, and she stared up into the darkness where he towered over her. A flare of lightning lit him in silhouette for the breadth of a second, then blackness swallowed his image as he put one knee upon the bed. Another brief flash created black hollows and white planes upon his handsome face as he leaned over her, but it was in total darkness that their bodies touched, their lips fusing like molten metal.

He slid his arms beneath her shoulders, both large hands tangled in the silk of her hair, and she lay beneath the long length of his body, knowing that she loved him, wanted him more than she had ever wanted anything. She moved her palms tentatively over his wide back, iron-hard muscles rippling fluidly with sinewy strength as he moved above her. She was overwhelmed by pulsating currents burning through her as his moist lips scorched a fiery path over her shoulder to the soft curve of her breast.

He rose above her, and lightning streaked the sky as Jillian felt a sharp pain. Her cry was lost in the harsh rumbling of thunder, and a wave of heat made the hurt into a fleeting memory. She gave herself to her husband, willingly and totally, breaths intermingled, bodies laced, until all awareness skidded to a standstill and the universe became a swirling mass of color and sound and fury as their union exploded, fusing their love with all the power of the storm that raged outside their windows.

Justin held her tightly in the moments afterward, his heart thundering within his chest. He had never experienced such sweet ecstasy in the arms of a woman.

Jillian, too, lay weak and sated. It was in those first moments of quiet contentment that she knew the depth of her love for this Englishman who held her so tightly, this man she hated and mocked and tricked. The significance of such a realization sent a flood of shame to stiffen her body, still soft and warm from his lovemaking.

Unable to bear her own guilt, she pulled away from him, and Justin lifted himself on one elbow as she moved to a miserable huddle on the far side of the bed. Her back was to him, her soft sobs raking his own emotions.

He frowned, feeling helpless, but reached across to lay a gentle hand upon the softness of her hair.

"I tried to be gentle. I am sorry if I hurt you," he whispered, but his concern only brought increased weeping. "Jillian, please tell me what is wrong. Let me hold you."

She drew away as he touched her arm, and Justin lay back, staring dully into the darkness. She had come willingly to meet his passion, and he was not sure how to handle her distress, but the pitiable sound of her muffled weeping was more than he could bear. He pulled her back to him, ignoring her halfhearted struggles. He held her firmly, and she felt tiny and soft and warm against him, her tears wetting his bare chest.

"I do not understand your torment, for you pleased me very much," he murmured softly, wiping the wetness from her cheeks.

Jillian's voice came very low.

"Aye, how could you understand? You have taken all that was mine to give and left me no pride."

"You are my wife, and you are with me as you should be," Justin replied against her hair. "Have I been so cruel that you cannot bear my touch without a fit of weeping?"

She was silent for a moment, then spoke quietly.

"I have betrayed my brothers by coming to you. I have willingly given myself to the man who claims their inheritance. Can you not understand my shame?"

"There is no shame in what happened between us. We are man and wife, and you cannot be blamed for the circumstances that brought me to you. Your brother is a man and will understand the ways of the world. He will not fault you."

Jillian raised her fingers to her throat, touching the spot where her Birthing Stone had been.

"Little does it matter now," she said, sighing. "For it will not be long before I take my last breath."

Justin's first thought was that she meant to do herself harm, and his muscles tensed beneath her cheek. His voice came sharply.

"Why do you say such a thing?"

Her lips moved against his furred chest. " 'Tis the ancient Druid teachings. If one's Birthing Stone is taken by force, one's spirit will follow its fate. It will surely be my fate to drown."

"You will not drown, dammit!" Justin gritted, his blood running cold at her calm resignation to such an ignorant tale. "And I will not listen to such nonsense."

Jillian closed her eyes and was silent, but she knew in her heart that her days upon the earth were short. Her tears flowed quietly to track down Justin's chest, making him aware that she truly believed the dire superstition, and it was not until his mouth settled upon her throat and shoulder that the heavy sense of doom was driven from her mind.

* * *

Jillian blinked as something cold dripped upon her face, and she fought off cloying strands of sleep to open her eyes. The heavy velvet draperies had been drawn wide, and sunshine flooded through the windows, filling the room with bright light. She raised her fingertips to the wetness on her cheek, squinting as she caught a sparkle of blue. Justin stood above her, her Birthing Stone dangling from his finger, still dripping with water.

She cried out in joy, scrambling up on her heels to take it in her hand, completely oblivious to her nakedness. Justin smiled as he sat on the edge of the bed beside her as she looked at the newly repaired chain, her throat clogged tight with emotion. Turquoise tears glittered in her eyes, and he took the amulet and carefully placed it over her head.

Jillian took the familiar weight in her palm, squeezing it tightly in one small fist.

"Now no more talk of drowning or evil spirits," Justin said, lifting her other hand to his lips, and she looked at him, gratitude brimming from the pure azure depths of her eyes.

"It is still my fate to perish in water, but you have surely lengthened my life."

Justin shook his head at her strange beliefs, but his gaze was drawn irresistibly to the blue stone resting upon soft swells of naked white flesh. His voice hoarsened.

"I shall surely keep you far away from water, then, my Jillian, because I will not lose you."

She smiled, her heart full, and she lifted a small palm to cup the hard line of his jaw. Love warmed her lovely eyes to a smoky shade as she placed her other hand lightly upon his chest, still damp from his dive. "I will love and respect you from this moment, milord, and be your wife in every way," she pledged softly. She hesitated, her eyes growing troubled. "And I shall pray that Brian will forgive me for betraying him. And Pierce, if he is alive."

Her words were earnest, and Justin grinned as he pressed her slowly back upon the silken pillows.

"And I shall pray for thunderstorms that send you running eagerly into my arms."

Jillian laughed softly, a lovely tinkling sound that was stopped abruptly as his mouth came down upon hers. She moved sensually to meet him, her soft breasts like hot velvet against his skin. Suddenly he moved away from her, sat up, and began to remove his boots.

"What are you doing?" she asked as his hands went to his belt.'

Justin quirked a quizzical brow. "What do you think, my love?"

"But it is day and the servants are about. It is not proper to stay abed and . . ."

Her voice died away in embarrassment as he tossed his pants away, his desire readily apparent to her shocked eyes. She stared at his hard, brown body and burning, silvery eyes for a mere instant.

"Nay, I cannot," she said, hastily removing herself to the other side of the bed, but Justin stopped her flight with one arm around her slender waist, drawing her back to him.

"You can and will, my sweet, for the sunlight upon your beauty only makes me more eager to have you in my arms."

" 'Tis indecent," she managed, her breath catching as he pushed her into the pillows and caught both her wrists beside her head.

"I am an indecent sort," he whispered, dropping his face to nibble warm kisses on her shoulder. Her pulse gave a decided leap as his lips followed the amulet's gold chain to quivering mounds of flesh. Her moan was indistinct as sweet fires crackled alive with newly learned passion, but Justin held her hands fast as his mouth inched with maddening slowness up the inside of her arm.

"Please," she choked, breasts heaving tantalizingly beneath his hot regard. "Release me."

Justin only smiled, continuing with the most enjoyable captivity of his love until the words he awaited were wrenched breathlessly from her as he tasted a particularly sensitive spot.

"I yield to you, milord," she managed, shivers dancing over every inch of her flesh. "I fear I've become as indecent as you."

Justin laughed and let her go, and she immediately twined her slender fingers in the thick, black curls at his nape. He rolled until she lay on top of him, her silky raven hair falling in a fragrant tent over his face and chest. All thoughts vanished as they climbed on the wings of love to heavens rent by starbursts of such white fury that they were both left trembling and shaken in its wake.

# EIGHTEEN

Jillian sat alone before her ornate gold mirror, staring at her reflection. Her eyes dropped dispassionately to the shimmering white silk gown that Justin had purchased for her to wear to the queen's ball. It was lovely; its neckline scooped low and was trimmed with glistening pearls that bared the smooth ivory skin of her shoulders. The sleeves were white lace sewn upon sheer white silk, fashioned to begin below the shoulder, then billow fully to the pearl buttons at each wrist. The deep expanse of naked flesh at her décolletage displayed to advantage a lovely choker of pure gold set with diamonds and pearls. Justin had given it to her for this night, and Jillian had pinned her Birthing Stone to her chemise so that she could wear his gift at her throat.

For hours she had sat motionlessly as Bridgit brushed heavy ebony tresses until her hair shone rich and lustrous, then threaded the fat black curls with ropes of pearls. Justin had spared no expense with her attire, and he had been equally lavish with the magnificent gown of emerald satin that Catherine would wear. But neither her beautiful gown nor the generosity of her husband gave Jillian pleasure.

She sighed, staring at the pearl-crusted white silk fan lying on the dressing table. Her delicate brows drew together as she wrestled with the conflicting emotions that tormented her.

In the time she had been at Waverton Hall, the Spensers had treated her with more warmth and kindness than she could ever have expected from an English household. Their affection had been freely given, and her days had been so filled with fittings for gowns and gifts of delicate lace and gloves that she hardly had time to think of her circumstances. And since the night of the storm, Justin had come to her each night, his lips like fire, making her forget the pain of leaving Ulster and the guilt of betraying her brothers. Shivers passed over her bare skin at the silken memories of his lovemaking, and upset, she stood and moved restlessly around the room.

She had tried so hard to be happy, to forget the fact that she had turned her back on her home and family. There had been no word from Donal, she knew not if he lived or died. Nor did she know if Brian fared well in his exile. And poor Pierce. Pain at his possible fate clouded her face again. Tonight she would be presented to Queen Mary, dressed in English finery, and she must act as if William of Orange had not ruined her family.

Anxiety mounted, setting her hands trembling, and she clasped them tightly before her. She could not go, she thought desperately; she could not willingly mingle with the very monarch against whom her father had fought and died. After all her attempts to thwart her arranged marriage, she had fallen in love with Justin, and now, though she loved him beyond reason, she could not obey his wish. She owed that much to her father and brothers.

Excited laughter rang from behind her, and Jillian turned as Catherine whirled in a graceful pirouette that rustled her shiny green gown. Her dark hair had been set into an elaborate coiffure of intricately arranged curls atop her head, all dusted with perfumed white powder. A jeweled beauty patch shone on her high cheekbone.

"How do I look? Will I find my true love this very night?"

Jillian looked at the other girl who was so close to her own age, wondering if she had ever been so carefree as her beautiful English sister-in-law.

"Did you not receive the powder I sent for your hair?" Catherine asked, looking at Jillian's jet-black ringlets draping over one shoulder.

"Aye, but Justin is not fond of the practice," Jillian answered.

"Nor will he don the powdered wigs the courtiers wear. Neither will Ryan for that matter. Aaron is the only one with any fashion sense, and he is not here to go with us. But do not worry, your hair is magnificent without powdering. Come now, we must go. It is a long ride to Kensington Palace."

Catherine bubbled over with enthusiasm, snapping open her fan and waving it to and fro.

"Justin has sent Milly up twice to prod us along."

Jillian looked away, her voice very low. "I cannot go, Catherine."

Catherine's fan stilled abruptly, her eyes confused. "But you are all dressed. Are you ill?"

"I am Irish," Jillian said quietly, and Catherine's voice softened.

"But you are a Spenser now, and already I love you like a true sister."

Jillian's eyes were unhappy. "And I have grown to care for you, and your brothers, but I cannot bow before the English queen. Her husband exiled my brother, Brian."

Catherine's face sobered, and she moved to Jillian, giving her a sympathetic hug.

"I understand how you feel, Jillian, and although I am sure Justin will be angry with you at first, he will get over it. He always does." She gave her impish grin. "For I am surely one to know his anger. I will send him to you."

As Catherine left, Jillian's resolve flagged somewhat at the idea of facing her husband with her decision. She moved to the fire and held her hands to the warming blaze, but even the flames did not dispel the coldness that had settled over her spirit.

She took a deep breath as Justin entered, then turned to face him. He stood by the door, his bronzed face a vivid contrast to the ascot of pure white silk, and his shoulders appeared immense, clothed immaculately in black silk. He looked devastatingly handsome in a waistcoat of azure blue stitched with fine gold thread, and his silvery eyes burned with an intensity that held her immobile.

Her heart raced with unreasonable panic, although she could see no trace of anger in his face. When he spoke, his voice was deceptively calm.

"You have to come, Jillian. Queen Mary has requested specifically to meet you."

She lifted her small chin and met his gaze with steadfast determination.

"I cannot."

"You do not have a choice. She is the Queen of England."

Jillian's teeth clamped, anger beginning to rise out of the quandary of her indecision. She hurled words at Justin that had lain dormant in the last few weeks beneath her love for him.

"She is not *my* queen! My family is loyal to James, not William of Orange. I did not ask to come here; I was brought to these shores when I could not protest! I will never grovel before the English throne."

Justin struggled to control his own annoyance but was only partially successful.

"James will never rule again, and you have to accept it. The Dutch and English navies crushed him and his French allies at La Hogue this past May. There will be no invasion to oust William and Mary." He paused. "And I am hardly asking you to grovel. You are the Countess of Wellingford now, and you will have every respect your position entitles."

"Do you think that an English title means aught to me? William's English army killed my father!"

Her voice trembled with unleashed emotion, her fingers curled tightly into her palms.

"If you will remember, I was with William at the Boyne," Justin reminded her quietly. "Am I forever to bear your hatred over a battle fought long before we met?"

Jillian swallowed hard, pain wrenching her heart.

"Nay, you are my husband, and you know that I love you."

"So you will come to my bed as a loving wife, but all the while you will curse my country and my king and queen," he continued relentlessly. "And if our union shall bear fruit, will you teach this hatred to my sons? Will you poison our daughters against me, and my brothers and Catherine, because English blood flows in our veins?"

"Can you not see how I feel?" Jillian cried, tears of distress brimming over. "Can you not see what your William has done to me? I am separated from my brother, who is all the family left to me! How can you expect me to swear allegiance to the very man who keeps us apart?"

Overcome by her grief, she dropped her face into her hands, and her heartbroken sobs brought Justin to her. He held her in his arms, murmuring soothingly against the top of her head.

"Do you think me so callous that I cannot understand your misery? Do you think I don't see the wistfulness in your eyes when you watch Catherine laugh with Ryan?"

Jillian continued to cry, and he spoke again.

"If you knew that I have requested the queen to intervene for Brian's pardon with William, would you stand willingly at my side this night?"

Jillian stiffened within his arms, and Justin watched as she lifted black lashes spiky with tears. Her turquoise eyes glowed.

"Is it possible? Could Brian come home to me?" she breathed, and Justin smiled tenderly, wiping away her tears.

"It is possible, but I cannot promise that the king will grant my petition. I had hoped to spare your disappointment until I knew his mind on the matter."

Sudden fear replaced the hope in her eyes. "Will William have reason to deny Brian's return?"

"I cannot say, but the fact that the Devlins

are practicing Protestants will be in your favor, as will be my past loyalty to the king. And I think you will find a formidable ally in the queen."

"But I do not even know her."

"But she rules beside a husband who wars with her father, much as you have been forced to do. I have heard it said that she requested James's estates in Ireland be made into schools for the Irish poor, although William refused her. But you must not give her a reason to refuse to help us. You must come with me tonight and show her respect."

Jillian's lovely face hardened with resolve. "I will do anything to bring Brian home. Anything the king wishes me to do," she stated with such conviction that Justin gave a wry smile, his eyes sweeping her bare white shoulders and the provocative swell of her breasts.

"You may say as much to Mary, but I pray you, love, do not make such a rash statement if you should meet William. He will surely forget even his mistress, Betty Villiers, and it will be my certain fate to be hanged defending your honor against him."

Jillian smiled as he draped her cloak around her shoulders, her heart remaining light as he led her downstairs and out to the elaborately appointed carriage where Catherine and Ryan awaited them. They had to pass through the dark and narrow streets of London, and it took a good bit of time to reach Kensington.

The palace was surrounded by huge gardens set out in formal rectangles of fountains and avenues, and as their coach and six entered the tree-lined road that would take them to the entrance, Jillian began to feel no small amount of trepidation.

She was grateful for Justin's supporting hand upon her waist as they crossed the wide courtyard and were taken by a crimson-liveried servant through a vaulted hall with a black-and-white marble floor and gigantic crystal chandeliers.

They stopped at the top of a wide staircase of gilded marble that descended into a cavernous ballroom where tall gold mirrors reflected thousands of glittering candles. Richly attired men in velvet and lace-edged jabots paid court to ladies resplendent in jewels and satin, and Jillian's nerves quivered alarmingly as she remembered tales told in Ulster of the wicked debaucheries practiced in the royal courts of England.

"Earl and Countess of Wellingford."

The tall, courtly servant's imposing baritone sounded imperiously, and Justin took his wife's hand with possessive pride as he led her down the steps. A sea of faces lifted to stare curiously at them, and Jillian was aware that many of the elegant English ladies eyed her tall, handsome husband with undue interest, making her wonder how many of them had known the ecstasy of Justin's touch.

As they walked along the velvet chairs lining the walls, Jillian's eyes found Eleanor Marlowe, who stood on the arm of a handsome blond man with a neatly trimmed mustache and beard. Jillian hazarded a furtive glance to see Justin's reaction to her. Her fears were allayed somewhat when he nodded coldly toward her, although Eleanor looked most beautiful in a low-cut gown of russet silk with matching lace.

Justin frowned darkly as they passed Eleanor and Winston Grannier. Eleanor's rudeness when she barged into his house and demanded that he punish Jillian and Catherine for their trick on her had made him furious. As far as he was concerned she well deserved his abrupt dismissal of her that night. But at the moment it was Grannier who made him angry by inclining his head in an obvious salute to Jillian's beauty. Justin still boiled inwardly at how the other man's eyes had openly devoured his wife's face and bare shoulders. Grannier was a notorious rake who had often killed on the duelling fields. Any lady of beauty was fair game in his eyes, married or otherwise, and Justin meant to keep Jillian far away from him. And Catherine too.

He glanced over his shoulder at his sister, following on Ryan's arm, and grinned; she barely gave Grannier a haughty glance as he bowed low before her. Catherine's disdain made Justin's role as her guardian a good bit easier.

He kept Jillian close beside him, his hand

riding upon her tiny waist as he presented her to more acceptable acquaintances at Court. Catherine soon joined the dancing with a suitable young man, leaving Ryan free and eager to renew associations of a more intimate nature among the beauties of the Court.

The queen sat on a throne draped elaborately with red velvet, her ladies-in-waiting surrounding her, and Justin pressed Jillian's hand reassuringly as they approached her. He had a disquieting surge of foreboding as he led his wife forward, for if anyone had experienced the full extent of Jillian's pride and loyalty to family, it was certainly he. He relaxed slightly as she dropped to a graceful curtsy before the queen.

Justin bowed, and the queen gestured for them to come closer. She was gowned magnificently in gold, tall and majestic despite her stout build, and her brown eyes were kind, if slightly red-rimmed and watery.

"I have looked forward to meeting you," she said to Jillian. "Many stories of Lord Spenser's devotion to you have circulated throughout Whitehall these past weeks." She smiled, glancing at Justin.

Jillian stared at her, finding it incredible that she stood like a docile child before the detested English ruler.

"I understand your brother bore arms against my husband at the Boyne," Queen Mary said, looking at Jillian. "Are you aware that I have a petition in hand to pardon Brian Devlin's crime against the Crown?"

"Aye, it was my husband's doing, for I sorely miss my brother, and surely that is the only act that will give my undying allegiance to you and the king."

Justin winced but breathed easier as the queen chuckled. He smiled as Mary bent twinkling, dark eyes on him.

"Your Irish bride does not insult me with flattery as do so many petitioners," she said, then looked at Jillian again. "Your honesty becomes you, my dear. It is most refreshing. I will talk to the king about your brother when he returns from his campaign."

Jillian's smile was brilliant, and Justin bowed respectfully as they backed away. Then he led Jillian across the floor to an ornate pillar gilded with scrolls where they were afforded some privacy.

"The queen appeared to be pleased with you," he whispered. "Perhaps she will be able to convince the king."

He smiled at her happiness, but his lips parted in surprise as she pressed herself eagerly against his chest, disregarding the people nearby.

Her spontaneous passion pleased him greatly, and he gave a low laugh, steadying her hoop with his palm as it threatened to rise dangerously in the back, giving the men behind them a tantalizing view of her legs.

"Come, sweet, dance with me before I lose

all control and answer the invitation in your eyes." A saraband was beginning as they approached the floor. Jillian curtsied prettily before him, and they turned, bowed, then touched hands in the delicate steps of the dance. Her smiling turquoise eyes ever on her husband, she was entirely unaware of the sensation she caused among the male dancers. Justin was not, and he frowned as the music took her to a different partner.

He barely acknowledged the lady in front of him. He mechanically performed the steps, annoyed that he would have to face several other ladies before he would reach Jillian again.

He grimaced as Eleanor Marlowe appeared as his next partner. She curtsied very low, intentionally presenting him with a brazen view of her ample bosom, and Justin wondered at how he had ever become involved with such a woman. As they met for a turn she managed to press her breasts wantonly against his arm, which affected Justin only in that it elicited a sudden worry that Jillian's partner might brush her lovely form in a similar fashion. His frown deepened as he caught sight of his diminutive wife partnered with Winston Grannier. The man lingered over his wife's dark head, his eyes roaming freely over her soft décolletage, and Justin went rigid with anger.

"You are as beguiled by the Irish witch as they say," Eleanor hissed through set teeth, peeved at his obvious fascination with his wife. Justin looked down into a false, vindictive smile that came nowhere near her brown eyes.

"Do not spread false rumors about my lady, Eleanor, or you will surely answer to me for it."

"She and Catherine have made me the laughingstock in London with their trick," Eleanor snapped furiously.

"A circumstance you well deserved, but be warned, do not attempt to blacken Jillian's name with your ridiculous stories of witchcraft or I will see you regret it."

Eleanor shivered under the icy threat in Justin's eyes as he disentangled her fingers from his arm. He moved away, humiliating her again by interrupting the dance, and she bridled under the twittering laughter of those who witnessed his insult to her.

Her jaw clamped with fury as Justin made his way to his wife's side to take her hand with gallant attentiveness. Justin Spenser erred by making a fool of her, she thought venomously, and she vowed that if it took her a lifetime, she would separate Justin from his witch-wife.

A vague idea fluttered alive in her mind, and she smiled absently as Winston Grannier stopped beside her, his fingers brushing the soft swell of her breast. They would both suffer as she had, she decided, but perhaps her plans of vengeance should be put aside until they returned to Kent where the peasants would not look kindly upon the evil ways of an Irish witch. Content to wait, she allowed Winston to lead her upon the polished dance floor.

# NINETEEN

The meadow of Runnymede stood alongside the River Thames southwest of London, and the early October weather brought throngs of townsmen and aristocrats to the auctions held there. Eleanor Marlowe stood in her crimson finery in front of the slave block. The white silk scarf draping her wide-brimmed hat flapped in the breeze from the river as her eyes examined the people around her, latching eventually on a tall, broad-shouldered man in the next pavilion where fine Arabian bloodstock was being shown. Her upper lip curled contemptuously, and as Justin Spenser leaned down attentively toward his small wife, her eyes froze into pure hatred.

Damn them both, she swore viciously beneath her breath, glancing back to the slave upon the low platform in front of the crowd. It was a Negress this time, perhaps of ten and five, and Eleanor watched without interest as lecherous old men prodded and poked at her firm young body.

She looked at her groom where he stood nearby, holding their horses. François Dubois was barely nineteen, and though his young face was impassive, his eyes were much older than his years. A red welt stood out upon his clean-shaven cheek where she struck him with her whip the night before.

Eleanor had purchased him when he was sixteen, solely to amuse her during Justin's long sea voyages. The boy had been proud at first, but she had finally broken his spirit with cruel floggings until he was reduced to whimpering for mercy under her anger. She no longer enjoyed him.

She found Justin's place again, memories of his open contempt rankling enough to bring spots of color to her cheeks. Soon he would suffer, for her plan for revenge was already set in motion. Her lips curved in a malevolent smile as she thought of the eagerness with which the scandalmongers of Whitehall had accepted Grannier's accounts of the Devlin woman's infidelities. Soon all of London would whisper the lies they had spread so diligently. She noted with satisfaction that a pair of fashionable ladies near the Spenser couple spoke guardedly behind their hands, their eyes upon Jillian. Justin would have a difficult time indeed stifling such juicy gossip about his wife, and when the common populace of Kent heard the stories of Jillian Devlin's witchcraft, it would be nearly impossible for him to prove otherwise. She smiled, eager at the thought of poisoning the minds of the villagers around the Spenser estates. She had already decided upon the perfect man there to help her in her vengeance.

She turned with interest as a different slave was brought forward for sale, her eyes sharpening when she saw it was a man, tall with a firmly muscled physique. He wore only a dark loincloth, his skin burned bronze, his dark hair long and unkempt. But even more interesting to her was the fact that he was heavily shackled, which was most unusual in an auction place. The chains clanked as he slowly climbed to the platform, but his gait was neither shuffling nor subservient. He was prodded to turn, and the crowd gasped as his back was revealed, horribly marked from the lash. Some weals were recent, raw and open, and a sensual thrill coursed through Eleanor as he was cruelly jerked by the chain upon his neck to face the crowd.

She stepped closer as the slave master slipped the man's manacled wrists over posts on either side of him, outstretching his arms. He was muscular, though very lean, most likely from starvation, a common tactic used to bring a rebellious slave to heel. Eleanor often used it herself. His face was covered by a week's growth of black beard, and Eleanor pushed her way to the front, wanting a better look at him.

The slave master was obese, his legs short and stubby, but the unsavory appearance of John Lutes hid a crafty cleverness that allowed him to read Eleanor's interest in a slave he feared would be hard to dispose of. He eyed her expensive gown, then grinned as he stepped off the block and sidled close beside her.

"Ye be needin' a goodun fer ye fields, milaidy?"

Eleanor glanced distastefully at his discolored teeth as he drew back fat lips in an ingratiating smile.

"Perhaps," she replied haughtily, stepping up to walk slowly around the bound slave. "The scars upon his back mark him to be a troublemaker," she commented, drawing the end of her riding crop none too gently along one of the rawer-looking wounds. The man did not flinch, and Eleanor smiled.

The slave master's words spilled out hastily. "Aye, 'e's spirited and o' strong Irish stock, 'e is. Look at 'is legs, strong as a bull, and feel 'is arms, like rocks they be. 'E'd work a long day fer ye, milaidy."

Or a long night, Eleanor thought as she ran a gloved finger over his lean ribs. The beatings had certainly been harsh, and she wondered if he was a broken man.

"I would know if he is properly obedient before lining your palm with my gold," she said, tapping her quirt thoughtfully in her palm.

The slave looked straight ahead now, and Eleanor spoke to the rotund slaver.

"Bid him to look at me."

"Look at the laidy, ye mangy cur," Lutes growled harshly, then became enraged when the bearded slave did not obey. The thought of losing such a lucrative sale drove Lutes into jabbing his rod viciously into the man's exposed rib cage.

"Damn ye, look at 'er or ye'll wish ye 'ad!"

Eleanor's heartbeat increased emphatically as the bound man turned his head slowly to focus dark blue eyes on her face. They burned with cold, intense hatred, and Eleanor's breath caught with excitement.

"Kneel, slave," she commanded, brown eyes glittering, but he did not move, his blue eyes delving into her with visible loathing. Before anyone could react, Eleanor brought her crop slicing down upon his naked chest, and the man tensed against his chains, his jaw tight with fury. He made no sound as blood trickled from the gash she had opened.

John Lutes sputtered in alarm at the lady's action.

"Now, milaidy," he entreated her in a whine. "There be no need to mark 'im up, 'e'll do yer biddin'."

Eleanor completely ignored him, her eyes on her victim's face.

"There is nary a one in this crowd who will purchase a mutinous slave to stir their servants into discontent. I must know his temperament. Stand aside."

Just yards away, Jillian watched as Justin moved around a beautiful black Arabian stallion, his hand patting the sleek flanks with knowledgeable admiration. They had stopped at Runnymede on their way to the country to choose bloodstock for the stables of Spenser Court. Their coach and riders waited not far away, but the newly acquired horseflesh would be taken back into London until Ryan brought them when he traveled to Kent later in the week.

Jillian looked around for Catherine, wondering where she had gone, and her eyes fell upon the dappled gray mare that Justin had purchased for her. One of the Spenser grooms held the beautiful horse, and Jillian smiled with pleasure at her husband's thoughtfulness.

She turned as a low moan arose from the people just behind her. Justin still haggled with the stallion's owner, and she moved curiously toward the slave block, slowly making her way to the low platform at the front of the crowd. She stopped when she recognized Eleanor Marlowe, then gasped as the blond woman ruthlessly struck the man chained before her. Appalled, Jillian's eyes darted to the slave's face. Her heart stopped.

"Pierce!"

Her whisper was strangled, her eyes widening with horror as Eleanor raised her arm to inflict another blow.

"No!" she cried, rushing to throw herself against her brother's chest. Pierce Devlin's first shock fled him, and as Eleanor brought the whip downward, he jerked his chains in a desperate attempt to protect his sister. But the whip was already in motion, and the quirt found its mark across Jillian's fragile collarbone.

She cried out in agony, and Eleanor's face

whitened at having unintentionally struck a woman. When she realized it was Jillian, her face hardened, and rigid with hatred, she pulled back her arm, her eyes on Jillian's face.

Before she could accomplish the marring blow, fingers of steel closed over her wrist. Eleanor cursed, jerking furious eyes to whoever dared to stop her. She blanched when she saw Justin's silvery eyes, now black with rage. A terrible fear overwhelmed her as his grip tightened relentlessly until her arm went numb to the shoulder. The bloodstained whip fell from lifeless fingers, and Justin fought his overpowering desire to knock her to the ground. Eleanor pulled back, terrified at the dark fury on Justin's face, then sagged in relief as he pushed her away in contempt. He leaned over his wife, where she lay huddled at the slave's feet. He lifted her carefully, his face still tensed in anger at what Eleanor had done to her.

"Are you hurt?" he asked tenderly, but Jillian had no thought of her throbbing shoulder; her joy at finding Pierce alive rose in her throat until she could not speak.

"I will have this slave," Eleanor demanded from behind them, and Jillian panicked.

"Nay, nay, she cannot have him!" she cried wildly, grabbing at the lapels of her husband's coat, then before Justin knew what she was about, Jillian had dropped to her knees in front of him, her arms encircling his legs, her upraised face white and stricken.

"Please, please, I beg you, Justin, do not let her take him. You must stop her, please, I implore you."

Justin had never seen, nor had he ever expected to see, Jillian beg for anything, but his initial astonishment fled quickly, leaving him appalled by her desperate display.

"Wait," he barked sharply to Lutes, gently pulling Jillian back to her feet.

"You need never beg for anything, Jillian," he told her softly, his eyes moving to the bound slave, who watched Jillian.

"Why do you want this man?"

Emotion swelled in Jillian's breast as she stared at the beloved face of the brother whom she feared dead. He was filthy and gaunt, and blood trickled down his chest. Her eyes filled with tears as she struggled to speak her heart.

"Because he—"

She stopped as Pierce's eyes narrowed in warning, and despite her distraught condition, she realized that he did not want their kinship known. She strove for an answer as Justin's frown deepened.

"Because he is Irish, and she is cruel. She beats him whilst he is helpless."

Justin's eyes dropped to the blood on the bearded man's chest. "What is the price of this slave?" he demanded of the fat slave master.

Eleanor stepped forward, determined to have the man that Jillian had pled for so pitifully, if only to spite Justin.

"I have already claimed him," she insisted.

John Lutes listened to their exchange, a calculating gleam sparking in his bulbous black eyes. It was not often that two rich buyers argued over a mere field hand, and he smiled greedily.

Justin turned his eyes to Eleanor, his look so deadly that she flinched.

"Then make your bid, Eleanor, but know from the beginning that I intend to have this man. Do not forget that I have leave to spend as I will, but your father's solicitor will not look kindly upon such extravagance. He holds the purse strings until your twenty-fourth birthday, does he not?"

Eleanor frowned, knowing full well that Justin knew of her financial restrictions. She hesitated as Justin stared at her with utter disgust. A moment passed before she smiled in bitter capitulation, but her words were barbed to pierce and infect.

"I withdraw then." Her eyes went to Jillian, where Justin's arm held her protectively close to his side. "And I compliment your Irish bride on her taste. He is a handsome specimen, to be sure, but I am surprised at your generosity. Few husbands would purchase their wife's lover for them. You have become most indulgent since you wed."

A muscle jumped spasmodically in Justin's lean cheek as her cutting words sent a shocked ripple through the onlookers behind them, and Eleanor arrogantly tossed her head with satisfaction before she disappeared among the spectators.

Justin looked down at Jillian to find her smiling tenderly at the chained field hand. His muscles tensed, but Jillian turned to him almost at once, hugging both arms around his waist; he heard her choked whisper against his chest. "Thank you, milord, I will always be grateful for this kindness."

Justin's black brows drew into a vee, and his face was set in consternation as he took her arm and helped her down the step. Jillian's backward glances toward the bearded Irish slave did not help his mood as he led her toward their waiting coach.

Catherine stood before a group of gaily costumed tumblers who performed for the amusement of passersby, and at Justin's sharp summons, she ran to join them.

"What has happened?" she asked upon sight of their grim faces.

She listened in amazement as Justin related the details of Eleanor's actions, all the while proceeding with long strides toward their carriage.

"That woman is a monster!" she said with venom. "How could she be so cruel? Does your shoulder hurt terribly, Jillian?"

"It will be all right. 'Tis the slave who suffers."

Jillian's concern grated on Justin, as did her reaction to the sight of a Spenser groom leading Pierce to the servant wagon. She started toward him.

"His wounds must be tended. There is room with us in the coach."

Catherine darted a shocked look at her, and Justin's rebuke came swiftly.

"A slave does not ride in the master's coach, Jillian, nor does the lady tend his wounds."

"But I am skilled in such things, and I can—"

"No!" he said sharply. "A serving wench will see to him, and he will travel later when Ryan brings the other servants."

His last words left no room for argument, and Jillian looked longingly at the cart that would take her brother back into London. Justin handed her into the coach, and she leaned back against the upholstered seat, unable to think of anything other than the fact that her brother was alive and near her. She had no idea why he warned her to be silent, but the desire to share such wondrous news with Justin and Catherine ate at her newfound joy.

"Where did that she-devil strike you?" Catherine asked, leaning forward to gently unfasten the neckline of Jillian's brown velvet gown. She gasped aloud at the long bluish mark on her creamy shoulder.

Justin's whole body tensed to granite when he saw the ugly bruise, and he found he could not speak at first, so deep was his anger at his wife's being attacked in such a way. He reached out and touched her cheek as Catherine carefully rearranged her dress.

"Eleanor will pay for hurting you," Justin muttered gruffly, and Jillian pressed the back of his hand against her cheek.

"You have saved the Irishman from a most terrible fate; that is all that matters."

Jealousy tightened into a hard knot in Justin's chest, and he removed his hand to turn brooding eyes on the passing landscape as Eleanor's caustic words about his wife's lover ran in a never-ending refrain through his mind.

# TWENTY

The gallery windows at Spenser Court were large and lofty with chiseled stone mullions stretching to the beamed ceiling. Late-afternoon sun left angular patches of dusty light on the black-and-crimson Persian carpet that led to a wide staircase, its carved wood darkened by over a century of use.

Jillian sat on a low bench covered with black velvet cushions which ran along the base of the windows, her eyes on the sculptured gardens far below with their graveled walkways and tinkling fountains. Justin's ancestral home was truly enormous, built in the shape of an *E*, the white stone now a slate-gray. The long hallways and spacious rooms were furnished magnificently with fine furniture and magnificent carpets and tapestries. Since they arrived, Justin had shown her many of the treasures he brought from his sea voyages to faraway lands like Cathay and Aleppo in Syria.

She found Kent to be most beautiful with its neat hedgerows and tilled fields, but since their arrival three days before, Justin had been busy overseeing the estates with Aaron, and Catherine had spent most of her time galloping over the countryside on her black stallion, which was named Sultan.

Jillian welcomed the solitude, and had spent hours in the window seat waiting for Pierce to come. Each day she watched the front avenue lined with ancient oaks that led to Spenser Court for his arrival, anxious to know what had happened to him and how he became a slave, although it distressed her to think what terrible things he must have endured.

Now that the small caravan of carts and horses had finally come into sight, she felt almost giddy with excitement. Since Justin had ridden with Aaron to inspect the tenant farms along the River Stratham, she would have time to see Pierce alone. Her smooth brow furrowed as she thought of Justin's behavior since their arrival. She had sensed a certain reticence in him, one that had not been there before. Only at night, when their lovemaking made them forget all else, did he seem himself, and she knew she had to persuade Pierce to let her tell him the truth. She no longer liked to keep secrets from her husband.

She sat impatiently, her hands fidgeting as the team of wagons seemed to crawl past the distant granaries and smokehouses. When they finally entered the cobblestone road to the stables, she hurried up to the third floor of the east wing where Catherine kept her apartments. She knew that one of the bedchambers overlooked the bricked courtyard by the stables, and she entered it, crossing quickly to open the window latch. She leaned over the casement where activity abounded below. Servants scurried about, and she watched with bated breath as Ryan led the small procession across the courtyard, the wagon wheels rumbling loudly on the red bricks.

A happy laugh escaped her as Pierce stepped down from the rear of one of the wagons. He wore simple attire, a white linen shirt and brown breeches atop dark hose, but she was relieved that he no longer suffered the weight of shackles. One of the grooms motioned for Pierce to follow him, and Jillian waited impatiently as they disappeared into the carriage house at one end of the stables.

Nearly a quarter of an hour later the groom reappeared to stride across the court, and Jillian left the window, her heart fluttering. She went directly to the room she shared with Justin and retrieved the salve she had mixed for Pierce's wounds; then, holding the covered bowl tightly, she moved quickly along the ground-floor corridor.

She passed a housemaid who curtsied respectfully to her new mistress, then went back to polishing a huge silver urn. A clattering of pans and cutlery amidst loud voices came from the kitchens at the rear of the house as she stepped cautiously outside. She looked around, aware that she would attract unwanted attention by crossing the courtyard to the carriage house, so she hurried instead to the hedged walk on which Catherine had taken her the day before to see her horse.

The Spenser stables were spacious and impressive with blue-and-white Dutch-tiled walls and bright yellow stalls and troughs. The interior was dim, motes of dust glistening in narrow shafts of light from the high apertures above each stall. The air hung heavy with the dusty odor of straw and horseflesh, and Jillian paused just inside the door, then moved to the stall where her own mare stood.

"Sssh, Pearl," she whispered, and the gray whinnied and stamped one foot as Jillian left her to glide stealthily along the shadowy central corridor. She had ducked into an empty stall when she heard a low crooning voice, and a moment later a stableboy about ten years old rounded the corner, leading a chestnut gelding. She waited until he was safely outside, then headed on toward the adjoining carriage house. She stopped short when she saw Pierce polishing the ornate gold fittings on one of the carriages.

"Pierce, Pierce!" she cried, and he jerked around as she ran into his arms. She sobbed into his shirt, and he held her, his soothing Gaelic words like a balm upon her soul as he pulled her behind the coach.

Pierce's heart constricted painfully as Jillian raised tearful blue eyes, and his voice was choked.

"I never expected to see you again."

Tears rolled down Jillian's cheeks. "I know.

I prayed this day would come, but we thought you had drowned at sea."

Pierce's face hardened, pinpoints of hatred brilliant in the depths of his dark blue eyes.

"The English bastards pulled me from the wreckage, only to sell me into bondage."

Jillian laid her palm against his cheek. "It must have been terrible for you. But what of your wounds? Are they healing? I have brought ointment."

"I was well tended in Londontown, but tell me of Brian. Where is he? And Mauve and Donal? Are they all right?"

Jillian laid her head on his shoulder, and he put his arm around her.

"Oh, Pierce, I have only bad news to tell you. Brian has been exiled from Ulster, and I know not where he is. And Mauve is gone from the plague. Donal is in Ulster, but I know not if he lives or dies."

Tears flowed faster as she looked into his eyes. "I thought I would die when I saw you chained up and whipped."

"Do not weep, Jillian. I am all right now."

He brushed away her tears, and she looked at him with pleading eyes.

"You must let me tell them who you are. They are—"

"Nay! You would surely suffer if our kinship were known. The English treat the Irish as dogs to chain and beat."

"But Justin is lord here, and his family have been very kind to me since we were wed."

Pierce's eyes grew cold. " 'Tis hard to believe that you married an Englishman."

Jillian could not bear the disgust in his voice, and she dropped her eyes, her words low.

"I had no choice, for the king gave me in marriage to him. He controls our lands in Ulster now."

Pierce did not answer, and Jillian's guilt spilled forth. "I knew not what else to do, Pierce. You must believe me! Neither you nor Brian were there to help me. I was alone, and Mauve and I tried to keep him from me, I swear—"

Pierce stopped her urgent words with a finger against her lips. "Forgive me, Jillian. You cannot be blamed. It was Mary who usurped her father's throne and set the Orangemen upon us."

Jillian raised steadfast eyes. "I have petitioned William to pardon Brian so that he can return to Ulster, and I will do the same for you. Then we can be together again."

Pierce's fingers tightened around her arm. "Nay, I tell you, we must fight the English for our rightful lands."

The man with eyes burning with fanatical bitterness was not the brother Jillian remembered, and the change in him broke her heart.

"Justin would treat you fairly if he knew you were my brother. He would free you, I know he would. He loves me and treats me with respect."

She raised her chin, knowing her next words would bring more of his condemnation.

"And I love him."

Pierce stared at her, his jaw moving into a harder position. "Then you have set your course, but I will never pledge allegiance to William or accept the heel of slavery upon Ireland."

His next words were almost a sneer. "Will your husband's love for you overlook that bit of treason? Will he harbor one sworn to fight against England until his last breath? I warn you, sister, do not tell him, or I swear I will flee this cursed land and leave you in the arms of your English lord."

Hurt ripped through Jillian at his harshness.

"Please, Pierce, I beg you, do not leave here. They will surely hunt you down and hang you if you escape. I cannot bear the thought of being without you again."

"Then swear to me you will not tell him," Pierce insisted, his eyes intense.

"I will not tell him, I swear it," she murmured brokenly, and Pierce's expression softened at her distress. The sorrow in his face was deep and terrible to look upon.

"I have often dreamed of the soft greens of Ulster and the misty light that lingers over the meadows and fields at twilight, and in truth, such dreams were all that kept me alive these last three years."

"We will be together with Brian someday,"

Jillian said, trying to smile. "And things will be good again."

Pierce smiled for the first time, but it was not the roguish smile she remembered from before.

"You must go now, Jillian, before we are seen together."

He led her to the door and looked down at her. "Remember your promise?"

Jillian nodded, and Pierce squeezed her hand.

"I will go first," he said, turning, but Jillian stopped him with a hand on his arm. She reached up to touch his cheek.

"Go with God," she whispered in Gaelic, sighing as he disappeared into the courtyard. She turned, gasping as her eyes collided with an icy, silver stare.

Justin stood a few yards away, his face like carved marble, his cheek working furiously. Neither spoke at first, Jillian too stunned, Justin too furious. The charged silence held, until Justin's voice came deceptively calm.

"What is that man to you?"

Gooseflesh rose to ripple down Jillian's arms, for it had been many days since she faced Justin's anger, and he had never looked at her as coldly as he did now. She had nothing to tell him but lies, and she nervously wet dry lips.

"He is but a countryman—"

"Dammit, Jillian, do not lie to me! I saw the way you touched his face! You know him from Ulster! Who is he? Your lover?"

Jillian paled under his cutting accusation, but her own ire rose from the insult.

"And when were we lovers, pray tell?" she gritted out, her blue eyes glittering angrily. "In the last few moments? I have scarcely been out of your sight since we've been in England, and I knew no man before you, as you well know."

Justin continued to be ruled solely by jealous anger, and he was only able to think of the tenderness with which Jillian had touched the Irishman. His jaw remained tense, his fists doubled tightly at his sides.

"Then you will not mind if I send him away," he said with a growl, but Jillian did not let him finish the threat.

"Please, do not! I knew him in Ulster, I admit to it, and we played together as children. 'Tis all, I swear to you!"

Justin turned from the anguish in her eyes, pacing a few steps away.

"What is his name?" he asked sternly, not looking at her, and Jillian swallowed hard as she stared at his forbidding back. She hated lying to him, hated the deception into which she had been forced.

"Brennan," she said falteringly, falling upon her brother's second name. Justin said nothing, and Jillian tried again, her voice trembling despite her efforts to steady it.

"I came here to see if he was well and to bring him dressing for his wounds, nothing more."

Justin turned suddenly and gave her a long

look; then, without another word, he walked out, leaving her to stare helplessly after him.

The evening meal was unbearably strained with Justin stony-faced and withdrawn at the head of the table while Jillian sat in subdued silence beside him, totally miserable. Aaron's dark eyes took in one, then the other, in concern, uncomfortable under tension thick enough to carve, and even the cheerful banter of Ryan and Catherine deteriorated as the meal progressed.

Thinking that perhaps time alone would benefit the quarreling couple, Aaron finally pushed back his chair and looked at Ryan.

"What say you we ride into Wellingford? 'Tis rumored that the barmaids at the Lion's Claw are both comely and accommodating."

Ryan nodded and rose, more than ready to leave such grim company. "That sounds like an agreeable way to pass the evening."

"I will come as well," Justin said abruptly, and Jillian looked at her lap, hurt curling in a tight band around her heart. Never before since they had been wed had Justin joined his younger brothers in their drinking and wenching, and her pain increased as he strode past without looking at her.

Ryan and Aaron exchanged a look, and Catherine frowned as Justin left the room. Jillian could not meet their sympathetic eyes, and she mumbled an excuse and hastened to the sanctuary of her bedchamber.

Bridgit was stoking the fire when she entered, and Jillian dismissed her, looking away from her maid's inquiring eyes. There was little secret as to why Ryan and Aaron frequented the inns; Catherine often teased them about it. Jillian closed her eyes upon the torturing images of Justin with another woman. She could almost see him holding her, kissing her, pulling her down upon his lap.

She fought back her grief at the thoughts, blinking away tears as she unlaced her gown and stomacher, then loosened the heavy black coil at her nape. She brushed her hair as she sat in a chair before the fire, dull eyes on red-orange flames that licked around the burning logs. When the fire began to dwindle, she climbed into the high bed, feeling very alone. She missed Justin terribly, and she struggled with her need to tell him the truth. But she had given her word to Pierce, and although Justin's rejection broke her heart, she could not contemplate the thought of losing her brother again.

It was very late when Justin returned to his bedchamber. The room was very quiet and dim, and he leaned his back against the door, his eyes on his wife. She lay upon his bed, her hair swirled over his pillows in a silky, black cloud. He squeezed his eyes shut, never having felt so desolate. He had gone with his brothers as in the days before he met Jillian, fully intending to sample whatever feminine charms came his way. But the maids who swung their hips so enticingly before him and pressed wantonly against his thighs, though pretty, could not compare with Jillian's exquisite beauty. He found no pleasure in looking at hair less black and shiny, or at eyes less blue and warm.

He quietly undressed, pausing again at the side of the bed to gaze down at her. She had captured him so thoroughly that no other woman would ever take her place in his heart. Yet her obvious feelings for the Irish groom pierced his chest like slivers of ice.

He slid into the bed, his fingers sliding beneath the ebony silk of Jillian's hair, and when she stirred, he pulled her back against his chest, his breath catching at the feel of her. To his surprise she turned in his embrace, her arms going around his neck. The softness of her lips brushed the ridged muscles of his chest, but his doubts threatened the ecstasy of the moment. He spoke low words against her temple.

"Do you love the Irishman?"

Jillian raised serious eyes, and her gaze was unwavering.

"Aye, I love him, but as a sister would love a brother and nothing more. I could not love otherwise, my husband, for I have given all my love to you."

Her sincerity could not be denied, and their lips met gently, caressingly, and each moaned beneath the fierce and familiar passion that overtook them. Justin stopped the kiss as her lips grew hungry, holding her face in his palms.

"I have wronged you, I think." His words

were barely audible, his eyes warm upon her. "The sight of you with him took away my reason, but my words were ill-spoken. Your friend from Ulster is welcome here, and you are free to treat him as such."

Jillian smiled tremulously, her heart swelling with relief and gratitude, her eyes fluttering weakly as his lips came to hers, hot and hungry. She pressed herself against him wantonly as his fingers worked to loosen the ribbons of her gown, then moaned as their bodies touched, his hands threading through silken tresses, his mouth a fiery brand upon her neck. She quivered with joy as his hard body pressed over her, and she slid her hands over the sinewy strength of his broad shoulders, pressing moist kisses upon his neck, his chest, until Justin thought only of her mouth and skin and heated response.

"I love you," he said, groaning against her ear, and Jillian rose to meet his embrace, giving all her love, all her loyalty to her husband, until time stopped in a sparkling starburst of pure bliss that entwined their hearts into one.

# TWENTY-ONE

The sun was warm upon their heads as Jillian stepped upon Pierce's interlaced hands to be lifted into her sidesaddle. She smiled down at him as he handed Ebony up to her. The small cat disappeared immediately into the deep pocket of her skirts, then turned until her slanted eyes peeked from the folds of royal blue velvet.

Catherine sat astride her huge black stallion, looking lovely in a riding habit of dark gold velvet, despite her mannish posture. Jillian shook her head in wonder. She had never seen a lady ride in such a way, and it looked to be most uncomfortable, but Catherine adamantly refused to heed her brothers when they chided her for unladylike behavior.

Pearl was gentle and easy to handle but still slightly squeamish under the hand of a new mistress, so Jillian held her with a firm rein. The air was crisp, and she inhaled deeply, pleased to be outside on such a gorgeous October day.

Catherine held Sultan to a walk until Jillian was abreast with her, and they proceeded together down the sun-dappled road through huge oak trees, spectacular in their scarlet autumn splendor.

"The man Brennan is certainly a handsome one," Catherine commented, glancing back to where the new groom stood watching. "But his eyes are like wintry ice and it is even worse when he looks at Justin or my other brothers."

"He has been ill-used by Englishmen," Jillian reminded her. "But he cannot help but see how kind you are after he is here a time."

She fervently hoped her words would prove to be true, so she could tell Justin the truth. Perhaps then the heavy weight inside her chest would dissolve. It had been nearly ten days since Pierce had come to Spenser Court, and Jillian had been careful not to be seen with her brother too often, because, despite Justin's permission, she had felt his frowning regard upon her when she actively sought Pierce's company.

Catherine chattered on in her usual ebullient manner as they crossed through a tall hedgerow, and Jillian followed Catherine's lead, spurring Pearl into an invigorating gallop across a grassy meadow. Becoming color flushed her cheeks as they slowed to a canter.

Vast fruit orchards stretched out before them, and they meandered through the long rows of apple trees, the limbs barren now from the recent harvest. They came upon a rutted coach road that would take them into the town of Stratham, then on to Wellingford Cross.

Sunlight was swallowed by shade as they entered an old covered bridge, the horses' hooves clopping hollowly upon the wooden planks until they burst again into the sun. They slowed, and Jillian looked at the wide, brown river flowing swiftly beneath the rock piers of the bridge. A crumbling bell tower stood visible above the treetops perhaps a quarter of a mile up the riverbank, and Jillian gestured toward it with her riding crop.

"What ruins lie yonder?" she asked, and Catherine twisted in the saddle to follow her direction.

"The old Catholic abbey. Cromwell razed most of it, but come, I'll show you what is left of it."

They followed the main road until a narrow path veered off to the right, then took the weed-choked way through a thick copse of trees. Jillian looked around in interest when they reached a maze of low walls surrounding the old stone tower. An arched colonnade was half-destroyed and overgrown with vegetation, and Jillian walked her mare along it to another low wall that was built parallel to the riverbank. A heavy, triangular stone stood on the bank, a cross carved on either side, and she looked curiously at an oaken plank that was attached to it in a seesaw fashion. One end lay half-submerged, the part in the water green with river slime as currents and small eddies rippled and swirled around it.

She pulled back on her reins and looked at Catherine.

"Did the priests use this to draw water?"

Catherine laughed. "Not hardly. That is the ducking stool of the witch hunters. We are fortunate we live in enlightened days, or the trick we played upon Eleanor Marlowe might have earned us a ride on it. But it would have been worth the wetting, I think, to see her flee in such terror."

Jillian smiled, looking at the rotted beam.

"I have never heard of such a thing. Did they truly duck the witch into the water?"

"Yes; indeed, there used to be a chair upon the end of the board there, and the heretic was held beneath the water until she confessed. Then they would hang the poor soul."

A violent shudder undulated up Jillian's spine as Catherine went on.

"But it was a better fate than others suffered. It is said that they bound some victims hand and foot and tossed them into that deep hole yonder."

She pointed at a spot just past the ducking stool. "If they sank to the bottom, their innocence was proved; but if they floated, they were deemed guilty."

"But would not the innocent drown if cast into deep water bound in such a way?" Jillian asked, horrified eyes on the dreadful contraption.

"Yes, the victims of the witch hunters rarely survived one way or the other."

Jillian shivered, and Catherine laughed again. "Do not worry, there are no witch-hunters in Kent. But come on, we must hurry on to Stratham Green because all manner of tinkers and entertainments will be arriving for next week's Harvest Feast."

Ebony stirred in Jillian's pocket, and Jillian held her close, unsettled by the stories of witch-hunters and ducking stools. The crumbling ruins seemed eerie and foreboding, and she could almost hear muffled screams and choked gurglings as helpless women were plunged into the river. Cold chills stood up on her flesh, and she was pleased to leave the shady abbey behind as they crossed once again into sunny fields.

Stratham was the closest hamlet to Spenser Court, and most of its townspeople helped with the vast harvesting of wheat and corn and hops that had to be done on the Spenser estates. But even with their help, workers came from afar for the seasonal work. The Spensers were known for their fair wage and the Harvest Feast where all were treated with food and ale and an evening of lighthearted entertainment.

Wide fields of cropped grass hugged one edge of the town near the church spire, and a frenzy of activity abounded as eager common folk, newly compensated for hard labor, moved among brightly colored wagons and tents where all sorts of wares were displayed. A mood of merriment pervaded the crowd as acrobats leapt and tumbled and puppeteers delighted crowds of happy children.

Catherine and Jillian dismounted beneath the wide branches of an immense oak tree. Several village women curtsied when they recognized Catherine Spenser, then smiled a shy welcome at their lord's beautiful bride. Jillian had met few of the peasants or laborers of her husband's lands, and she nodded, pleased at their friendliness.

She and Catherine walked slowly among the different stalls where bolts of shimmery Oriental silks and the softest of velvets were set out beneath fluttery canvas canopies. Jillian's eyes sharpened with interest when she caught sight of a bright yellow wagon whose large red letters proclaimed strange and powerful spices from the Far East and medicinal herbs from Bombay. She moved under a low canopy whose purple fringe snapped and fluttered in the brisk wind. The extensive selection of roots and plants excited her, because many were quite rare, and as she searched through them, Catherine wandered desultorily around the tables, unable to fathom her sister-in-law's fascination with dirty roots and dead leaves.

A smaller table was set at one side near the back entrance of the wagon, and Catherine stopped beside it, looking at the gold and silver jewelry that lay upon a length of plush black velvet.

The proprietor of the wagon stood nearby,

clothed in the flowing white robes of an Arab. Catherine barely glanced at him as she lifted a slender chain to examine a heavy silver medallion. She turned it, intrigued by the strange half moon and stars entwined with oddly formed letters.

"What is the cost of this trinket?" she asked the Arab, who watched Jillian as she browsed through the tables with Ebony at her heels.

He turned to Catherine as she spoke, and she gasped as pure azure eyes glowed from a darkly tanned face. She stared at him, thinking he was undoubtedly the handsomest man she had ever seen. His gaze dropped to her bodice in a slow, insulting appraisal that seemed to strip her naked, though in truth, her décolletage was quite modest. Angry color rose in her cheeks as he calmly recaptured her eyes.

"To one of such beauty, the necklace is a gift from a humble merchant."

He spoke in flawless French, and his deep voice fell pleasantly upon her ear. But when his eyes continued to roam her face and hair, resentment flared in her.

"You are not an Arab," she said coldly, bristling as the blue eyes lingered for an insolent moment on her lips.

"Nay, I call no country my own, nor as yet any woman."

His eyes made another rude circuit of her fine features, and her flush deepened. He took the necklace from her, his fingers intentionally brushing hers.

"The symbols tell of an ancient legend of the necklace. Allow me to fasten it around your neck."

He smiled as he placed it over her hair, and Catherine lifted it in her gloved palm.

"What is this legend?"

"It is said that the wearer will languish with love for the one who places it upon her throat."

Catherine darted startled green eyes toward him, then jerked off the chain and tossed it angrily back upon the table.

"You are impertinent," she said sharply, moving quickly away from him, inwardly infuriated by the man's low laugh.

In a tent just across the way Eleanor Marlowe barely glanced at Catherine Spenser as she stalked away from the Arab peddler, her brown eyes narrowed and cold upon Jillian and her cat.

"She is the one, I tell you," she said softly, turning to look up at Jack Harkins.

He was very big, with the broad, square-shouldered build of a common laborer, and his close-set, dark eyes followed her pointing forefinger to a small black-haired woman. He grinned, his breath fouling the air, and as he spoke, he revealed broken and yellowing teeth.

"She looks a laidy to me eyes, not a witch."

"I have seen her make fire smoke and leap at her victims, and she has help in her evil deeds. See there, a black cat follows her every movement. It is her familiar, I tell you."

Jack Harkins was a mean and selfish man with no qualms about his life as a highwayman. He led a mangy crew of cutthroats and murderers who plundered and robbed throughout the whole of Kent, and it was just this reputation of unscrupulous greed that had brought Eleanor to him. But he was not as stupid as he was greedy, and he contemplated the fine lady's story of witches and spells. His eyes narrowed as the cat across the way leapt into Jillian's arms, then seemed to vanish into thin air. Eleanor smiled as Harkins caught his breath.

"Did you not see her magic with your own eyes just then? I risk her wrath upon myself to tell of her wickedness. It is said that she caused a terrible plague upon her home in Ireland. She bears the evil eye and none can escape her black deeds."

"There is sickness in Tombrane," Jack muttered, and Eleanor nodded, her eyes glittering.

"That is her doing, for she passed through Tombrane town on her way from London. We must rid our countryside of her before she brings doom down upon us all."

Harkins looked at her, the cast in his left eye giving him a bizarre look. He scratched at his unkempt black beard, then his pate, which had receded in baldness to mid-skull. His expression was crafty as he lifted the emerald necklace she had given him.

"And what else must I do to earn this? Surely spreading tales of 'er witchcraft is meager toil for such a goodly reward."

Eleanor smiled. "There will be a greater reward when I claim my inheritance within this year. But we will have need of your men if my plan is to succeed."

He nodded. " 'Twould serve the good people hereabouts well to rid 'em of 'er evil spells."

Eleanor's laugh was malicious. "Await my word for the time and place."

Jack Harkins pocketed the heavy necklace, then joined the jostling crowd outside the draped tent, and Eleanor's eyes found Jillian again.

"Your days are numbered, Irish witch," she whispered, her smile as brittle as crystal. "No one makes a fool of me."

She lifted her cowl to disguise her features, then left the tent from the back where François Dubois, her French groom, awaited with her horse.

Jillian exclaimed in delight when she found a ginseng plant. She glanced around for Catherine, surprised to find her gone. The tall Arab was walking toward the back of the wagon, and Jillian carried her prize toward where he had disappeared, holding Ebony securely in her pocket. She carried no coin with which to buy the ginseng, but she felt sure Justin would give it to her if the tinker would come to the Harvest Feast.

Low wooden steps led to a red silk curtain

over the door of the wagon, and Jillian called a greeting. When the man did not appear, she looked around hesitantly, then climbed the steps.

"Hello, is anyone—"

Strong hands grabbed her shoulders, shocking her to silence, and she began to struggle as a hand clamped tightly over her mouth. He dragged her bodily inside the wagon, her screams muffled by his hand.

"Jillian! Do not be afraid. It is Brian!"

The soft Gaelic words made her go limp with astonishment, and as she was released, she turned quickly, her eyes wide with disbelief.

"Brian, Brian, is it really you?" she breathed, her voice catching. They hugged with wordless joy until he released her, grinning down into her incredulous face.

"So you have recovered. Donal told me you were very ill when the English ship took you away."

"Have you seen Donal then? Is he well? Or here with you?"

Her eager questions would have gone on, but Brian quieted her with a low laugh.

"Nay, he is back in Ulster. I sailed there to see if you were safe, but the English earl had already followed you here."

Ebony stirred in the warm pocket at the familiar masculine voice, then came quickly outside to jump into Brian's lap. Jillian smiled as her big brother cuddled the purring cat.

"I have missed you so much, Brian. I prayed every day that you and Pierce were safe."

Brian hugged her shoulders again, his voice low.

"I have been well enough, except for the worry about you. I command the *Windward,* which lies in anchor at Harwich. I've come to take you home. You are all I have since Pierce is gone."

Jillian pulled back, her eyes alive with the news she had for him.

"Nay, we are not alone, Brian, for Pierce is alive! And well!"

"Pierce is alive?"

Jillian laughed at his stunned expression, quickly telling him of her chance meeting with their brother at the slave auction.

"God be praised," Brian murmured, his voice gruff with emotion. "I knew not if it would be my fate to ever see either of you again."

" 'Tis a great risk you run to come here or even to Ulster," Jillian whispered, suddenly realizing his danger. "The English will surely hang you if you are caught. You must go quickly."

"I will not leave you alone again, nor will I leave Pierce to languish in chains."

"But you do not understand. I have grown to love my husband and his family. His sister has become most dear to me. She is here with me today."

"Aye, I have met that green-eyed beauty."

Brian's smile was strange, but Jillian did

not pause to consider it as she laid her hand on his arm.

"Justin has asked the king to pardon you and lift your exile. Does not that tell you of his kindness? And he would do as much for Pierce, but Pierce refuses to let me tell Justin of our kinship."

"Jillian! Where are you?"

Catherine's worried voice came from outside, and Brian pulled Jillian up, pushing her toward the door.

"Go quickly, and I will pack my wagon. If I come to the Harvest Feast, will I be able to see Pierce?"

Jillian nodded, and they hugged again before she descended the steps, holding Ebony close, her heart so full of joy that she felt it would burst.

# TWENTY-TWO

The banquet hall was the most ancient part of Spenser Court, dating from long before the reign of Henry VIII. It formed the entire bottom floor of the western wing with huge oaken beams, darkened by smoke and age, vaulting the white plaster ceiling. Enormous stone fireplaces rose with majestic grandeur at each end, with ancestral shields of bronze and copper displayed above one while ancient crossbows and swords graced the other.

On the night of the Harvest Feast fires roared in openings taller than most men stood, and long trestle tables laden with bountiful food and plenteous ale skirted the inner walls in a *U* facing a windowed wall. A magnificent black-and-gold tapestry hung on the wide stone mullion separating the windows, the twin winged lions glittering silvery in the torchlight.

The Earl of Wellingford sat on an elevated platform before the Spenser coat of arms with his family. A curved table draped with silk and set with silver was before him, and Justin observed with satisfaction the multitude of guests enjoying the bounty of his harvest.

Round platters of roast pig lay on each table alongside others of beef and mutton, and bowls of boiled vegetables and meat pies were offered with baskets of crusty bread. Wine and the hearty beer from the Spenser breweries flowed plentifully. There were musicians on a balcony that overlooked the festivities, and the loud laughter and din of voices bore evidence of hearty appetites and good spirits.

The Harvest Feast had been celebrated for over a century by the Spenser family, and the weeks Aaron had spent with preparations were not lost on the laborers who came from the faraway shires each fall.

Justin's eyes hardened as his gaze swept past Eleanor Marlowe. Her presence was unwanted, but her family had been their nearest neighbor for years, and he could not force her to leave. Instead she had been snubbed by his family, given a place at the tables far below her rank. He had been surprised that she had not stalked out at the insult, but he really didn't care what she did, as long as he did not have to abide her. He looked at Aaron, who sat on his right, deep in conversation with Sir Henry Wright, a gentleman who shared his passion for farming. They discussed the various crops and the new methods of rotation, and Justin's eyes soon sought the fairer one who sat on his left.

Jillian wore a soft velvet gown of pale blue, and her slender hand rested upon Ebony, who lay in her lap. Her husband leaned back, content to look at her as she spoke with Catherine at her other side.

He raised a silver goblet and drank, his eyes moving down the graceful curve of her throat and then across high cheekbones faintly flushed with pink. In the last few days he had noticed a subtle, inexplicable change in her, one that heartily met his approval. A deep serenity had settled over her, bringing her soft musical laughter more often and, even more important, erasing the melancholy he read in her eyes so often since he joined her in England. She seemed content and happy, and that made him so.

She caught him looking at her, and her open, loving smile totally devastated the man beside her. He reached out and lifted a silky black curl, smoothing it tenderly over her shoulder, and Jillian closed her eyes as his knuckle ran over the soft curve of her cheek in the softest of caresses.

She had never felt so happy, and when Justin pressed her hand to his lips, she shivered at the silvery promise lying deep within his eyes.

"Yonder comes the insolent Frenchman from Stratham Green," Catherine muttered sourly from behind Jillian, her dislike more than obvious, and Jillian reluctantly dragged her eyes from her husband. She instantly picked out Brian in the flowing white robe, and at her delighted smile, Justin swung his eyes to the man she watched. He was aware that the Frenchman's eyes lingered for an extra moment upon Catherine, though she pointedly ignored him.

"Lord Spenser, I beg leave to compliment you on your bountiful hospitality," the man said in fluent French, and Justin stared at him as he bent slightly from the waist. A faint familiarity nagged at him. "Have we not met before, sir?" he asked, his eyes intent, and Jillian stiffened in alarm, darting a dismayed look at Brian. She breathed easier when Brian smiled and answered without pause.

"Nay, I am Jacques Dehaven, a stranger to these parts. But it was my great honor to meet your lovely wife and sister at the stalls at Stratham this week past."

Justin glanced at the two women, not having heard of the encounter, wondering again at Catherine's hostility toward the man. He turned back as the Frenchman spoke again.

"The kindness of your lady has brought me here with tidings that I fear may cause you some displeasure."

His last remark brought Aaron's attention from horse breeding, and Justin's eyes narrowed with renewed interest.

"What tidings?"

"I have been in Stratham for over a fortnight now, milord, and I have heard many disquieting rumors concerning the lovely Lady Jillian, especially in the last few days. It is said"—he paused apologetically—"that she is a witch and has caused an outbreak of fever in a nearby village."

His words had scarcely left his mouth when Justin's fist came down hard on the table, rattling the cutlery and causing many heads to turn.

"Who tells such lies?" he growled harshly.

"A man called Jack Harkins stirs the people the most, an ignorant fellow with a cast to one eye," Brian answered calmly. "But the belief is most widespread, I fear. So much so that were I the lady's husband, I would be afraid for her safety."

Justin's jaw locked, and Jillian looked down as several people stared openly at her. Aaron's hand settled on the tensed muscles of Justin's arm.

"The peasants are superstitious, Justin. As lord lieutenant of Wellingford it is your duty to stop such rumors before they spread further."

Justin controlled his anger, wondering if Jillian would always be called witch, no matter where he took her.

"You have my thanks for coming to me," he said to the Frenchman. "And I shall certainly heed your warnings until we have squelched such ignorant prattle."

Brian inclined his head, giving Catherine a brief glance.

"And if I may speak again, perhaps caution may be served by restricting the activities of your sister as well. I have heard her name bandied about, though not to the same extent."

Catherine's face flamed, and she sputtered with outrage, her green eyes flashing fire.

"How dare you presume to tell me what to do! A common peddler—"

Brian interrupted, which acted to incense Catherine further.

"I think only of your well-being, milady. I am a brother myself and often worry about my sister. She was once a willful child as you seem to be."

Aaron hid a smile behind his hand, but Catherine exploded with wrath.

"Willful child! Why, you arrogant, ignorant—"

"I thank you for your warning," Justin interrupted before she could get started. "I assure you that both Jillian and Catherine will be well protected."

"Justin! You can't take the word of—" Catherine began again furiously as the Frenchman moved away, his white robe billowing behind him, but Justin's eyes stopped her short.

"I can and will. Neither you nor Jillian will leave the estate until I can contact the justices of Wellingford and Stratham."

"But what about riding Sultan?" Catherine protested.

"You will not ride until we can stop such dangerous talk. Is that clear?"

Justin's voice brooked no refusal, and Catherine clamped her jaw, indignation welling up as she turned a scathing glare on the

Frenchman, who had taken a seat at the end of a table only yards from her chair.

Jillian said nothing. Although she felt sorry for Catherine, she knew that if Brian risked a conversation with Justin, he was very concerned about the rumors. Her fine dark brows dented into a small frown as she wondered how such talk had started. The common people she had encountered outside Stratham on the green had been most kind to Catherine and her. She looked at Brian and found him staring at Pierce, who leaned against the wall behind the tables, aloof and hard-faced. Brian's face reflected Jillian's own concern for Pierce, and she sighed. Pierce was so very different now than in the old days in Ulster, when he had been happy and carefree. It had always been Pierce who swung the prettiest serving girls in a dance and laughed until everyone joined the fun. Her eyes went to Ryan where he stood in the midst of a merry group, one arm around the waist of a pretty maid. He threw back his head, his laughter audible above the music in the hall.

"Do not be upset over the peddler's words, my sweet. I will let no harm come to you."

Justin's whisper close to her ear dissolved the worried lines on her face. She smiled into his eyes.

"I am used to such talk. But I cannot imagine the people of Stratham harming me or Catherine. They treated us with much friendliness when we walked among them."

"You were well known in Ulster, love, and protected by a powerful family. But here you are a stranger to the land. Fear and ignorance are dangerous when they are coupled, and I will take no chance with your safety."

Justin lifted her fingers and brushed his mouth along the back of her hand. The sweet scent of her perfume sent a tingling into his core. He wanted her now as he always did when he touched her or looked at her. Each time they came together it was like the first time, a sweet, thunderous passion that at times almost frightened him.

"Do you not grow weary of this endless din, milord?" Jillian murmured, pure turquoise eyes half closed in invitation.

Justin's mouth went dry, and without hesitation, he stood. Jillian wasted no time, either, pushing Ebony off her lap as she eagerly put her hand in her husband's. They neither saw nor cared about the knowing smiles that passed between many at the surrounding tables as he led his wife from the dais. Justin missed Jillian's quick backward glance at Brian and the smile they shared.

Across the room another took note, and Eleanor Marlowe's eyes rested speculatively on the handsome Arab peddler for a long, thoughtful moment. The two had met before at his wagon; she had witnessed that herself. Perhaps the Irish witch had already tired of the groom Justin had bought for her and had taken a new lover. Eleanor smiled at the idea of Justin Spenser being cuckolded by a lowly tinker, though a handsome one he was. She stood and moved toward him, her mind already contemplating various uses he might play in the final stage of her revenge.

Brian Devlin raised his tankard of ale, his light blue eyes roaming over the crowded hall. It was quite obvious that his little sister was in love with Justin Spenser, and he was glad, since the marriage had been forced upon her. And he had to admit that her English husband treated her with the utmost respect and kindness. In truth, Lord Spenser's eyes rarely left his wife, which boded well for them and gave Brian rest on Jillian's well-being. The rumors, however, were ugly indeed, and heard by his own ears. It had been difficult to restrain himself when Jack Harkins tried to stir the fear of the patrons of the taverns with his vicious descriptions of Jillian's evil powers. Through discreet inquiry Brian had found that Harkins was an unsavory character who was the leader of a motley crew of highwaymen.

Brian had not yet determined just why the man maligned Jillian in such a way, but intuition told him that there was more to his motives than met the eye. But now that he had met Jillian's husband, he could relax about her safety. Instead it was Pierce who troubled him more.

He looked again to his brother, who still stood alone, his cold, expressionless eyes on the merrymakers. Brian had searched him out the day before, and as they planned an escape to Ulster, Brian had been appalled at his younger brother's bitterness. The hatred he displayed was all-consuming and vicious, the kind that would burn into his soul to destroy him. Pierce remained resolute in his opposition to William even after Brian had told him of James's defeat at La Hogue. Brian had been there himself and well knew it unlikely that the French would launch an invasion.

Pierce talked of fighting for their lands and rights, but Brian was of a more practical bent. He pondered long and seriously Jillian's talk of a pardon and had almost decided it was possibly the only way to reunite his family in Ulster. After all, they were Protestants as were William and Mary, and they could be a greater help to a tolerant Ireland as powerful landowners there.

"May I sit with you?"

The feminine voice caught Brian completely off guard, and his fingers closed automatically over the dagger hidden beneath his robe. He relaxed again as he gazed into the face of a young woman gowned in red. She was a lady by her dress, quite lovely with elaborately curled blond hair. The expression in her large brown eyes gave him some pause, or perhaps, he suddenly realized, it was the lack of expression that caused his wariness.

"It would be my honor, milady." He rose as she sat very close beside him.

"I am Lady Eleanor Marlowe, and a very good friend of Lady Spenser."

"I am most honored to make your acquaintance. I am Jacques Dehaven."

Eleanor's eyes moved to Jillian and Justin as they threaded their way toward the staircase at the far end of the room.

"She is most lovely, don't you agree?"

Brian was careful to be indifferent. "It appears that her husband thinks she is," he remarked, gesturing toward the stairs where Justin had swept Jillian into his arms before they were completely out of sight.

He watched the woman's face harden, and he knew at once that Eleanor Marlowe was no friend to his sister. His eyes remained shuttered.

"You seem very special to her as well," Eleanor probed, innocent brown eyes intent on his face.

Brian's expression did not waver.

"I am afraid you are mistaken. I hardly know the lady. We met but once before this night."

Eleanor studied his handsome face; his vivid blue eyes were unreadable. A spark of desire glowed inside her as he gave her a slow, faintly mocking smile. She knew that he was a man who would not be controlled or manipulated, and he reminded her of Justin in that way.

She jerked back, startled, as Jillian's black cat leapt between them, arching its back against the Arab robes, its purr low and content as Brian stroked its back.

So the Frenchman is no stranger to the

witch's cat, she thought triumphantly. The Irish bride had surely taken a lover, and the familiarity with which he fondled her pet only proved it. Brian watched her eyes grow assessing and wily.

"Since you are a stranger hereabouts, perhaps you will need a companion with whom to while away the night," she murmured, running the tip of her tongue in a slow circuit of her scarlet-painted lips, and Brian's gaze dropped to her moist mouth for an instant, then met her eyes again. She was giving him the most blatant invitation he had in many a month, and he sensed somehow that she might know something of Jack Harkins's lies about Jillian. Perhaps her interest could be to his advantage.

"I am most honored by your kindness, milady, and accept your company with pleasure."

Eleanor smiled, an inner thrill of satisfaction running through her.

"There is a private garden near the stables with high brick walls. I will go there shortly and await you."

She rose and left him without further comment, and Brian followed her retreating back with troubled eyes, quite sure she was an enemy, both to him and to Jillian. But now he had been afforded an opportunity to learn more of this Eleanor Marlowe, and he meant to take it.

He drank, his eyes gradually straying to the curved table before the hanging tapestry.

His eyes clashed like a clang of cymbals with fiery green ones, but Catherine Spenser's fury only enhanced her beauty to near magnificence in his eyes. He was a little surprised by his strong attraction to the young Englishwoman. She was obviously a brat, spoiled and pampered by her doting brothers, but as he raised his tankard toward her in a salute, she arose and, tossing her black curls contemptuously, swept away in an angry swirl of lavender silk.

Brian grinned, his admiring eyes on the sway of her slim hips, and as he divined her intention to leave the banquet hall through the courtyard, he took a different path through the rowdy crowd, a slight smile lifting one corner of his mouth.

Catherine was still seething over the damned idiot of a peddler and his interference, when she stepped out into the cool night air. The fact that he sat and chatted with Eleanor Marlowe was proof enough that he was a rogue and a libertine as well as a fool. She took a deep draught of fresh air into her lungs, trying to calm the riot of resentment that boiled her blood. She was sick and tired of men running her life and telling her what to do! None of them were a whit smarter than she was! They were just bigger and stronger and wore breeches instead of skirts!

"Good evening, milady. Lovely night, don't you agree?"

The low voice was instantly recognizable, and Catherine swung around.

"How dare you follow me out here!" she cried, and Brian met her wrath with an unruffled white grin, his amusement obvious beneath the lantern glow.

"I was here before you stepped out, I believe, so it must be your wont to follow me about."

"Oh! You are the most vile and contemptible man I have ever met," she gritted out with low, venomous contempt, and the way Brian's eyes calmly roamed her face and heaving breasts infuriated her even more.

"And you are the most beautiful angel I have ever seen," he said, very low. "It is a pity that no one has ever thought to tell you that you are a woman and should calm your bad temper and behave as such. But, perhaps if I am lucky, that task will be my pleasure to perform."

Catherine's eyes glittered green rage at his calmly uttered insult.

"And perhaps it will be my pleasure to tell you that you are not man enough to show me that nor anything else."

She lifted her skirts, her slim nose even higher, as she hurried away, and Brian watched her go, deciding in that moment that he would have the saucy wench. He walked toward the gardens to meet Eleanor Marlowe, wondering how he would win Catherine Spenser over to him.

# TWENTY-THREE

It was nearly dark. Shadows crouched on black haunches around the sculptured shrubbery where François Dubois watched Jillian Devlin Spenser. She walked along the finely graveled walk of the formal gardens of Spenser Court where he had hidden nearly all day, waiting for an opportunity to speak to her without being seen. He had to succeed in his errand or Eleanor Marlowe would flog him without mercy.

Dark hatred twisted the young groom's face into an ugly mask. His mistress was cruel, truly a demented woman, and he knew full well that she had evil plans for the Lady Spenser. He thought the small, black-haired Irishwoman approaching him was very beautiful, and he admired her courage. He had often thought of the day she suffered Eleanor's blow to protect the chained slave, but his fear of Eleanor ran deep. He had no choice but to obey her commands.

Jillian had no idea of the groom's presence so very close by as she hurried toward the east wing of Spenser Court. She had walked for a long time in the mild weather, hoping the exercise would get her mind off her husband's absence. It had not, and she smiled to herself because he had only been gone since early that morning. He had ridden with Ryan and Pierce to speak to the justices in Wellingford about the accusations of witchcraft against her. It pleased Jillian that he had chosen her brother to accompany them, and she hoped the long ride together would soften Pierce's opinion of Ryan and Justin. But she was lonely without them and did not relish the thought of occupying the huge canopy bed alone.

"I have word for you, milady."

The low words in French broke into her thoughts, and Jillian spun with fright. She peered into the darkness, but no one stepped forth from the shadows. She backed away warily, glancing at the armed guard who followed her at a discreet distance.

"Who is there?"

She frowned as the man spoke again, very low.

"I bear urgent word from the peddler of the yellow wagon. He begs you to await him this night at the old abbey."

Bushes rustled faintly as the clandestine messenger moved away, and Jillian stepped forward.

"Wait, please, I must know more."

Running footsteps gradually faded from earshot, and she stared into the deep twilight, thinking that Brian's dilemma was most dire if he should summon her so secretly. She could not understand why he would not come himself or whom he trusted enough to send with his message. The man had spoken French, so it might possibly be one of his men from his ship. She debated possible reasons for the summons as she crossed the drive where several other guards stood on duty.

Since Brian's warning last week at the Harvest Feast, Justin had commanded a constant posting of sentries on the grounds. She had been in sight of at least one man all day except inside the house, at Justin's express order during his absence.

The wide downstairs hall was quiet and deserted, since most of the servants were dining in their quarters in the back, and when she passed Aaron's study, he was bent over his desk, hard at work on his ledgers. She briefly wondered where Catherine was as she hastily climbed one of the back staircases to the lord's wing. Her sister-in-law had sulked endlessly over Justin's decision that she could not ride Sultan, but Jillian's mind could not dwell on that with Brian's cryptic message in her thoughts. She was worried about him, for something truly dreadful was amiss. Perhaps the king's men had found his whereabouts, and he was preparing to flee England. The idea of such danger sent her heart pounding, but even if she tried to meet him at the abbey, how would she leave the estate undetected?

She entered her sitting room and pulled off her cape to fling it carelessly upon a chair.

She began to pace, trying to decide what she should do. If she waited for Justin to return on the morrow, it might be too late. Brian would be gone. And even if he were not, she would have to convince Justin to accompany her to meet him, and she could not do that without telling him the truth about Brian.

She retraced her steps, her brow knitted with worry. If only Pierce had not gone with Justin, he could ride to meet Brian. Nerves already skittish, she whirled around as her door opened. A young boy stepped inside and quickly shut the door behind him. Jillian backed away, afraid.

"What do you want?" she gasped, and a low laugh erupted. Jillian stared at him, ready to scream if he took a step toward her. Her mouth dropped as he moved into the candle-light.

"Catherine! You frightened me!"

Catherine laughed again, and Jillian's eyes dropped to the brown linen shirt and matching breeches she wore, then on to the shapely legs in dark, masculine hose. Jillian had not seen her sister-in-law in such garb since the day she regained consciousness in London, and she stared openmouthed at her until Catherine spoke.

"I am tired of Justin's silly orders. I have not ridden Sultan for an entire week, and I'm going to exercise him this night. I've brought clothes so that you can come, too, if you wish."

She held up a pair of boy's breeches.

"These were Ryan's when he was little. They were the smallest I could find, but you'll look like a stableboy in them."

Jillian stared at Catherine, a ghost of an idea hovering in her mind, despite the half-hearted protest she uttered.

"But we would surely be recognized by the guards."

"No. I have done this many times when Justin or Aaron imposed some ridiculous restrictions upon me. No one has ever found out yet, except Ryan once, and he didn't tell."

She laughed then and did a quick jig. She looked utterly preposterous in her outlandish attire, but Jillian remained sober.

"Catherine, I must talk to you. 'Tis most important."

Catherine stilled, her smile disintegrating at Jillian's serious tone.

"What is it? Is something wrong?"

Jillian hesitated. "You must swear to me first that upon your sacred honor you will not tell a soul about this. Especially Justin."

Catherine's eyes widened, more than surprised that Jillian would keep anything from her husband. She often marveled at the undying devotion Jillian showed to Justin since they had settled their differences.

"Of course, I will swear, Jillian, but I hope you are not in trouble."

"Nay, but I must ride to the old abbey ruins at once, and I do not think I can find my way there alone. No one must see us."

"The abbey? But why? That lies far off the

estates," Catherine protested, having intended only to ride in the inlying meadows.

Jillian considered briefly, then decided to tell her as much of the truth as she dared. Catherine had proven herself a loyal friend more than once, and Jillian trusted her implicitly.

"I must meet the Frenchman, Jacques Dehaven."

Catherine's mouth dropped agape, the green of her eyes darkening with dislike.

"You cannot do that. He is naught but a rogue, a scoundrel. . . ."

"I have known him before in Ulster," Jillian said quietly, cutting short Catherine's diatribe. "And he is not one to summon me thither without good reason."

Catherine studied her, thinking it too much to believe that she planned a tryst with the peddler, not the way she felt about Justin.

Jillian easily read her expression and answered her unasked questions.

"We are not lovers, but he is dear to me, and if he needs me, I must go to him."

Catherine began to shake her head, for the first time considering Justin's reaction to such a clandestine rendezvous by his wife—to meet a man, no less.

"Justin would have my head if he found out, and I shudder to think what he would do to you! He's even jealous of Ryan and Aaron!"

"He cannot find out. He won't even return from Wellingford until tomorrow."

Catherine frowned, somehow sure that nothing good could come of Jillian's idea.

"Please, Catherine, 'tis most important to me."

Jillian's pleading eyes decided Catherine, despite the premonition of disaster that rose inside her.

She finally nodded. "All right, but we best hurry before Aaron leaves his study for the night."

Jillian smiled gratefully, quickly stepping out of her gown and into the black breeches that Catherine held out to her. They swallowed her petite figure, and the rough fabric felt alien upon her bare legs. She slipped slender arms into the wide sleeves of a loose linen shirt, then stood docilely as Catherine wound her hair into a tight knot atop her head. Jillian pulled on the shapeless wool cap Catherine gave her, hardly recognizing herself in the mirror.

Now that she had committed herself to Jillian's scheme, Catherine's love of adventure was stirred, and she led the way, boldly confident that she could get them outside without being seen.

"Come, we will sneak through the grand gallery, and if we rub dirt on our faces, it will be all the harder to recognize us."

Jillian followed her, quite nervous, although she had to grin at the most convincing boyish swagger that Catherine affected once outside the house. She obediently smeared a handful of grime upon her face as they ducked behind bushes to escape the notice of the guard on duty at the courtyard entrance. They took the hedged path through the gardens to gain entrance to the rear of the stables. No one was around so late, and it took only moments to saddle their horses.

"We'll sneak out through the breeding corrals," Catherine whispered, and Jillian nodded, then whirled fearfully at a sound behind her. She released her pent-in breath at the low mewling in the darkness as Ebony's paws touched her legs. She scooped up her cat quickly, then stepped up on a box to mount her mare.

It felt most strange to straddle a horse, and she shifted uncomfortably on the hard leather saddle as Catherine opened a gate and led Sultan through, then closed it behind Jillian. Ebony settled into place against the pommel, and only moments later they gained the road to Wellingford.

The moon was full, its white light casting elongated black patterns on the road behind them, their shadows seeming to keep silent chase. The land took on a different cast in the dark of night, and Jillian was grateful for Catherine's lead. She felt completely lost as they took a shortcut through one end of the orchard, and she shivered in the chilly rush of night air as they galloped toward the abbey.

It seemed a very long ride before they reached the covered bridge, and they walked their horses at a dull clop to the other side. Catherine drew Sultan to a stop as they left the overhang, and Jillian reined up beside her. A faint glow was visible somewhere in the abbey ruins.

"That must be the peddler's fire . . ." Catherine began, but her words died as several dark figures lunged at them from the shadows of the bridge.

Jillian gasped in fright, trying to control the spooked mare as a hand grabbed at her bridle. Another man grabbed Sultan's trappings, and the spirited stallion reared slightly and pranced sideways.

"This ain't no Irish witch," came a gruff voice, and the ominous words goaded Jillian into action.

She jerked her reins, but the man held them fast. She slapped at him as he grabbed her arm, and in the ensuing struggle, her cap was torn loose. Pins fell with it, and her hair tumbled down her back. The coarse laugh that followed sent fear spiraling through both women.

"So, the witch takes the shape of a boy. Get her!"

Catherine kicked her steed before the man could pull Jillian from the saddle, bringing her crop down hard upon the one holding Sultan. The robber screamed in pain, and Sultan jumped forward. Catherine's whip fell again with a sharp whack upon the flanks of Jillian's mare, sending the horse into a gallop, and Jillian clutched Ebony close, leaning low upon the horse's neck.

Her heart hammered furiously as she dared

a backward glance at Catherine. In the bright moonlight she could see the black stallion's front legs flailing in the air before he gained his footing and raced down the riverbank away from the abbey. Relieved that Catherine had escaped, Jillian concentrated on reaching Brian. It was her only chance because the robbers now chased her on horseback.

She cut into the path to the abbey, sobbing as she headed toward the fire at the river. She cried out in horror as she rounded the tower, blundering into the very encampment of the highwaymen who pursued her. She tried desperately to turn the mare, but countless rough hands grabbed at her, and she screamed as she was pulled bodily from the saddle. Her eyes darted around in terror as a tall man with a straggly black beard jerked one arm around her waist to hold her off the ground. He picked up Ebony by the scruff of her neck, holding the terrified cat high above his head.

"Look 'ere, me lads, the witch has brought 'er familiar to us!"

Jillian jerked against his grip as a crowd of men pressed close, their eyes bright and glittering with excitement, their faces flushed with ale. Her heart pounded wildly as they poked and prodded at her body, feeling like a hundred hands clutching at her. She slapped at them hysterically as the man carried her toward the river, ignoring her kicking struggle.

It was then that Jillian saw Eleanor Marlowe, who waited at the bank, the flames illuminating a wicked, malicious smile. Her blood ran cold as Eleanor's eyes glittered with insane brightness. Her gaze darted to François Dubois at Eleanor's side; his eyes were dark with helpless compassion as Jack Harkins lowered her to the ground, then caught her back against his chest, one massive arm tight around her neck.

He held Jillian tightly in the flexed crook of his arm, then raised the black cat high.

" 'Tis proof of witchcraft! She rides at night with 'er cat, performing 'er evil spells upon us. The devils must burn!"

To Jillian's stark horror he hurled Ebony into the fire, and Jillian screamed shrilly as the screeching cat hit the blazing logs, twisting frantically to escape the fiery death. The highwaymen laughed as the tortured animal streaked past them in flames, her shrieks of agony terrible in the night. Jillian sobbed uncontrollably, crying out in pain as Jack Harkins grabbed a fistful of her hair and cruelly jerked up her face.

"Confess, witch," he demanded, his bad eye gleaming obscenely in the reddish light. "Confess yer work of Satan!"

The men around them stilled for her answer, tankards of ale clutched in meaty fists.

Jillian's voice trembled with denial. "Nay, I am not. I am not a witch."

Her captor frowned, his voice harsh. "Confess, I say, or suffer the fate of yer devil-cat."

Jillian shook her head helplessly, tears streaming down her face. "I am innocent, I swear it!"

"She lies!" Eleanor stepped forward, her face hard. "But she will confess after a ride upon the stool!"

"No, no . . ." Jillian cried, but the mob roared approval, and Jack Harkins dragged her to the ducking stool on the riverbank. Great waves of sick horror engulfed her as she realized that the rotted plank she and Catherine had seen had been refitted with a sturdy board, and a rough-hewn chair was lashed by ropes on one end.

The horrifying accounts of the witch-hunters came flooding over her, and Jillian fought wildly as Jack Harkins shoved her roughly into the seat. Hands held her cruelly as Harkins tied her back to the chair, her arms at her sides, knotting the ropes so tightly that she could barely move.

Eleanor laughed as two men lifted the heavy board up on the stone fulcrum, and Jillian groaned in mindless terror as the board was thrust out over the river. She stared with horrified eyes into the cold, black water below her, and the two men lowered the plank until her shoes dipped into the rippling current. She pulled desperately at her bindings, and the chair wobbled slightly where it was attached to the end of the board.

Jack Harkins's yell echoed over the river. "Confess yer crimes, witch!"

A hush descended, and Jillian looked over

her shoulder at them, her voice shaking until she could hardly form her words.

"Nay, I am innocent, please, believe me!"

The big man was silhouetted against the roaring flames, and Jillian watched with cold dread as he lifted his fist and slowly turned one thumb downward.

Jillian's breath left her as the board dropped abruptly, and the sudden plunge into the ice-cold water shocked her system to a standstill. She held her breath as the board slowly sank deeper beneath the water, the pounding of her heart filling her ears. The depths of the river were dark and totally silent, and the chair moved with her as she pulled and twisted against the ropes, her eyes open and panic-stricken.

Seconds ticked by, and she stared upward as the surface of the river, rippling from her plunge, gradually stilled into a calm mirror. She could see the wavery image of the full moon above the river, and her lungs burned for air, the pressure slowly filling her chest with lead.

Justin, Justin, help me, her mind cried, but she remembered then that her fate had been foretold when Justin had tossed her Birthing Stone into the spring. Jillian knew in that moment that she would die here in the dark, cold water.

A strange resignation settled over her, and she stopped fighting the cords and waited, her consciousness gradually growing dusky blue around the edges. Just when she had given up all hope, her lungs ready to burst, the board jerked upward, and she broke the surface, gasping and choking, taking in the wonderful air in great, harsh gulps. Her dull eyes found Eleanor Marlowe's place upon the bank where her pale blond hair glinted white in the moonlight.

Her smile was very cruel. "Do it again."

The board dropped, and Jillian moaned in despair as she again sank into watery depths as dark and silent as a grave.

# TWENTY-FOUR

Justin's thoughts were grim. He had been appalled at the extent of the gossip that had pervaded the surrounding villages and towns. As far away as the hamlet of Clairbarn, on the other side of Wellingford Cross, the constables had heard talk of Jillian. It was very dangerous, but even more than that it was surprising, since the persecution of witches had been nearly nonexistent in his lifetime. He couldn't understand it, but he made his displeasure felt, and the constables had assured him that they would end all talk and curb the growing hysteria. The discoveries of the day had made him so uneasy about Jillian's safety that he had started home instead of staying the night in Wellingford.

They rode through the darkened village of Stratham now, and Ryan rode at his side with the Irish groom, Brennan, behind them. Justin glanced back at him, wondering at his perpetual silence. He had said nothing the entire day, and it made Justin uncomfortable. He already berated himself over the fact that he'd brought the groom only because of a very keen reluctance to leave him behind with Jillian. Although he trusted his wife, he did not like to see her with the man.

When they left the whitewashed houses behind, and rode alongside the Stratham green, Justin noticed that the yellow wagon of the Frenchman stood nearby at the edge of a wood. A dim light shone from a small window, and Justin turned Caesar toward it, curious if Jacques Dehaven had heard other threatening rumors concerning Jillian.

The peddler appeared at the back of the wagon before they could dismount. He no longer wore the white robe, and Justin's eyes dropped to a sword buckled at his side. A brace of flintlock pistols was tucked in his belt.

"Greetings," Brian called, holding out a lantern, his eyes resting for a moment on Pierce before settling back on Justin Spenser's face.

"We are journeying back from Wellingford. We have alerted the justice there and they have agreed to hunt down Jack Harkins and his men and end their troublemaking for my wife."

"That is good news indeed, then," Brian returned. "And is your lady well?"

"We go to her now but stopped to inquire if the rumors persist in Stratham."

"Since the man Harkins has been absent these past few days, much of the talk has ended, but I now have reason to believe that another is behind his actions. A lady by the name of Eleanor Marlowe."

"Damn the woman," Justin gritted out, wishing he could get his hands on her if indeed she was the cause of the trouble.

They all turned as a dull thud of hooves against grass came to them. Justin thought at first that it was Sultan who approached, but the rider who skidded to a stop before them wore breeches. It was not until Catherine cried out that he realized it was his sister.

"Justin, Ryan, thank God!" Catherine gasped breathlessly. "You must come quick! They've got Jillian!"

Justin's muscles turned to stone, his voice coming harshly. "Who? Who has her?"

"Highwaymen! They stopped us at the old bridge, and they chased her into the abbey! I circled around here to get help!"

Her eyes left Justin's white face, and she gasped when she saw Brian.

"What are you doing here? Jillian's message was to meet you at the abbey!"

"I sent no summons to her," Brian said, his eyes darting to Pierce before he jumped to the ground and slung his saddle upon the back of his horse.

"Go get Aaron," Justin barked to Catherine, wheeling his steed, his fear welling so strong as to block his very breath.

Ryan and Pierce spurred into a gallop behind him as Catherine thundered off in the opposite direction toward Spenser Court. Brian closed the gap before they were a mile down the road, and they rode hard, each afraid of what might have already happened to Jillian.

When they finally rounded the bend that overlooked the river, Justin's eyes went with a terrible dread to the orange glow painting the dark night sky. Clouds of gray smoke and sparks climbed with the heat, and Justin's stomach knotted and held. He had faced death in battle or at sea many a time but never with such devastating fear as he felt when he visualized Jillian, pale and lifeless. His throat constricted until he could not breathe at the thought of losing her. He loved Jillian, loved her deeply and passionately. She had become an integral part of him now, and if she were gone, if— He could not finish the thought, and cold dread locked his heart inside an icy crust.

His face set in granite, he pulled his sword free, and Ryan and Brian followed his example, unsheathing their weapons as they thundered across the covered bridge toward the abbey.

They ignored the road, urging their horses along the narrow riverbank toward the fire. They jumped their horses over the low wall enclosing the abbey, and the scene that met their eyes was like a passage from hell. Justin's eyes were riveted on the bonfire, but his relief at seeing no woman staked in its midst was short-lived as he saw Jillian on the ducking stool.

Rage and fear exploded together in a surging, boiling current that fired the depths of his soul. A terrible, bloodcurdling battle cry ripped from his lungs. The highwaymen turned from their grisly work as his yell echoed in terrifying reverberations over the ruins. They forgot their victim then, and pulled their weapons as the four horsemen descended upon them.

Brian followed Justin toward Jillian, pistol in hand. He aimed at Jack Harkins, who had drawn his sword, and the bullet struck the outlaw's shoulder, knocking him to his knees. He dropped his sword to grab his wounded arm, and Eleanor backed away from him, her fingers tightly gripping her groom's arm. The two men holding the plank dropped it and fled for the woods, and Justin groaned in horror as he saw Jillian plunge into the water.

He swung his blade in complete desperation as the highwaymen closed their ranks around him, blocking his path to her. He was hardly aware that Pierce had grabbed the sword tossed to him by Brian, covering his back as Justin cut a bloody swath toward the riverbank. His eyes were wild with horror, and he knew but one purpose, to reach Jillian before she drowned.

His sword rose and fell with deadly accuracy, leaving men maimed or dead in its wake, until he reached the ducking stool and threw himself from his saddle. He dropped his sword and reached for the end of the plank, pulling the heavy board down with all his strength, completely oblivious now to the men fighting all around him.

Jillian came up choking, and Justin frantically tried to pull the plank over the fulcrum toward the bank. He turned as Pierce yelled a warning from behind him, but it was too late. Jack Harkins grabbed him by the throat, his thick fingers crushing into Justin's larynx, pressing his back against the board. Justin quick-wittedly grabbed his wrists.

He managed to get his knee between them and thrust Harkins back, then sent a steel-knuckled fist against his wounded shoulder. The man fell, clutching his arm, and Justin grabbed the board again.

"Hold on, Jillian, hold on," he yelled as Jillian screamed his name over and over.

Eleanor cursed as Harkins struggled to his feet and ran for the woods, then grabbed her jeweled dagger from her belt. She ran up behind Justin, her face contorted with madness as she screamed profanities. Justin turned at the waist, still trying to hold the board. He raised his arm to deflect her blow, groaning as the sharp metal opened the meat of his shoulder. Eleanor jerked it out to stab at him again, and in the struggle to stop her, Justin lost his grip on the plank. He yelled Jillian's name in black horror; her terrified scream echoed in his ears, stopping abruptly as the water swallowed her cry.

Justin turned to Eleanor, his fingers holding her wrist, then doubled his fist to backhand her, but her eyes stared at him unseeingly, bulging in the glaze of death. He looked down at the point of a sword that protruded from her stomach. Blood gushed from the front of her gown as her French groom slowly pulled out the long blade. The corpse slid lifelessly to the ground at their feet, but Justin was already struggling to raise the stool.

François Dubois let the sword fall and helped him, both staring with horrified eyes as the end of the plank broke the surface. The chair was gone.

Justin went crazy. He dropped the board and took the river at a run. Oblivious to his wound, he dove into the dark water, his eyes open and searching the black depths.

Tied to the heavy chair, Jillian would have sunk to the bottom, and he pulled himself downward with all the strength in his arms, feeling desperately along the bottom. Cold mud oozed through his fingers, and soon his air was gone. He broke the surface for a breath, then dove again, arms waving frantically in a blind search.

He could not find her, and each second that passed meant less chance of her surviving. He was sick with helpless panic when his fingers touched her hair waving eerily in the current. He grabbed a handful, feeling his way across her face as he struggled to get his knife out of his scabbard. He hacked hysterically at the ropes holding her to the chair, and when he finally freed her, he fought his way to the surface, holding her tightly against him.

Most of the highwaymen were dead or had

fled when Aaron had thundered into the abbey with a contingent of armed riders, and Pierce watched anxiously from the bank. When Justin's head burst from the surface, Pierce got a hold on Jillian's limp body and hauled her out of the cold water. Justin pulled himself out, his eyes dark with despair as he pushed Pierce away. He turned her on her stomach, pressing his hands upon her back. Water ran from her mouth, and he turned her over again.

"No, no, no, live, live," he muttered hoarsely, taking her pale face between his palms. Her eyes were closed, her body cold, and he forced down his growing hopelessness, lowering his mouth to her icy lips, determined to make her live, determined that she would not die. He blew his own breath into her over and over, unaware that Brian and Ryan had dropped to their knees beside Pierce, bloodstained swords still in their hands. With stricken eyes they watched him work over her, refusing to give up, until he finally stopped and put his ear to her bloodless lips.

He groaned with the blackest of grief, dropping his face against her breast. And then he heard the faint beat of her heart, and he pulled away as her lips trembled. She coughed up water, gasping; her eyes fluttered slightly, and raw emotion rose in Justin's throat as she began to breathe. He clutched her limp body tightly against his chest, rocking back and forth, his sobs muffled in the wet tangles of her hair.

Hours later Justin sat on the window seat of his bedchamber, his eyes on the far horizon where streaks of pale gold crowned the night. He stared unseeingly at the glory of the sunrise, trying to make his mind blank.

He turned his head to the bed. Jillian lay quiet at last, and he shut his eyes, leaning his head against the wall. When he finally revived her, he wrapped her trembling body in his mantle and rode home with her in his arms, not wanting anyone else to touch her.

He had left Ryan and the others to deal with the dead and wounded, his only concern for Jillian. She sobbed weakly against his chest during the ride, and through the long night hours he held her close in their bed, his jaw tight with contained rage each time she awoke, screaming with terror.

Even now his fists were clenched, the muscles of his arms forming hard ridges as he thought of what Jack Harkins had done to Jillian. He knew now that Eleanor Marlowe had instigated it, and Justin felt her death was a just revenge for what she had done. But Harkins had escaped, like the coward he was, and Justin swore a sacred oath to hunt down the animal and every other man who had stood by and watched Jillian tortured. They would pay dearly for what they had done to her, if it took him his entire life to find them.

"Justin!"

Jillian's frightened cry brought him to his feet, and he crossed quickly to the bed. She was sitting up, hugging her shoulders, her eyes wide with remembered horror. He smiled reassuringly, taking the hand she held out to him. It felt small and cold between his large palms, and the rage began again as he thought of her total defenselessness against the men who had hurt her.

"Here, sweet, drink this," he murmured softly, his voice odd, and Jillian obeyed, still so weak that she welcomed his supporting arm at her back.

"What is it?" she asked.

Justin set the cup aside, then stretched out beside her, gathering her into the warm circle of his arms.

"Only a sleeping potion. Catherine brought it while you slept. It will help you rest better."

"As long as you hold me I will be fine." Jillian sighed, snuggling closer to his hard body, and Justin turned on his side, nestling her head into the curve of his arm where he could look at her. His face grew serious as he raised a finger to a discolored bruise upon her forehead. He lightly traced a long scratch that stood out in an angry red line on her smooth cheek, and pain swelled around his heart. He pulled her close, squeezing his eyes shut. She was so small and good and kind, and he had almost lost her. It had been too close: only a few moments longer in the cold water and her loving warmth would have been gone forever. Extreme fury gouged his mind and stiffened his limbs as the need for revenge ate like acid into his soul.

He swallowed, hard and convulsive, his whisper low, muffled in her soft black hair.

"I have to go after them, my love."

Jillian tensed all over. "No, please, don't leave me alone."

His arms tightened protectively, and he forced a smile as he tenderly brushed silky hair behind her ear.

"I remember a time when you told me that one had to do certain things because it was in their heart. It was the night you went to Mauve, do you remember?"

He waited for her nod, then went on. "That is how I feel now, but you will be safe here until I return. I have posted a guard at your door, and one will remain with you every minute that I am gone. The animals who hurt you must be caught."

"I don't care about them," Jillian breathed against his chest. "I only want you here with me."

"They must be punished."

His words were hard as granite, and Jillian sought his face, her fingers on the grim lines etched upon his brow.

"I am afraid for you."

"Do not worry, because I take both Ryan and Aaron with me, and many of our men. I will stay here with you until you sleep, and I promise I will be back before you are strong enough to be up and about."

They were quiet for a time, Jillian's ear resting upon the softness of Justin's shirt, lulled by the strong and steady thud of his heart. She knew she could not change his mind, but it tore at her heart that he had to leave her.

"Why did you go to the peddler, Jillian?"

His voice was low, with a strange vulnerability that she had never heard before. Tears welled up in her eyes, and she knew that it was time to tell him the truth. She leaned back to look at him.

"Because he is my brother, Brian."

Justin stared at her in shock, and she continued, "He came here to find me and take me home with him to Ulster. And the groom I protected is Pierce, my other brother. It was God's will that I found him. They made me swear not to tell you, though I begged them to let me."

She began to cry, and Justin's voice was gentle.

"Do not weep, for now I can understand many things that troubled me greatly."

He smoothed her hair with his palm, and Jillian felt as if a terrible weight had been lifted from her shoulders as his mouth found hers in a tender kiss.

They did not speak again, and soon, drugged sleep rose in billowing clouds to hug her into a deep, white peace where she was not haunted by flickering fires and leering faces and lungs screaming for air.

"Jillian, Jillian, wake up. . . ."

Jillian opened drowsy eyes, trying to focus on the bleary face just above her, as insistent fingers shook her by the shoulders.

"Brian? What do you want?"

Her next thoughts touched on her husband, and she struggled up in fear.

"Is Justin all right?"

"He is fine, but I will help you to dress. We must go now while he is away."

"Go? Where?" she mumbled, still not quite awake, as he jerked back her covers.

"Ulster. Hurry now, before the guard is found."

Confusion reigned in her sleep-drugged mind as Jillian located Pierce beside her door. His sword was in his hand, and one of the Spenser men lay on the floor beside him.

"You have killed him!" she gasped out, and Brian's words were hurried as he propped up her back with his arm.

"He is not dead, just unconscious. Come on, I'll help you to dress."

"I cannot leave here," Jillian protested, her voice growing stronger. "I cannot leave Justin!"

"You have to now, while he and his brothers are gone."

"Nay, nay, I will not!"

"Hurry," Pierce hissed impatiently from his place at the door, and Jillian put a weak hand against Brian's chest as he was about to lift her.

"Go if you must, but I will not leave him. I love him."

Brian paused, his eyes softening.

"Do you really think we would leave you here, little sister? Where the English hate you enough to tie you to a board and drown you like a rat? Nay, you must come with us."

"Justin will protect me."

"Justin can only protect you within these walls. Is that how you want to live?"

"I only want to live with Justin, and nothing else matters to me."

She tried to pull away, and Brian sighed.

"Dammit, Jillian," Pierce growled harshly. "Do you want us butchered here and now? Get dressed like Brian said!"

"I have told Justin who you are, and he will help you to gain your freedom," Jillian cried, her eyes filling with tears.

Pierce cursed then, and Brian shook his head.

"Think, Jillian. Now that Justin knows who we are, he will have to tell the king or be faced with treason. And William will not think kindly upon Justin's harboring of an exile. Do you want to risk the king's displeasure falling upon Justin and his family? Do you want them disgraced with the loss of their lands? And if Justin does tell, I will surely be hanged. Do you want that?"

Jillian stared at him, then dropped her face into her palms, sobbing because it was true, all of it. Brian put a comforting arm around her shoulders.

"Don't you see, Jillian? You will be safe in Ulster, and it will be less likely for us to be arrested. When Justin finds you have gone, he will surely come to you."

"But he will never understand! I cannot go, I cannot!"

"You have no choice, sister. I am sorry, but I am taking you with us."

Jillian struggled against him as he picked her up and pulled a blanket around her. The sleeping potion had robbed her of her strength, and she could only weep as he carried her down a deserted stairway to a back entrance where Bridgit waited with their horses. After Pierce had mounted, Brian lifted Jillian carefully into his brother's arms, then swung into his own saddle. They rode along the wide stone portico facing the side gardens, and just as they were ready to strike out toward the river, Catherine rounded the corner, looking for Jillian.

"Wait, where are you taking her?" she cried frantically as Pierce and Bridgit rode past her; Brian spurred his horse as well.

Catherine ran after them, yelling for help, and a few yards away, Brian frowned and jerked his horse around, galloping to where Catherine stood. He leaned down and caught her around the waist, pulling her up against him.

"Tell your brother that Jillian returns to

Ulster with her brothers, and we will take good care of her there."

"Brothers?" Catherine repeated, pushing against his hold as his horse's excited prancing clattered against the stones. "I don't believe you, let me go!"

Brian laughed, his grip tightening. "Aye, I am Brian Devlin and my brother Pierce rides with Jillian."

"But . . . but you can't just—"

Her words ended abruptly as Brian's mouth came down hot and hard over hers, doing exactly what he had wanted to do since the first moment he had seen her. Catherine hung limp and breathless against him when he finally raised his head and grinned at her.

"And as for you, Cathy, love, curb your wild ways and obey your brothers, because I will be back for you someday."

He kissed her again, more tenderly this time, then carefully lowered her to the ground. He smiled down at her, pulling a small pouch from his vest and tossing it at her feet. With a small salute he kicked his horse into a run toward the others.

Wide-eyed, Catherine stared after him until he had disappeared from sight. She reached down then and retrieved the black velvet bag, lifting out a slender chain hung with a silver medallion engraved with a half moon and stars. She looked at it for a moment before she raised trembling fingers to touch her lips, still warm and throbbing from Brian Devlin's relentless kisses.

# TWENTY-FIVE

"I worry about Pierce. It grows late, and his patrol has been out since morning."

Jillian lifted her eyes from the tiny black kitten in her lap to gaze at Brian. They sat in the drawing room of Devlin Manor, and she watched as her brother rose and moved to the front windows.

"Pierce has returned after dark many times since we've been home. And Donal rides at his side," Jillian answered, scratching the cat's ears. Pierce had given the kitten to her in place of Ebony when they arrived in Ulster, but each day since she'd left England nearly a month before, her heart had twisted into a tighter knot. Her loneliness for Justin had become like a pendulum cutting at her insides with sharp, never-ending slashes.

She had sent him a letter when Philip Hammond had sailed home to England a week ago, explaining that her brothers had forced her to leave. She had begged him to believe her, because she knew he would never forgive her if he thought she had willingly deserted him.

She closed her eyes, fighting back the endless tears she had shed. Ever since they had been home, Sean Flanagan had engaged Brian's men in relentless skirmishes, one raid upon Devlin lands after another. But Jillian no longer cared, not about the properties or the Flanagans. She wandered about listlessly during the days, missing Mauve as well as Justin, then tossed endlessly upon her bed, awakening each morning queasy and tearful.

"My God," Brian muttered, and Jillian opened her eyes to find him staring past her. She turned in her chair, expecting to see Pierce, but her heart stopped in midbeat.

"Justin," she gasped, rising to her feet without knowing it. Joy blossomed in a swelling wave that blotted out all else, but it faltered as her husband stared at her, his eyes like the November frost upon the windows.

Her smile receded uncertainly, and he looked away from her. Jillian's heart lurched, her fingers seeking a steadying grip on the chair back beside her.

"The king has granted your pardon," Justin said without preamble, and Jillian listened to his deep voice, having prayed a thousand times for the day that she would hear it again.

"Both you and Pierce are now free to live in Ulster as before," Justin continued. "His only condition is that you swear never to bear arms against his Crown. I have brought the documents for your signatures."

Jillian and Brian both stared incredulously

at him, then Brian grinned as he met Jillian's happy smile.

Justin did not look at Jillian again; he drew off his leather riding gloves as he moved across the room.

"We are most indebted, Lord Spenser—" Brian began as he was handed the contracts, but Justin interrupted.

"Your brother saved my life that night at the abbey, and you fought at my side to save Jillian. I owe you more than this pardon. Therefore, I have deeded the Devlin properties back to you as your rightful inheritance. I ask only that you sell your goods at a fair price to my merchant ships."

Brian could not hide his shock, and his words were thick.

" 'Tis a most noble and generous thing you do for our family."

"And Catherine sends this to you." Justin reached into the pocket of his vest and retrieved the silver medallion. "She said you'll have to put it on her neck yourself before she'll wear it. She mentioned a legend and said you would understand."

Brian grinned as he took it and dangled it from his finger.

"That I will gladly do. Is she well?"

"Aye," Justin answered, and Brian glanced at Jillian as her husband continued to ignore her. He looked at Justin.

"Perhaps you would like a moment alone with your wife," he suggested, and Jillian's eyes grew hopeful until she heard Justin's reply.

"The Flanagans have brought me here."

Hurt hit Jillian with such force that she sank miserably into her chair.

"Did Philip Hammond not give you our letters?" Brian asked quickly, and Justin shook his head as he sat down before Brian's maps and strategies.

"I have not seen Philip since I sailed from here last August. Has the fighting worsened?"

Brian looked sympathetically at Jillian's stricken face as he sat across from Justin. His face sobered.

"The Flanagans have burned villages and slaughtered cattle without pause since my return, and although we've regained some ground, they now outnumber our men."

"Not anymore," Justin told him. "I have brought my own men here to stand with you. Ryan rides here with them as we speak."

Jillian listened to them, her eyes never leaving Justin's beloved face. He looked the same, darkly tanned and handsome, though tired lines etched his eyes. She knew he thought his anger justified. He was a proud man, and he believed she had walked away from him, but it was wonderful just to see him, to listen to his voice and know he was well and safe. She sat still, her heart aching with bittersweet pain. Her desire to run to him and make him understand was a staggering force inside her, but she knew she must wait. Later, when they were alone, she would make him listen to her. She had to.

Her attention left his face only because of a noise from the foyer. Donal appeared, his clothes rumpled, his face streaked with dirt. Justin and Brian stood at once, and Jillian sat straighter at the dire expression on Donal's face.

"Where's Pierce?" Brian asked, moving forward in concern.

Donal gestured wearily, his signed explanation bringing a gasp from Jillian.

"What did he say?" Justin demanded sharply, and Brian looked at Jillian.

"Sean Flanagan wiped out their patrol, and he has Pierce. He intends to kill him if his demand is not met." Brian hesitated, worried eyes on Justin's face. "He wants Jillian. He has learned from a captive that her beauty resembles our mother, whom he once loved. He says he will not harm her, and he will free Pierce only when she willingly comes to him."

There was a momentary silence until Jillian moved. "I will go and prepare myself to leave—"

"No!" Justin's voice was harsh, uttered through clenched teeth, and Jillian's eyes shot to him.

"I must, if Pierce is to be saved."

"You will not, I say," Justin ground out succinctly, his eyes hard upon her face. "I am still your husband, and although you see fit to disregard that fact, you are subject to my authority. For once, madame, you will do as you are told."

"But he will kill him!" Jillian cried, and Justin's jaw went rigid.

"Of course, she cannot go," Brian interjected quickly. "Such a thing is totally out of the question. We will have to rescue Pierce another way."

"Is the Flanagan stronghold well fortified?" Justin asked then, and Brian nodded.

" 'Tis a castle, centuries old, but one side is virtually defenseless. We could take it very quickly with enough men."

The two men moved back to the table, leaving Jillian to stare helplessly after them. Neither looked at her again as they made their plans, and she turned numbly and left the room, her fear for Pierce mingled with the terrible hurt of Justin's cold rejection.

By the time she reached her room she had made up her mind what she was going to do, and she bathed leisurely, then donned a gown and matching robe of rose satin and delicate lace. She sat docilely as Bridgit brushed her hair into a gleaming black mantle over her shoulders, then walked purposefully down the hall to the bedchamber that her husband would occupy. She sat down in a high-backed chair before the crackling fire and folded her hands to await him.

It was very late before she heard him approach the door, and her nerves wavered precariously as he entered. Their eyes locked as he saw her at the hearth, but his face remained impassive.

"What do you want?"

His cold words cut into her, but Jillian raised her chin a fraction.

"I am your wife. I belong here with you."

Justin stared at her for a long moment, and his short bark of laughter was devoid of humor.

"That was not your thought in England," he reminded her caustically, and Jillian swallowed dryly.

"I had no choice, as you had no choice but to capture Jack Harkins and his men."

"And I did, if it interests you. They were hanged at Wellingford Cross."

Justin moved away, laying his sword aside as he pulled off his leather vest. He untied his cravat, glancing sidelong at Jillian where she sat watching him. Her hair gleamed in a blue-black luster where the firelight touched it, and her turquoise eyes were so full of sorrow and love and hurt, he had to force his eyes away from her. He wanted to grab her, to bruise her lips under his mouth, to savor the feel of her skin, but his mind would not forgive the nights he had lain alone at Spenser Court, her perfume still lingering on his pillow until he thought he would go mad. He paced angrily to stand before the window, staring into the darkness, fists doubled at his sides.

The soft carpet muffled Jillian's footsteps, and Justin jumped slightly as her hand settled lightly on his back. He whirled, his breath catching as he stared down into the beautiful blue of her eyes. He tensed all over as she placed both palms upon his chest.

"Please, please listen to me, I beg you. I love you, my husband; every moment away from you has been torment to my heart."

His hands trembled with the desire to pull her into his arms, and he came very close to giving in to the overwhelming need. But his pride had been battered, and the wound was still raw and oozing around the edges. He moved away from her to take a stance at the fire.

Jillian looked after him, tears brimming, and the terrible hurt she felt began to give way to desperation.

"I had to go! Why can't you believe me? Pierce and Brian would not leave without me, and both you and they would have been in danger there! They forced me to go with them!"

Brian had told him the same earlier, but the hurt ran deep, and Justin still did not speak, choosing instead to stare silently into the grate. Jillian gritted her teeth.

"Then harbor your hatred for me, for I will never grovel at your feet! I will leave you to your stubborn pride and be sorry that I ever met you!"

She ran for the door, only seconds before bursting into helpless tears, but she did not reach it. Justin's hands caught her and swung her around.

"You will leave when I bid you to leave," he ground out, his face red with fury, and as Jillian's tears began to spill over with the hurt he'd wanted her to feel, his lips came down upon hers. The kiss was hard and punishing, and Jillian struggled to free herself, but in her heart, she knew that this was what she wanted, his arms around her, his mouth upon hers, even in anger.

She slid both arms around his hard waist, pressing herself against him eagerly as his mouth continued to twist hungrily over hers, his hand snarled in her hair.

"Damn you, damn you for leaving me," he muttered huskily as he lifted her from the floor, but his words were no longer hard or angry, and Jillian's heart thundered as she slid her hands up beneath the back of his shirt over muscles that rippled as he carried her to the bed.

He pulled at her gown in his haste, tearing loose ribbons and lace, flinging it to the floor, one strong arm around her naked waist as he fell upon the bed with her, his mouth on lips he had caressed over and over in dreams and daydreams, his fingers touching flesh as smooth as the fine satin he had ripped asunder.

She moaned with pleasure, caught in the vast, uncontrollable spiral of fire that took her heart, her soul, and soldered it to his. They moved together, bodies warm and eager, breaths ragged until the immense love they shared conquered the long, empty days and nights apart, the anger and hurt and loneliness. All was forgotten and cleansed and purified as they renewed their love, melding them again into one heart and one destiny.

It was almost noon the next day as Jillian sat with her back pressed against silken pillows, watching Justin as he dressed. He strapped a molded black breastplate upon his chest, then positioned his sword at his hip before looking back at her. Her face was so sorrowful that he sat down and touched her cheek in a light caress.

"Try not to worry, sweet. Sean Flanagan will surrender to us. He is outnumbered and he will know it."

"And what of Pierce? Will Sean let him live?"

"I cannot promise that he will, but there would be little reason to kill him. It would only worsen Sean's own fate."

Jillian looked down, her words low.

"And what of you? What if I am left a widow after this day?"

"I will return to you because I will not allow anything or anyone to separate us again."

Jillian suddenly clutched him to her; his armor was hard and cold against her bare skin.

"When do you have to go?"

"We march soon."

They held each other tightly, and Justin's

kiss was long and infinitely gentle, both palms cupping her face.

"They wait for me," he whispered finally. "I must go, but you must promise me that you will wait here until I return."

Jillian looked away, and Justin raised her chin until their eyes met. His silvery eyes were intent.

"Promise me, Jillian."

"I promise," she murmured with lashes down, and Justin smiled and kissed her lightly.

She sat very still as the door closed behind him. Her promise to him rebelled with her conviction that she was the only one who could save her brother's life. Sean Flanagan would not hesitate to kill Pierce if his demands were ignored, and she knew it. Such thoughts tortured her, and a shudder of revulsion coursed through her as she remembered Sean Flanagan's ugly, scarred face and unkempt red hair. Bile rose in her throat as she thought of Pierce at his mercy; Pierce, who had suffered so much already.

She arose and dressed quickly in a simple dress of white linen with a white satin stomacher, then pulled on a warm fur-lined cloak. She had to get outside in the fresh air where she could breathe.

She walked aimlessly for a time in the gardens, ending up near the open pasture behind the stables where Justin and Brian had assembled their fighting men for the march upon Flanagan Castle. Her nerves were brittle with worry over the outcome of the coming battle, and she stared dully out over the field.

While she stood there a horseman suddenly appeared against the trees, and she shielded her eyes from the sun. She did not recognize the rider until he rode closer and she saw his red beard. Startled to see Patrick Flanagan so near to Devlin Manor, she looked around to see if the guards had spotted him.

There was no one in sight, and she ran forward to meet him.

"Patrick! What are you doing here?" she cried, grabbing his bridle as he drew up beside her.

"I've come to help you in the fight against my father," he said, then smiled grimly at Jillian's shocked face. "I have seen my father lapse into complete insanity over his hatred for your family, and I cannot stand his cruelty or brutality any longer. I am ready to stand against him."

"Does he know you have come to us?" Jillian asked, reading the anguish in her friend's dark eyes despite his bitter words.

"He would kill me if he knew. I have come secretly to tell your brothers of a hidden tunnel that leads from our family's crypt into the castle yard. It is the only way they can save Pierce Devlin if they are going to attack us."

Chills rose on Jillian's arms. "Then Pierce is still alive?" she breathed, her eyes frightened.

"He is alive, but my father will kill him. I

knew I could trust you, and only you could make your brothers listen to me."

"But it is too late! Brian and Justin have already started their march! Over an hour ago!"

"Then come, we must cut through the woods and try to catch them!"

Jillian did not hesitate but grabbed the arm he held down to her, and Patrick swung her up behind him. He spurred his horse, knowing that they had little time to reach the Devlin force before they launched their attack. They rode hard, cutting across the thickly forested hills of the Flanagan land in the hope of intercepting Justin on the road to the castle.

They were very close to their destination when they heard the sound of riders. Jillian jerked her eyes around to find a small band of men, armed and helmeted in the scarlet and green of the Flanagans, approaching them. Patrick pulled up on his reins as the leader recognized him, well aware he had no chance to outrun them.

"Do not speak," he whispered to Jillian as the soldiers surrounded them. "I have captured Jillian Devlin," he said louder. "I take her to my father now."

Jillian saw the initial surprise on the faces around them, but they saluted their lord's son and fell in around him. Her apprehension grew as they reached the fields outside Flanagan Castle. High, gray walls were manned by armed guards who peered down at them as they stopped in front of an immense wooden gate, and her heart thundered as they rode through the opening. The heavy wooden doors closed into place after them, and a heavy log dropped into iron crossbars.

She shivered, prickles of fear moving up her spine as she contemplated their danger. She was in the very castle of which she had been warned all her life, surrounded by the sworn enemies of her family. The guards dismounted and led the way, and Patrick took her by the arm.

"I will try to protect you from him until I can get you out through the tunnel," he whispered.

One of the soldiers pulled open an arched door that led up steep steps, and Jillian and Patrick followed him up through the darkness to where a heavy curtain hung across the top. Patrick pulled it aside to reveal the Great Hall of Flanagan Castle, and Jillian gasped in horror when she saw what they had done to Pierce.

Her brother hung spread-eagled above the gigantic stone fireplace at the far end of the hall like a living trophy. He wore only breeches, and his wrists were secured to iron spikes, his feet tied to a wide mantelpiece. He struggled impotently against his cords when he saw her, but his words were muffled behind a gag.

Sean Flanagan sat in an enormous carved chair across from Pierce, and as Jillian turned to him, he stared in stunned disbelief at her face.

"Maire," he breathed, and Jillian shuddered as his eyes crawled over her like the most repulsive of insects. Her voice rang clear and firm.

"I am Jillian Devlin."

She stood very still as he rose, seeming gigantic in his scarlet vest. He walked toward her, but when he lifted a lock of her hair where it lay upon her breast, she pulled away in aversion.

Sean's face went livid, and growling with sudden rage, he grabbed her up with both hands, fingers biting cruelly into her arms.

"Do you find me less than pretty, you haughty little bitch? Your father gave me this scar and took my Maire from me, but now I will have you in her stead! You will act the whore for me to use as I see fit, and your brothers will die as my slaves!"

Muffled sounds of rage came from Pierce, and when Sean turned to laugh contemptuously at his futile attempts to break free, Jillian wrenched from his grasp. Before she could dart away, Sean had caught her by the hair, and Jillian cried out in pain as he flung her to the floor. Patrick tensed, his hand going to the hilt of his sword.

"Let your brother watch your dishonor," Sean cried as he held her down. "For I will wait no longer to have my Maire!"

Jillian screamed as he caught her neckline and ripped it, and she clawed frantically at his maimed face. Sean laughed at her wild struggles, his huge hands tearing at her skirts. Pierce went crazy in his bondage, jerking with all his strength against the restraints. He managed to free one hand as Jillian cried out again, and he worked desperately to loosen his other wrist.

The terror in Jillian's voice pushed Patrick past endurance, and he ran forward, grabbing his father's massive shoulders, somehow managing to pull him off Jillian. He drew his sword as Sean came to his knees, his eyes flaming with fury.

"Damn the whelp of my loins! So you want the wench for yourself, do you? You'll not be man enough to service her, you thankless cur."

Sean drew his weapon, brandishing it lethally at his son, and Jillian scrambled away as they squared off to face each other. Sean advanced, swinging his long sword in heavy, confident swipes, gradually maneuvering his son's back to the wall.

Faraway trumpets sounded attack, and Sean paused in his anger, but only to bark harsh orders to his men, who had drawn their swords to come to his aid.

"Get to your posts, damn you, whilst I finish my treacherous son. Then I will deal with the Devlin brats."

The two bodyguards ran to where the clash of battle was already audible, and Sean's sword came down hard. Patrick managed to parry it with his own blade. Metal clanged, and Patrick backed away under a fresh onslaught, no match for his father's strength.

Jillian had wasted no time getting to Pierce who still struggled against his ropes. She looked around urgently, her eyes lighting on a long oaken table, still set with cutlery and half-eaten food. A knife lay near a platter of meat, and Jillian grabbed it and tried to find a foothold on the wall so she could climb high enough to cut the rope holding Pierce's right foot.

Father and son fought desperately behind them, Patrick steadily losing ground under the experience of the older man. He was finally pinned, and Sean took swift advantage of his immobility; one swing of his immense fist sent his son sprawling in a heap against the wall.

Sean turned then, his face contorted with hatred as he advanced toward Jillian. She had cut the cord holding Pierce's foot, and he clawed at the rope around his neck as Jillian climbed down, still holding the knife. Sean was upon her before she could escape; he caught her by the nape, the point of his sword in the hollow of her throat.

He gave a snarling sneer, and Jillian closed her eyes, then, with every remnant of her strength, drove her blade into the meat of his thigh. Sean groaned in agony and staggered backward, only to meet another sharp blade.

He turned to stare into the eyes of his son, then crumpled to his knees at Jillian's feet. She began to shake uncontrollably as he fell sideways and lay still, and Pierce jerked the last rope free and jumped to the ground. He took Jillian in his arms as the thunder of booted feet and hoarse cries came from the outside. Justin and Brian burst into the room together, swords drawn, several armed men behind them.

Justin stared in astonishment at Jillian as she rushed into his arms, while Patrick stood in shock over his father's corpse. Justin took in the scene for another instant, then held Jillian away from him, his eyes dropping to her torn bodice.

"How did you get here?" he demanded tightly.

Pierce spoke up from behind her. "She came for me and would have been killed if it had not been for him." He pointed to Patrick. "He fought Sean when he attacked her."

"Thank God," Brian murmured. "For we would have been too late to have saved either you or Jillian."

Jillian pulled away from Justin and went to Patrick, whose face was ashen as he stared at his father's blood dripping from the point of his sword.

"You saved our lives, Patrick," she said gently. "You had to do it."

"I have hated him since I was a boy. I wished him dead a thousand times. Yet now I feel only sad." Patrick's words were nearly inaudible, and Pierce moved to Patrick, putting both hands on his shoulders.

"Let us end this war between Devlins and

Flanagans. Both of our fathers are dead. There is no longer a need for such hatred between our clans."

Patrick nodded numbly without speaking, and Brian came forward to shake his hand.

Jillian smiled, carefully avoiding the sight of Sean Flanagan where he lay in a pool of blood. She felt a hand close over her shoulder and gasped as Justin took her by the hand. His steps were long and angry, and Jillian ran behind him as he nearly dragged her outside into the courtyard.

His face was set in rock as he lifted her into his saddle and swung up behind her, ignoring Ryan as he rounded up the Flanagans who had survived the assault. He was so angry that he dared not speak for fear of shaking her senseless, but Jillian lay against his strong chest, truly happy. Pierce was safe, as were Justin and Brian, and the long and terrible feud had come to an end. All was well as it had never been before, and although she knew Justin was furious, she was not afraid of him. She smiled, feeling secure in his embrace.

Justin rode to the Enchanted Pool, hoping the ride would calm his seething temper. It did not work. He slid off Caesar with Jillian in his arms, then strode several paces away from her, running angry fingers through his black hair. He turned to her, his silvery eyes blazing.

"Damn it, woman, you broke your promise

to me! You could have been killed, don't you understand that?"

"Patrick came with his offer to help us save Pierce, and we were on our way to you when we were captured," Jillian told him calmly. "Surely you cannot fault me for wanting to help you win your battle and save my brother's life."

"You could have sent one of our men after us instead of endangering yourself as you did! Will you *never* learn to consider your own safety? My God, what must I do to keep you from harm? Lock you in a garret?"

Jillian met his glare, her lips curved in a wicked smile.

"You would have your son born in a garret, milord?" she inquired sweetly, laughing as Justin's angry expression dropped like lead.

"My son?" he repeated dumbly, and Jillian's eyes grew warm at the pleased grin that slowly lit his face. He came to her in one stride, pulling her into his arms. He shook his head.

"Jillian, my love, my stubborn, willful witch, you have me in your spell, and if it takes a garret to keep you out of trouble, I will gladly build one."

Jillian smiled, her lips against the rapid pulse of his bronzed neck as he carried her to a private, grassy bower, for she knew that even if she were truly a witch, she could never weave a love spell as powerful as that which bound her to Justin Spenser. He was her life, her love, her destiny, forever.